THEN A BRIGHT FLARE POPPED OVERHEAD,
SHOWERING THEM WITH SPARKS AND DRENCHING
THE AREA WITH A SICKENING GRAY GAS.

Angel heard Sam fall into a coughing fit, and he couldn't see his own hand in front of his face. It was mass pandemonium as the combatants collided with one another, trying to make their escape. Angel thought he saw Buffy slice through the fog to deliver a firm kick to one of them, but it might have been a hallucination. He dropped to the ground and began to crawl out of the fog, finally making his way to a stretch of clear air over the rocks of a sunken grave.

When Angel could finally see again, he almost wished he were still blinded. There stood Buffy with a flashlight in her hand, training the beam on Riley, who held his wife in his trembling arms. Sam was covered in a mass of blood that seemed to ooze from every pore of her body, and she wasn't moving.

"She's dying!" croaked Riley. "She's bleeding to death."

Buffy the Vampire Slayer™

Available from POCKET BOOKS

Angel™

City Of
Not Forgotten
Redemption
Close to the Ground
Shakedown
Hollywood Noir
Avatar
Soul Trade
Bruja
The Summoned
Haunted
Image
Stranger to the Sun
Vengeance
The Longest Night, vol. 1
Impressions
Sanctuary
Endangered Species

Angel: The Casefiles, Volume 1—The Official Companion

The Essential Angel Posterbook

Buffy / Angel™ crossovers

The Unseen Trilogy
    Book 1: The Burning
    Book 2: Door to Alternity
    Book 3: Long Way Home
Monster Island
Seven Crows

Available from Pocket Books

For Randy, much thanks

**Historian's Note: This story takes place in an
alternate seventh *Buffy* season timeline.**

First Pocket Books edition July 2003

Copyright © 2003 by Twentieth Century Fox Film Corporation
All Rights Reserved.

POCKET BOOKS
An imprint of Simon & Schuster
Africa House
64–78 Kingsway
London WC2B 6AH

Printed and bound in Great Britain by
Cox & Wyman Ltd, Reading, Berkshire

2 4 6 8 10 9 7 5 3 1

A CIP catalogue record for this book is available from
the British Library
ISBN 0-7434-6865-1

Buffy
the vampire slayer™
ANGEL™

seven crows

By John Vornholt

POCKET
BOOKS

New York   London   Toronto   Sydney   Singapore

One crow sorrow,

Two crows mirth,

Three crows a wedding,

Four crows a birth,

Five crows silver,

Six crows gold,

Seven crows a secret,

Which must never be told.

CHAPTER ONE

Santa Ana wind blew grimy sand and the prickly scent of creosote across the Sonoran Desert. Despite the heat, Paco shivered as he stood in the darkness beside a rusty metal fence topped with crushed barbed wire. Like ghosts, pathetic figures assembled in silence, gathering around a jagged hole in the ten-foot-high fence. From a distant *cantina* on the dirt road behind them, a *corrida* song of lonely trumpets and wailing voices punctured the night. Farther in the distance on the U.S.A. side of the border, real coyotes laughed and chattered in the black hills.

The coyotes have caught a rabbit, thought Paco, *and they're tearing it to pieces.* A splinter of moon glimmered among the wispy, fast-moving clouds, but it did nothing to dispel the darkness, or the young man's fear. It wasn't fear of living in El Norte that made him shiver—it was the fear of the journey to his new life. In these foreboding hills, many had perished of heat and thirst or, even worse, bandits and vigilantes. With the border patrol cracking down on entry points near the cities, would-be immigrants had been driven to remote stretches of wasteland along the Arizona border. Out here in the desert, only one law mattered: the urgent need to find shade and water before the sun rose, baking the sand to 115 degrees.

Paco looked around at his fellow travelers—a taciturn group who included two gray-haired old men, three brawny workers like himself, two stocky women, and a slim young mother with a three-year-old child clutched to her breast. His heart instantly went out to the mother, who must have been desperate to bring a young child on this dangerous crossing. Was her husband already in the north, working construction or tending the fields? Was she pregnant, determined to have her next child born a citizen of the U.S.A.?

She noticed his attention, gave him a fleeting smile, then lowered her head demurely. *No husband,* Paco decided, *and not pregnant.*

Finally an engine whined above the distant music, breaking the uneasy hush at the wall. A dark shape like a bread box bounced along the rutted terrain, its springs and suspension squealing in protest. The van cast no headlights upon the desert until it was almost upon them, then the lights shone only long enough to catch the figures huddled by the fence. With hope, fear, and expectation pounding in their hearts, the pilgrims pressed forward. One by one, they climbed through the hole in the metal fence and shuffled forward to meet the idling gray van, a Ford Econoline of ancient vintage.

Two lean, long-haired men stepped from the front seat of the van, and Paco recoiled in fear. He had met these two men before, of course, when he had made the deal to smuggle him into the U.S. Along the border, those who performed such services were called coyotes—for they had to be as crafty and cunning as their namesakes. Still, there was something chilling about these two . . . and their cold-eyed, languorous gaze.

The taller man was named Machete, and he had a grizzled, hawkish face with a drooping black mustache. The smuggler wore a fringed leather jacket and frayed jeans that looked as old as the timeless hills around them. True to his name, a well-used machete hung from a fringed sheath on his belt. The other one, Raul, was even scarier, because his baby-handsome face was countered by a worldly ruthlessness behind his olive-green eyes. He was dressed like a dandy with a bolo tie, dark suit, and huge chunks of turquoise jewelry on his gnarled hands. His long-nailed finger bobbed as he counted the waiting passengers.

"*Muy bueno.* Everyone is here," he said with a

cold smile. When Raul talked, his voice was a hiss, like the hot wind that rustled across the desert. His Spanish was oddly proper, as if he were from the old country, Spain. "Seven hundred dollars," he said, holding out his hand. "American, in advance."

Machete grinned and opened the back door of the van. In the dim moonlight, Paco saw that it was configured like a commercial vehicle—no seats, only a few filthy blankets and pillows. Instinctively, Paco moved closer to the young mother and her wide-eyed daughter. She gulped and seemed to welcome his protection, however meager it would prove against these two rattlesnakes. The others were in a hurry and quickly coughed up their wads of American bills—life savings for most of them, or money collected from their villages or families. Like cattle, they vaulted nervously into the back of the van.

When the young mother reached the door, Raul took her money and frowned. "Seven hundred?" he rasped, gazing at her squirming child. "But there are *two* of you."

The woman looked stunned, apologetic, then very afraid. "But I . . . you said that a baby didn't count. I will watch her . . . she will be no trouble."

To complicate matters, the child began to whimper, deepening Raul's frown. Paco stared at the lump of cash in his own hand, knowing he had only fifty dollars more than his expensive fare. He was about to offer the fifty when the other smuggler, Machete, stepped forward.

The grizzled *vaquero* put his hand to the child's face and smiled darkly. "Oh, let her go, Raul. I *like* children, and this one will be quiet, I'm sure."

The mother recoiled in fear, but the little girl smiled at Machete, entranced. With a weary sigh, Raul motioned them aboard. "She had better be quiet. Next."

Paco produced his money, and the two smugglers eyed him appreciatively. "A strong, handsome young man," said Raul. "You will do well in America if you get rid of these *peón* clothes. You could have a great future."

"I hope so," answered Paco, trying bravely to meet their disturbing stares. He jumped aboard with the others and squirmed among many torsos and legs to find a seat in the crowded compartment. With relief, he found himself sitting next to the young mother and her daughter, who was now humming quietly in her mama's lap.

Paco smiled just as the door slammed shut, plunging them into darkness. The only opening was a small window in the divider between the rear compartment and the front seat. "My name is Paco," he whispered.

"I'm Anita," she answered quietly, "and this is my daughter, Sofia."

"Pleased to meet you," said the young man. "Where are you going—"

His voice was drowned out by the strangled growl of the van's engine, which sounded as if it had seen

5

better days and badly needed a new muffler. With a rough jolt they were suddenly moving, and they bounced rudely over a path that would only last until the next hard rain. All of the passengers groaned and muttered as they were jostled about, the grimy blankets and pillows doing little to protect them from the bumps and hard edges of the van's interior. Someone found a plastic jug full of warm water, which they passed around, and the pilgrims settled in for a hot, dusty, uncomfortable journey.

"Where are you from?" Paco asked Anita.

"Guaymas," she answered. "My family are all fishermen. My brother is in Colorado—he says it's very beautiful, and they have lots of work. Many hotels."

"That's a long way to go," answered Paco. "I want to try California. When my English is better, I would like to be a policeman. Or a security guard."

They shared small talk about their dreams and ambitions for as long as the brutal ride would allow. Often the squealing springs and laboring engine would drown out their words, but the noise never dimmed their hope. The coyotes had promised to take them as far as Tucson, where they would be able to catch a Greyhound bus to distant destinations, and Paco had a cousin in Tucson to help him. But first they had to brave this endless desert, where the rugged terrain often reduced their speed to a crawl. Once they reached the highway, Paco hoped it would be smooth traveling for the rest of this long night.

With boredom and bruises taking their toll, the

young man decided to stretch his limbs. Whispering apologies, Paco maneuvered over the legs of the other passengers until he reached the divider between the rear compartment and the front seat. He wanted to hear what Raul and Machete were talking about, plus he wanted to look out the tiny window—to see something else besides blank faces. To his disappointment, there was nothing to see but the black hills and endless stands of prickly pear, cholla, and gnarled mesquite trees. He was shocked to realize that they were still driving without head-lights, even though enormous saguaro cacti loomed on every side of them.

Raul drove with such reckless abandon that Paco was certain the van would crash any moment. Paco had no idea how the smugglers could navigate in this vast wasteland, with no landmarks or civilization to guide them. He supposed they made this trip fre-quently enough to know the way.

Suddenly a pair of headlights bounced over a hill in front of them, and Raul spun the steering wheel, nearly pitching them into a ditch. With tires spinning and much cursing, Raul managed to regain control of the overloaded van. As they lumbered up a steep hill, spewing dust and rocks, Machete drew his long blade from its fringed sheath. At this point, Paco knew they had been spotted by the authorities and were trying to escape.

The van careened wildly through a rocky arroyo, reaching such a high rate of speed that Paco was afraid they would become airborne. He turned to look at the frightened passengers, who already knew they were in trouble. He was the one near the window— the one who could talk to the coyotes—and they looked pleadingly at him. When his eyes lit upon Anita, clutching her daughter protectively, he knew he had to do something. *"¿Qué pasa?"* he yelled at their insane guides. "Why are we going so fast?"

"¡La migra!" Machete shouted back. "Keep quiet back there, or we'll throw you out!"

The vehicle took such a lurch that Paco was dumped into another man's lap. The van felt like a cork being tossed upon the ocean, and both women and men began to wail. Feverish prayers rose like a litany of the damned, and passengers gripped his arms and legs, looking for a handhold, help, support . . . anything. The mad chase through the dark night seemed to go on for an eternity, until the careening vehicle smashed hard into an unseen rut. Metal in the undercarriage snapped, and the van tipped over and fell to its side, like an elephant felled by a rifle shot. Screaming, the passengers were pitched on top of one another, and Paco was suddenly fighting for breath at the bottom of a squirming mass of humanity. Over the din, he heard Raul and Machete cursing their blasted luck, and a door banged open.

Paco pleaded for calm, but nobody seemed to hear him until the rear door crashed open. Feeble moonlight slipped into the van and its twitching pile of arms and legs, and the wailing began to hush. Paco could see the slim figure of Machete pulling people out and tossing them to the ground like so much garbage. Anita managed to hold on to her child, even as she was rudely hauled out the door. Miraculously, none of the unfortunate passengers seemed to be dead, or even badly injured, and they were grateful to escape from the overturned vehicle.

Out of fear—or an instinct for survival—Paco decided to play dead. Since he was at the front of the storage compartment, there was no way for Machete to reach him unless he crawled into the van. The young man lay still in the shadows, trying to quell his labored breathing and thudding heart. Whether Machete didn't see him or didn't care if he was dead or alive, he shut the door without dragging him out. Its hinges creaking loudly, the door refused to latch all the way shut, and about an inch of starlit desert shone through the open crack.

As Raul and Machete bellowed orders, Paco crawled forward to see what was happening. Brandishing knives, the smugglers herded the benumbed passengers away from the wreckage into the black desert, warning them to be quiet. Dust swirled everywhere, adding to the sense of chaos. In the distance, headlights peaked over a hillside dotted with scrub brush and prickly pears, and Paco imagined that the border agents were calling for backup. At least, that's what he would have done.

With muted weeping and limping, the survivors of

the crash staggered into the darkness. "Stay under cover!" ordered Raul. "Nobody follow us!"

Machete stared angrily at the headlights on the hill, until the passengers were out of sight. Then he growled, "Let's go deal with them." To Paco's surprise, he sheathed his machete and walked up the hill with his hands raised, as if he were surrendering. That didn't seem possible for either one of these two, but Raul also raised his hands and marched through the dust.

Paco knew he should jump out of the van and run for his life. There was a half-empty jug of water tipped on its side, and he grabbed it. As he slid from the van onto the crusty sand of the desert, guilt overcame him, and he couldn't flee. How could he leave Anita, Sofia, and all the others? It was better to turn themselves in to the authorities, as Raul and Machete were doing. *If that's what they are doing.*

Then he knew he had to follow the smugglers. Paco crept forward, keeping low among the scraggly creosote and desert broom. The heat, the dust, and a strange uneasiness made his skin tingle, and his stomach was knotted with apprehension. Would the police return his money? he wondered. It was clear that none of them was going to make it to Tucson on this accursed night.

Silhouetted in the headlights of their green and white Jeep Cherokee, he saw two border patrol agents with rifles in their hands. Slowly, their arms upraised, Raul and Machete approached them.

"*¡Alto!*" shouted one of the agents in accented

Spanish. "Stand still, and keep your hands where we can see them."

"We mean you no harm," said Raul in a friendly manner. "We need help—we've had an accident."

"We're unarmed," lied Machete. Then he said something else in what sounded like English.

The agents took aim with their rifles and again called for the smugglers to stop. Neither one of the coyotes slowed down; in fact, they seemed to move faster up the hill than before. With no one's attention on him, Paco swiftly followed them, only he kept low among the brush. Aided by a clump of prickly pears and several barrel cactuses, he was able to get close enough to see the border patrol's faces. They were young, about his age, and both appeared to be *gringos*. Clutching his jug of water, the young man crouched down behind a large yucca plant with spiny topknots, looking like some kind of multiheaded visitor from outer space.

When the smugglers continued to advance upon the agents, one of them panicked and shot his rifle straight into Raul's chest. Paco gasped—certain the coyote was dead. But no . . . Raul staggered for a moment, then he grinned as his face underwent a horrible transformation. No longer was it boyishly handsome—now it was the wild-eyed, thick-browed visage of a demon. Machete's face also twisted into something inhuman and insane, and both creatures moved in a blaze of speed. They fell upon the border agents, whose screams lasted only a second before these monsters pulled them down into the dirt. They hunched over the prostrate bodies like wolves feeding at their fallen prey.

Paco shuddered and closed his eyes as slurping sounds filled the eerie night. The metallic smell of fresh blood assaulted his nostrils, and he gagged, fighting the urge to vomit. Fear paralyzed him for a few seconds, but he knew he had to get out of there and warn the others. Crawling on his hands and knees, careful not to make any more noise than was necessary, the young man scrambled back down the hill. With a worried glance over his shoulder, he saw that no one was following him. The monsters were occupied with their kill.

Careful not to raise his voice, Paco said nothing until he actually found the frightened group of immigrants, huddled behind two giant saguaro cactuses. The saguaros' twisted green arms reached toward the black sky, like creatures begging for mercy.

"They're killers!" he sputtered. "They're animals— I don't know *what* they are. They killed those two border agents . . . we have to run for our lives!"

"*Tranquilo, muchacho*," urged one of the gray-haired men. "Are you *loco?* You make no sense."

"We heard the shot," said a woman. "What happened?"

"I told you!" Paco took a gulp of dusty air, telling himself that he was indeed making no sense. He had to slow down if he hoped to reason with these skeptical people. "Raul and Machete . . . bullets don't hurt them.

They killed the border patrol agents. We have to run!"

"Into the desert?" the old man asked incredulously. "Do you know what happens to people out here with no car and no water? You are food for the vultures."

"If they killed *la migra,* then we are safe," concluded another man.

"No, no!" Desperately, Paco searched for Anita and Sofia among the passengers, and he found them sitting on a rock. The young mother cradled her daughter in her arms, dabbing a dirty blanket at a spot of blood on the child's forehead. Both of them looked as if they were in shock.

He crouched down before them and pleaded, "Anita, you must come with me! We must escape before they get back. Look, I have water!" He waved the half-empty plastic jug.

She stared at him with moist eyes full of sadness and disbelief. "My daughter is hurt . . . we need help."

"Yes, we must get help!" agreed Paco. Suddenly he heard the roar of a car engine, and he turned to see the border patrol Jeep rumbling down the hill toward them. "*¡Vamos!*" he pleaded. "We must go now!"

Anita shook her head slowly, staring past him into the bewitching night. "No, not into the desert. It's already hot. . . . By noon, it will be a hundred and fifteen."

"*¡Mierda!*" muttered Paco, leaping to his feet. Tears streamed from his eyes. "You are all doomed!"

As the Jeep bore down on the cowering huddle of humanity, the distraught man staggered into the darkness. His legs and brain screamed for him to run as far as he could, as fast as he could, but his heart told him not to desert his fellow passengers. He ran until he thought his lungs would explode, then he crouched down behind a large barrel cactus. In the days that followed, he wished he hadn't stopped to witness what came next.

The screams began immediately, followed by terrified wails, thrashing, and growling. Two people tried to escape, but he could swear that man-sized creatures leaped like great elk and dragged them down. It seemed as if the killing went on for hours, but it was probably only a few seconds. Struggling to keep a grip on his sanity, Paco remained still until he was sure that the bloodletting had stopped . . . and the monsters were busy feeding.

Weeping for those lost, the lone survivor slunk away into the unforgiving desert.

CHAPTER TWO

Riley Finn stood in the scorching Arizona sun at midday in midsummer, staring at the decomposing bodies in the ruts of the arroyo. The sand was dark beneath them, and the mixture of death and heat brewed a potent aroma. The buzz of flies and mosquitoes was constant, like the babble of voices among the authorities gathered at this killing ground. Riley loosened his tie and wiped sweat from his neck and brow, wishing he had worn more sunscreen. The young man had seen more gruesome sights than most mortals, but this one was impressive: eight adults and one child torn apart by unknown forces. Even without taking a closer look, the scattered remains also told him that scavengers had been here, feasting on the carrion.

Had they been left here to die, he wondered, *or killed first and then left to rot?* His stomach queasy, Riley turned away to gaze at the stately saguaro cactuses lining the dry gulch—silent witnesses to this horrendous orgy of murder. That wasn't all. Two more mangled bodies lay up on the hill, and they were border patrol officers, which accounted for all this frenzied activity. Several big crows lay dead in the vicinity, their black-feathered bodies distinct against the bone-colored sand.

Seeming unaffected by the carnage, Samantha Finn circled the corpses, taking pictures with a digital camera. She brushed away the flies and focused her lens upon the neck of one of the women, who looked as if she had once been young and pretty. Near the woman lay the child's body, mutilated beyond recognition. Technicians in protective gear, masks, and rubber gloves were riffling the corpses, looking for identification and clues. They found very little of either, noticed Riley, while doing much to disturb the crime scene. Despite the number of authorities and vehicles on hand, there seemed to be a rush to conduct the investigation. Maybe, he figured, that was because of the unrelenting sun and flesh-decaying heat.

Two things were certain: a gray van had crashed nearby and had been abandoned. Plus the border patrol's Jeep was missing, and its tire tracks were hard to follow on the hardscrabble desert.

"Sheriff!" called one of the local deputies, running from his patrol car to a beefy man in a white cowboy hat. "They found the BP's Jeep near the border, over by Sasabe."

Sheriff Clete Barton nodded sagely and stroked his double chin. "That figures. Any evidence?"

"They didn't say," admitted the deputy.

"There's not much left to do here but load the meat wagon," concluded the sheriff.

Sam returned to Riley's side, brushing her light brown bangs out of her sweaty but pretty face. His wife's unflagging enthusiasm and energy always amazed him, because he could feel the weight of centuries of futility in this battle against supernatural evil.

With her khaki multipocketed vest, hiking boots, and sensible shorts, Sam looked as if she were on safari. "Look at this," she whispered, shoving the digital camera under his nose.

Riley looked at the small LCD screen and saw the clear marks of two puncture wounds on the neck of the young woman lying in the arroyo. Hers was one of the less mangled bodies, but he assumed they would find more puncture marks if they looked thoroughly.

"Just like the Nogales killings last month," said Riley. "It looks like the agency was right to send us here."

"Come on, let's wrap it up!" bellowed Sheriff Barton, dabbing a stained handkerchief to his thick, sweaty neck. He took off his cowboy hat and wiped the sweat out of the band, too. "You Feds can stay out here all day long if you want, but I'm getting a sunburn and a crotch rash! Me and my men are taking these bodies back to the cooler."

"But don't you want to determine the cause of death?" asked Riley, stepping toward the corpulent sheriff.

Clete Barton barked a hoarse laugh, then looked Riley up and down. The clean-cut young man was wearing a dark blue Bureau of Alcohol, Tobacco, and Firearms (BATF) windbreaker and badge, which wasn't accurate, but it did work as a cover. Everyone just expected agents to fumble around and keep to themselves, as did the INS, FBI, and other gathered officials. The windbreaker covered some special equipment he was wearing.

"You aren't from around here, boy, but we see this kind of thing all summer long," declared the local lawman. "It's a simple case of abandonment and death due to dehydration and exposure. We know the BP chased the people-movers and ran their van into a ditch. Somehow they got the drop on the officers, killed them, and took their Jeep. That makes it special, but these illegals were as good as dead the moment the smugglers left them here. We didn't find any water, anywhere—not even in the radiator—and that alone is enough to kill them."

"But the bodies are torn up," said Riley, trying to keep a calm, nonthreatening tone to his voice. He motioned to the obvious carnage in front of their eyes.

The old sheriff chuckled. "Let's see, we got coyotes, jaguars, bobcat, bears, and vultures out in this reserve. You can see their tracks all around the carcasses, if you boys haven't messed it up too much."

Sam jumped forward to add, "I think I saw a wolf print. Right over there, in the bloodstained mud."

"That's possible too," allowed Barton with an appreciative glance at the athletic young woman standing before him. "Your damn eco-nuts are always throwing zoo wolves out in the wild—to starve to death, or get shot near the hen coop. I bet you're real good at nature, little missy."

"I do my best," answered Sam brightly. "But you're the expert, sir."

"That's why you shouldn't feel bad . . . none of you!" declared the sheriff, waving to the other investigators, most of whom had stopped their work to watch him. "The scavengers found 'em before we did, and then they had the good sense to get out of the sun. So let's load 'em up and be done with it. I can tell you, you'll have a hard time just identifying the victims—these people can fall off the face of the earth and never be noticed."

Now Sam's eager smile looked frozen as she backed away from the sheriff and resumed searching for tracks. Barton motioned his men to take over, while the federal people sprang into last-second picture-taking mode. An FBI agent tried to argue about jurisdiction with the local lawman, but he made little headway. In truth, none of them had much stomach for fighting the decision to get away from these heaps of sundered bodies, rotting in triple-degree heat.

"What's with the dead crows?" asked Riley, pointing to the black carcasses dotting the hillside like murdered exclamation points.

"Don't know," snapped Sheriff Barton. "By the way, some of those birds happen to be ravens, but it's hard for an outsider to tell them apart. I know most of the Feds, but I've never seen you before. What's your name, and your pretty assistant's name?"

"Riley Finn, and her name's Sam," answered the young man, deliberately omitting their real relationship. "By the way, we'd like to see the coroner's report, when he's done."

"He could write this one in his sleep," Barton said with a smile. "Hey, Joe! Get those body bags!"

"Yes, sir!" answered one of the county paramedics.

Riley shrugged and strode to the muddy spot where Sam was crouched down, taking a plaster cast of a paw print. "Why do I think this investigation is being whitewashed?" he whispered.

"They might just be complacent," answered Sam, never looking up from her work. "The sheriff has his statistics right—they did have over a hundred natural deaths of illegal entrants along this border last year. He wouldn't suspect vampires when the sun and the heat usually do the job. You know, if animals had attacked them when they were alive, there would have been more blood." She looked up and added, "Unless they were drained of a lot of their blood first."

"Right," answered Riley absently. "Is that plaster going to take long to dry?"

"No, sweetie, not in this heat," answered Sam. "We'll be back in time to get a dip in the motel pool."

Riley frowned and looked up at a scraggly palo verde tree, so named because even its bark was green. On a bare branch sat a single crow, looking down sadly. He had to imagine that the fowl grieved for all the dead black birds, not the dead brown people. The sight of the lone crow reminded him of a poem he had heard as a child.

"One crow sorrow," he intoned. "Two crows mirth/Three crows a wedding/Four crows a birth/Five crows silver/Six crows gold/Seven crows a secret/Which must never be told."

"What?" said Sam, puzzled.

Riley shrugged. "Oh, just a poem my grandmother used to tell me. You have to believe in augury for it to make any sense."

"You mean telling the future from chicken bones and bloody entrails?" asked Sam skeptically.

"We've got plenty of bloody entrails," answered Riley, glancing at the mangled bodies in the wash. "I didn't used to believe in omens, but I've seen a lot of weirdness the last few years. Who's to say that nature isn't trying to tell us things? You seem to think you can learn something from that paw print."

"Well," said Sam, leaning back on her haunches, "a wolf's canine teeth make a puncture wound similar to a vampire's fangs. Maybe the old redneck sheriff is

21

right: It's tragic, but there's nothing unusual here."

"I would hate to think this is normal," answered Riley. He gazed solemnly at the grisly crime scene, which the locals seemed to hope would fade into the burning sun and timeless solitude of the Sonoran Desert.

Riley eased into the roiling waters of the hot spa beside the motel swimming pool. To his surprise, the water was barely warmer than the outside air, which had cooled only a little since the sun began to set. Here in southern Arizona, it seemed to take hours for the blazing sun to fade from the sky, even though they didn't observe daylight saving time. Gratefully, Riley put his arm around his wife, who was wearing the pink bikini he loved; he decided that any thankless assignment was bearable as long as Sam was nearby. He didn't even think he could pursue this crazy line of work anymore without her devotion.

The sweat beaded on his forehead and upper lip, and the pungent smell of chlorine burned his nostrils. But as Sam nestled her curvy body into his and laid her sweat-soaked head on his shoulder, there was no place on earth he would rather be. The dingy strip motel even began to look beautiful as the cerulean sky began to reveal its bejeweled treasure trove stars. The gurgle of the spa jets and the buzz of the insects blended into a strange lullaby, which relaxed Riley further. Mercifully, the horrible images of the day in the desert faded from his mind, and he began to think about what he and Sam could do when they retired to their nondescript motel room.

Sam's thoughts were never far from his own, and her hand stroked the hard muscles of his stomach while she gazed at him. Just as he bent down to meet her lips with his, a shrill ring issued from the combination phone-PDA two feet away.

"Oh, screw it," rasped Riley, pressing forward for his kiss.

"Can't screw it now," whispered Sam, gently pulling away from him. "We've been waiting all day for word from headquarters. Let me take it in the room, and I'll check all the e-mail. I'll be right back, sweetheart—keep your motor running."

Before Riley could protest, his lovely boss sprang from the spa, grabbed the PDA and the room key, and dashed toward the row of depressing motel rooms. Her lithe figure was gone before he could even feel the pang of missing her. Murmuring a few choice swear words, Riley sank into the churning bubbles of the hot tub.

He waited until his skin became as wrinkled as a five-thousand-year-old demon's hide, then he climbed out of the spa and sat at the edge of the pool, dangling his feet in the chilly water. It was probably ninety degrees, but it felt cool. With impatience, Riley stared at the door of their motel room. He even glanced at the sky, which had grown black and was sprinkled with an impossible number of stars. Distant galaxies seemed as close as the fingers on his hand, and the night air smelled like cactus flowers. Beyond the safe confines of their little motel, the desert was blacker than the sky, and Riley tried not to think about the desperate immigrants who were risking their lives to reach this mirage of paradise.

Finally he heard a door creak open and slam shut. He looked up hopefully and was thrilled to see Sam padding barefoot across the walkway. Only when she drew closer to the swimming pool did he realize how bummed she looked.

"I can't believe it," muttered Sam. "We've been ordered off this case."

"What?" said Riley, sitting up with alarm. "We just started!"

"I know." She plopped down beside him and dangled her own feet in the shimmering pool. "I can't explain it."

"Did they understand your report?"

She frowned. "Well, I did write it in English. And I sent numerous photos to illustrate it. By the way, they confirmed that *was* a wolf print, for all the good it does us."

Riley shook his head in amazement. "Did they say *why?* Our own research department spotted the similarities between this case and the Nogales incident last month."

"I know." Sam scrunched her face into a frown and blinked at him. "They said it was a jurisdictional matter."

"Jurisdictional?" Riley snorted derisively. "We're black-ops—we *never* have jurisdiction! We're always operating in the shadows. I bet that damned sheriff pulled some strings somewhere. I should've lied when he asked my name."

"You're a lousy liar, sweetie," said Sam, stroking his cheek. "But we're at loose ends now—we don't have any orders, or anyplace to go."

"We can't give up this investigation," grumbled Riley. "I *know* it was vampires who tore those people apart, no matter how many wolves and bobcats showed up later. This border is full of desperate people, who trust complete strangers with their lives. Out there in the desert at night . . . it's like a vampires' picnic. Plus we've seen this pattern all along the border. It could be just the tip of something bigger."

Sam tapped her chin thoughtfully and said, "If *we* can't investigate this—and kill them—maybe somebody else can."

"You want to call in a specialist . . . someone private?" asked Riley thoughtfully. "Someone who's used to killing vampires?"

"We could provide support from behind the scenes," added Sam. "And we've got money in our discretionary fund."

"You know who I have in mind," said Riley gravely.

Sam nodded. "Of course. Do you want *me* to call? I don't mind."

"Let's both call," answered Riley. "It would be more pursuasive coming from two different agents."

"I love you, Riley, because you care about people," said Sam in a husky voice. She gazed at him with startling blue eyes, and any more thoughts about vampires, redneck sheriffs, and illegal aliens were quickly forgotten. They kissed beneath the twinkling starlit sky as a flock of bats darted nervously over the shimmering lights of the swimming pool.

CHAPTER THREE

Sunnydale

Buffy Summers scowled darkly as she tried to stick the sequined trim onto the lumpy felt pillow, which was already laden with glitter and little animal appliqués. No matter how hard she tried, the glue kept coming off on her grimy fingers, and the trim wouldn't stick. Plus she was making a mess on her kitchen table. When she tried to brush a strand of honey-blond hair out of her eyes, the hair stuck to her fingers, and she almost pulled a hank of hair out of her scalp. At the sound of her scream, her younger sister, Dawn, burst out laughing.

"You've got glitter in your hair," said Dawn. "And sequins on your nose."

"I'm just going to decorate myself," muttered Buffy. "It's easier." She glanced at a pile of misshapen animal pillows that they were going to sell at the PTA Arts and Crafts Fair, along with a bunch of other pathetic homemade doodads. It was all for a good cause—to raise funds for the high school, which like every other school was perpetually short of money—but it seemed so futile when she could be doing . . . be doing *anything* else.

"I should've volunteered to bake something," said Buffy.

"Like you bake better than you sew?" Dawn moved away from the kitchen sink, where she had been mixing some papier-mâché. "Come on, where's your school spirit? We need this money to keep summer school going . . . to lower the drop-out rate."

"Whatever happened to taking summer off?" asked the counselor wistfully. "That's what we used to do when *I* was in high school."

"Fighting demons and the Hellmouth doesn't buy textbooks," Dawn pointed out. "And you're like a teacher—you're not supposed to goof off in the summer."

"You don't know teachers very well," grumbled Buffy. "In my day, they were the biggest summer slackers." She poked a sticky finger at the trim on the pillow, and a pile of sequins fell off in her lap. "I give up. Can't we just sell the house and donate the money to the school?"

"Where would we live?" asked Dawn, acting as if she thought her sister was serious.

Buffy sighed and rested her chin in her palm. "I don't know. Sometimes I just want to get away from it all . . . Sunnydale, the counseling, the responsibility of—" She stopped herself before she could add Dawn's name to the list of responsibilities. *No need to bring her down too*, she thought.

"Like you wouldn't miss everything," Dawn said skeptically.

"Like I wouldn't," echoed Buffy.

Just then, the telephone rang. Dawn moved to grab the cordless phone from its holder. "Hello, Summerses' residence," she announced efficiently.

A second later, she glanced curiously at Buffy, letting her older sister know that the call was for her. "Can I say who's calling?"

Whatever the answer was, Dawn's eyes grew as wide as basketball hoops, and she looked stricken with indecision for a moment. "Yes, she's here," the younger girl finally said. As she handed the phone to Buffy, she whispered, "It's Riley."

Buffy stared in shock for a moment, then she mustered enough brain cells to take the phone from her sister. "Hello?" she squeaked.

"Buffy, it's me . . . Riley," came the familiar voice. "I hope I'm not disturbing you."

"Oh, no," lied the Slayer, trying to wipe the glitter out of her hair, as if her old flame could see her through the phone line. "I'm just doing . . . counselor stuff."

"That's good," came the reply. "I heard you were working at the high school, trying to keep it in one piece. But it's summer break, so you should be off, right?"

"Right! I'm way off." Now she grew skeptical. "What did you have in mind?"

"I just have a case I'd like you to work on," answered Riley. "It's right up your line, and we've been told to back off."

"You were never very good at backing off," added Buffy with more meaning in those words than she had intended. "And how is Mrs. Finn?"

"Sam is fine," answered Riley easily. "We both would appreciate your help. It's not far away, just one state over. Ever been to Tucson? Or Mexico?"

"I think I did a spring break there once . . . girls get crazy, and all that." She frowned. "Isn't it real hot there now?"

"Yes, but they tell me the summer rains are coming, and it will cool off soon. Still, I think your usual bare-midriff look will work fine here." His tone grew businesslike as he added, "I've arranged a ticket for you at Pacific Airlines for a flight tonight at eight o'clock. I hope that's giving you enough time. We can pay you, too, out of some extra funds we have."

"Our tax dollars at work," said Buffy with a wry grin. "You're lucky, because I think I can drop what I'm doing." She tossed the gummy animal pillow into the trash.

"It will be good to see you," concluded Riley. "If

30

I'm wrong about what we've got here, it will just be a paid vacation. See you later tonight."

"Bye." The line went dead in her hand, and Buffy looked thoughtfully at the phone for a moment, scarcely believing what she had heard. The last time she had seen Riley, he had ignited all the old feelings, and it seemed as if they could start up right where they had left off. Of course, that was before she had met his gorgeous new wife, who was also Ms. Commando. After seeing them together, she had to admit they were a couple made for each other in militia heaven; Xander had called them Mr. and Mrs. Nick Fury.

Would it be awkward to work with my old flame? wondered Buffy. Probably not, if they kept it all business. As for Sam . . . well, she could make even the Slayer feel a bit inferior. Still, it was kind of flattering that they needed her help.

Another voice chirped over her internal monologue, and Buffy realized that her sister had been trying to get her attention. "Where are you going?" demanded Dawn. "What's happening?"

Buffy rose from the table with a smile on her face. "What's happening is that Willow is going to watch you for a few days. I'm going to Arizona."

"Can you take me?" begged Dawn.

"He didn't say he needed two Summers, just one." Buffy strode out of the room and headed toward the stairs.

"What about these stupid pillows?" asked Dawn.

31

"Maybe Willow can turn them into voodoo dolls!" shouted Buffy as she charged up the stairs, already planning what she would wear in Arizona.

Los Angeles

Angel sat perched on the edge of his desk, trying to keep from looking bored as Winifred Burkle read to him from one of the musty tomes in their office library. He knew that a certain amount of research was necessary in his supernatural private-eye firm, but it was his least favorite part of the business. Of course, no one could remember all the demons, monsters, fiends, and malignant spirits that occasionally visited this dimension—not to mention Los Angeles—but Angel would rather fight them than read about them.

"The Greater Lystagi has a venomous bite," intoned Fred as she adjusted her glasses, "and it's about fifteen percent larger than the Lesser Lystagi, or Common Lystagi. The venom resides in the saliva and acts as a nerve agent, resulting in numbness, atrophy, and even paralysis if the bite is severe enough—although this effect has been found to be temporary if a mustard poultice is applied to the wound immediately."

"A mustard poultice," repeated Angel, trying to sound interested. He had killed one of these things in less than fifteen seconds just the night before, and he hadn't needed a mustard poultice. "Do you think we can get a box of those at the drugstore?"

Fred frowned at him over her glasses. "Don't be facetious. It says here that the Lystagi usually travel in packs, so there are bound to be more of them. *You* might not need a mustard poultice, but the rest of us should be prepared."

"It doesn't matter." Angel pointed to the solid old telephone resting stoically on the desk. "That thing hasn't rung since Alexander Graham Bell was a baby. Just once, I would like to pick it up and find some well-heeled client on the other end. As Cordelia would say, somebody with some deep pockets that aren't full of lint."

As if in answer to his rant, the telephone jingled. Fred smiled at her boss and reached for it. "Hello, Angel Investigations."

After a moment, she frowned and said, "Yes, he's here, but I can take down the details and—" Fred paused, listening to the caller, then she shrugged. "All right, I'll put him on." As she handed the receiver to Angel, Fred whispered, "She's a damsel, but she doesn't sound in distress."

"Good," answered the vampire with a sly smile. "Angel speaking."

"Hello, my name is Samantha Finn," came the assured voice on the other end. "We have some mutual friends."

"We do?" Angel asked with a thoughtful frown.

"As in Riley Finn."

Now Angel stopped slumping and stood at rapt attention. He straightened his black leather jacket and asked, "Are you Riley's wife?"

"Yes, I am," she answered, "and we're still in the same business you're in. At the moment, we've got an assignment that we're unable to fulfill by ourselves, and we'd like a few days of your time. I've heard some good things about you, and I know you'll be discreet."

"You can rely on that," said Angel, flashing a grin and a thumbs-up to Fred. "I've got several associates, and we could—"

"Just you," answered the woman. "Riley and I will assist you. We've got some funding, and I don't think we'll have any problem meeting your fee. I know this is short notice, but we'd like to see you tonight in Tucson, Arizona. A ticket is waiting for you at the Pacific Airlines counter for an eight-thirty flight from LAX. I know you'd prefer to travel at night."

"Yeah," agreed Angel. "Uh, Mrs. Finn—"

"Please call me Sam."

"Okay . . . Sam. Are you sure this is all right with Riley?" He didn't want to mention that they had come close to killing each other a few times, and both had desperately loved the same woman.

"Yes. He was supposed to call you himself, but I guess he left it up to me," she answered. "We've talked before about using your services."

"Oh, you have?" Angel said with some pride. "I guess our services are rather unique."

"You're the one who's unique," she answered. "I'm looking forward to meeting you. Good-bye, Angel."

"Good-bye." The investigator handed the receiver back to Fred, who hung it up. "I'll be going out of town for a few days, but it should be good for the bank account."

"It sounded as if you were talking to an old friend," remarked Fred.

"Never met her," Angel answered thoughtfully. "But we do have mutual friends. And enemies."

That went fairly well, thought Sam Finn as she tucked her mobile phone into her oversized bag. *Now we've got somebody on the case who isn't likely to be caught or connected to us.*

She looked up at the sign hanging over the entrance to the Verdura Community Hospital, a small facility on the outskirts of a border town in the middle of nowhere. Like the town's name implied, this area was an oasis in the desert—with rolling hills, a nearby river, and majestic cottonwoods and cedars that coexisted with the misshapen cactus and mesquite. The hospital was situated next to a pecan orchard, and the tall, orderly trees seemed out of place.

Unlike the day before, Sam was wearing a conservative gray business suit, because today's investigation would take place indoors. In that morning's local newspaper, she had spotted a story about an illegal immigrant who had been found the day before wandering in the desert north of here. He had been near death from heat stroke and dehydration, but they had rushed him to this hospital in time to save his life. Of course, as soon as he was well, he would be shipped back to Mexico. It was a long shot to think that this patient was connected to the recent murders in the desert, because hardly a day went by when some illegal entrant wasn't rescued from the summer heat. Still, it was worth taking a chance to interview him.

Riley had gone to the county seat to get word on the coroner's report on the mangled bodies. Sam hoped he would be able to do so surreptitiously, because they were supposed to be easing off this case. Fortunately their methods never underwent much scrutiny from their superiors, who usually didn't want to know what they were doing as long as they produced results. Dead vampires and demons were the desired results.

Sam pushed open the door and walked into the lobby of the small hospital, and the frigid air-conditioning hit her like a blessed spring shower. She saw lots of law enforcement types standing around, both uniformed and plainclothes, which was kind of surprising. This was not a place to dilly-dally. Sam flashed her badge at the desk receptionist and strode into the place like she owned it.

Every room seemed to be occupied by two or three patients, which was also surprising for such a small town. She supposed this hospital served a rather large rural area, with a goodly number of retirees and border crossers. Harried doctors and nurses ran to and fro, and there were the usual beeping noises and pungent disinfectant smells. Sam didn't need to ask directions to the right patient, not with two sheriff's deputies standing in front of one room.

Before anyone could get a good look at her, she ducked into the women's rest room and headed straight for one of the stalls. Locking the stall door, she quickly pulled a white nurse's uniform from her big purse and began to switch clothes. Even the purse itself was reversible, turning into what looked like a garment bag.

Two minutes later, a nurse with glasses and pulled-back hair emerged from the rest room and walked briskly toward the door guarded by the deputies. She had left her garment bag hanging in the stall, hoping no one would bother it. At the door, she officiously checked her clipboard before walking in.

"Have to check his vitals," she told the deputies, who admired her form as she walked past. Sam cut that off quickly by shutting the door in their faces.

Lying in the bed was a handsome young Mexican man; he was alone, even though there was another bed in the room. Intravenous tubes fed him fluids, and his skin was chapped and sunburned—but otherwise he looked as if he would recover. Sam knew she had no time to waste, because a real nurse or doctor might show up any minute.

She looked at his chart and saw that his given

name was Paco Gonzales. She gently shook him awake and said, in serviceable Spanish, "Paco, can I talk to you for a moment?"

"Oh, hello," he said, sounding somewhat confused, but his face brightened when he got a good look at the new nurse. "Time to take more pills?"

"No," she answered, "it's time for you to tell me what happened to you out in the desert."

The man shifted uneasily in his bed. "I have told the others, but no one will believe me."

"I'll believe you," answered Sam. By the looks of the lawmen posted outside and the empty bed in the crowded hospital, others believed him too. "You were with those poor people when the gray van overturned."

He nodded warily, and Sam went on: "What happened to the border agents? How were they killed?"

Paco sat up, looking agitated, and a monitor beside him began to beep loudly. "The coyotes—the smugglers—they were not human! They became like . . . *wild animals*, and they tore the officers apart. I tried to tell the others to run away before the monsters came back, but they wouldn't leave."

"Calm yourself," said Sam soothingly, pushing him back onto his pillow. She had a feeling her time was running out. "How many smugglers were there?"

"Two."

"Did they have names?"

He nodded. "Raul and Machete."

"Where did you meet them?" asked Sam, just as the door creaked open behind her.

"Verdura, Mexico."

"What are you doing?" bellowed a voice from the doorway. "Who are you?"

Sam didn't need to turn around to see who it was, because she recognized the belligerent voice of Sheriff Clete Barton. "I'm almost done," she answered calmly, making notes on her clipboard. "He's doing much better."

Keeping her head down, Sam tried to escape from the room without anyone getting a good look at her face, but he held out a brawny arm to stop her. "Don't I know you from somewhere?" grumbled the sheriff.

"Yes," she said, affecting weariness, "I *work* here." Using her own considerable strength, Sam pushed away his arm and brushed past him. Aware of the guards' eyes on her again, she walked only far enough down the corridor to duck into another room.

There she found a rumpled, gray-haired doctor shaking his head as he draped a sheet over a patient's face. "Another one down," he muttered. "I want this room completely disinfected, and get me the lab reports as soon as possible."

"Yes, sir," Sam answered efficiently, planning to relay the orders to a real nurse before she left the hospital. The doctor barely looked at her as he shuffled out of the room, and the imposter finally had a moment to catch her breath.

She looked down at the words she had written on her clipboard: "Raul and Machete. Verdura, Mexico."

Sam knew that was the larger town directly across the border from here. It wasn't much to go on, but it was more than they'd had before. Plus they had an eyewitness who had identified the killers as vampires . . . or something equally dangerous.

No matter what headquarters said, this was definitely not a case they were going to abandon.

CHAPTER FOUR

About 9:30 that night, two flights arrived at Tucson International Airport from different parts of Southern California. Like any modern airport in these days of increased security, people meeting the passengers were not allowed to wait at the gates; they had to congregate like a mass of refugees outside the security checkpoint.

So it was that Buffy Summers didn't see anyone she knew when she disembarked from the airplane into a terminal that could have been in any city, not just Tucson. From another gate closer to the luggage return, a second plane was disengorging its passengers, and she merged into a slow-moving stream of men, women, and children, some empty-handed and some struggling with a ridiculous amount of carry-on luggage. Buffy peered out the windows lining the concourse and saw darkness broken by scattered pools of light and activity, with luggage vehicles snaking among the parked planes like huge serpents. She shivered, remembering a few huge serpents she had known.

Ahead of her in the herd of arriving passengers was a broad-shouldered fellow in a black leather jacket who reminded her a great deal of the former love of her life. Of course, it couldn't be *him*. What would he be doing in Tucson, Arizona, on a Friday night in the middle of summer? Of course, what would any of these people be doing here, if they knew how hot it was outside? Buffy had checked the national weather report in the newspaper before she left Sunnydale, and the low in Tucson was eighty-five degrees. The highs were in triple-digit figures best reserved for counting swear words in a rap song. She was encouraged, however, by the freezing air-conditioning in the airport. It made goose bumps on her bare midriff and arms.

As they passed the metal detectors and search tables on the other side of the short security wall, the crowd of arriving passengers narrowed to a crawl. Buffy slowed down as she neared the man in the black-leather jacket. Just beyond the security checkpoint stood a knot of waiting friends and family, and she craned her neck to look for Riley. She didn't see a stout woman in front of them drop an armload of parcels, and the man in the leather jacket had to stop suddenly. Buffy crashed into his back, dropping her own bag, and he whirled around, unsure who he should help first. Then his dark brooding eyes lit upon hers. "Buffy?" he said in amazement.

Both of them jerked upward, banging their foreheads together. "Angel," she muttered, massaging her aching cranium. "You have always had the hardest head. I mean that . . . in a good way."

"Of course," he said uncomfortably. "And it's okay with me if you're in Arizona. It's a big state."

"It's just so funny, both of us being here." Buffy lowered her head, at a loss for words.

"Move it along, will ya!" said an impatient businessman who was trying to force his way past them with enough carry-on luggage for six people.

"Just a minute," Angel said huffily, his old-world machismo rising to the surface. "She dropped something." He pointed to the stout woman crawling after her packages. "And *she* also dropped something."

"I'm going to drop my lunch if we don't get out of here," grumbled the businessman.

"I'm okay!" insisted Buffy, grabbing her bag and Angel's brawny arm and trying to steer him away from trouble. She whispered under her breath, "You aren't following me, are you?"

"Why should I do that?" Angel asked angrily. "It's normal for us to be here in . . . wherever we are."

"Tucson," snapped Buffy. "Did you bring your golf clubs? They have lots of golf courses here."

"I'm here on business," said Angel, once again

caught up in the flow of humanity headed for the luggage return.

"Me too," she answered, puzzled. "I don't think there's a vampire convention here, so it must be—"

"Some kind of mistake," he completed her thought. "Only the most evil, twisted people would throw us together."

"And that would be—" Buffy looked up to see Riley and Sam Finn giving them pained smiles. *Yes, they are definitely Mr. and Mrs. Nick Fury*, thought the Slayer. They even dressed alike in stuffy casual from Banana Republic.

"Buffy," Sam said uneasily as the other passengers flowed past them and down the escalators. "This is a surprise."

"And Angel," Riley said with distaste. "What brings *you* to Arizona?"

"I called him," answered Sam. She flashed Riley the kind of piercing glare that a wife reserves only for her husband. "You *told* me to call him."

"I told you to call Buffy," Riley said through clenched teeth. He pointed to the petite blonde. "*That's* Buffy."

"I know who she is," Sam answered angrily.

Angel clapped his hands together. "Well, now that we all know who we are, maybe somebody could tell us why we're here."

Buffy suppressed a smile, thinking it was quite entertaining to watch the perfect couple squirm. "We're here because *they* screwed up."

Angel folded his arms and furrowed his dark brow. "I think calling *me* was smart, not a screw-up."

"Don't you get it?" said Buffy. "They agreed to call in outside help. And *he* thought of me, and *she* thought of you. Or something like that."

"Exactly like that," Riley muttered with a sheepish look at his wife. "I guess we're not always on the same page."

"I think this case is big enough for both of you," said Sam quickly. "And we could use the help, because we're supposed to back off."

"Me work with Buffy?" Angel asked doubtfully. "I don't know about that. . . ."

"Is it any weirder than working with *me*?" responded Riley.

"I had my doubts about that, too," agreed the ages-old vampire. "Almost all the work I do is weird—this will just be a little weirder."

"I can go home," suggested Buffy, although she kind of liked being surrounded by hunky old boyfriends.

"No, please stay," insisted Sam, taking her hand. "There are no more flights back tonight, and we owe you at least a good meal and an explanation. I'm sure the Bates Motel can find another room."

"The Bates Motel?" Buffy said warily.

Riley managed a wan smile. "We just call it that. It's a little strip motel down by the border, in the middle of nowhere."

"Sounds delightful," said Angel.

"Are you sure the manager doesn't dress up like his mother and kill people in the shower?" asked Buffy.

"No, we're not sure of that," admitted Sam. "We're not sure of anything around here. It's an hour-and-a-half drive down to the border, and we'll tell you about it in the car. Have you got luggage?"

"Lots!" Buffy answered cheerfully.

"Not much," admitted Angel. "Just a bathing suit and some sunscreen."

Riley looked as if he would turn three shades paler, but he gamely said nothing as he led the way down the escalator. With a heavy sigh, Angel fell into place behind him on the moving walkway, and Buffy found herself descending with Sam at her side. "Really, I could go home," the Slayer told her hostess.

"No way!" Sam answered forcefully. "I didn't get enough time to spend with you before, and you're, like, my idol. Besides, I don't get many women to talk to in this line of work."

"You ought to move to Sunnydale," said Buffy.

Sam smiled and tossed her light-brown hair. "If we didn't know you were there, we would probably have to."

Buffy frowned thoughtfully, trying to choose her words. "It doesn't bother you that I'm his . . . that Riley and I were . . . an item?"

"Not much I can do about it," Sam answered with a shrug. "Now, if he introduced me to some bimbo and said this was his ex, it would be different. But you're the Slayer! I know you found each other at a vulnerable time in your lives. You were on the rebound, and he was being betrayed and manipulated. Maybe you could not have gotten through that time without each other. So you saved him for me—that's the way I look at it."

"I may be the Slayer," Buffy said with admiration, "but I don't have your self-confidence."

"Thanks," Sam answered as they stepped off the escalator into the cavernous luggage room, with its gleaming chrome conveyor belts and impatient people. The two men had already hunted down the luggage, as men will, trying to protect the bags before some rascal absconded with them. Angel had no problem recognizing the old but flowery gray-and-white luggage that Buffy preferred, and he also corralled his small valise and self-contained cooler.

As they walked outside and into the parking lot, the heat hit them like a body slam, and it made Buffy's skin tingle. Even though lovely palm trees were swaying in what looked like tropical breezes, the temperature had to be almost a hundred, and the breeze only moved the heat from place to place. Still, it felt good to be standing under the stars, thousands more of which were visible here in south Tucson than in the urban centers of California.

For some reason, Riley stopped abruptly and stared at two crows sitting on the cross beam of a light pole. Everyone else stopped to follow his gaze, although Buffy couldn't figure out why this sight required their attention.

"Two crows mirth," intoned Riley as he gazed at the birds on the pole.

"Two crows mirth?" Buffy echoed with a puzzled frown. "I don't know what's mirthful about two crows."

"Maybe they saw our meeting inside the airport," Riley answered with a smile.

"Don't mind him," Sam said dismissively. "It's just an old nursery rhyme his grandmother taught him. He thinks the crows are trying to tell him something."

"Those crows are just sitting there," observed Angel.

"At least they're alive," remarked Riley. "Some crows around here aren't so lucky." He shook off his strange reverie and pointed to the half-empty parking lot. "Come on, the rental car is over here. Next stop Verdura."

Angel squirmed uncomfortably in the backseat of the rented sedan, and it wasn't just because he missed the open air of his big convertible, or that he preferred to drive. The proximity of Buffy in the seat beside him was also having an effect. She glanced his way a few times, mustering a polite smile once or twice, but she preferred to talk to Sam. In fact, everybody preferred to talk to Sam, who was vivacious, knowledgeable, and wasn't a part of their complicated history. Sam seemed to realize that she would have to be the glue that held this foursome together, especially while they were trapped in a car for an hour and a half. It didn't help that the country-side was just that: wide-open country with few points of interest unless one really liked cactus and solitary mountains.

Sam gave them the rundown on the grisly discovery in the desert, plus her interview with the lone survivor. The coroner had given the bodies a cursory examination, backing up the sheriff's false conclusions. Angel didn't say anything, but this seemed like a run-of-the-mill vampire case, especially for people who lived in Los Angeles or Sunnydale. The setting was unusual, as were the number of deaths, but this was the sort of sport at which vampires played. Sam and Riley seemed more concerned about the fact that they had been ordered off the case than the case itself. Without that small detail, neither he nor Buffy would be here. Riley said very little, but Angel had the feeling that he was almost embarrassed to have called them in. It must have seemed like a much better idea when he thought just Buffy was coming.

On the other hand, Sam was almost giddy over their presence. To her, this was like an amateur rock musician sitting in with the Rolling Stones. Angel tried to tell himself that he was getting well paid to be here, and if he imparted some knowledge to these amateur Van Helsings, then so be it. He had done far more stupid things for a buck lately.

"Can I ask you one thing," Angel interjected quietly, bringing a hush to the crowded vehicle. "If you've been called off this case, why are you going against your bosses' wishes?"

Now the silence was so pronounced that they

could hear the tires rolling over the bumps in the rural road. They could hear the hot wind streaking past the sleek car.

"We're stubborn," answered Riley. "And somebody doesn't want us to be here."

"I respect that," answered Angel. "But are you ready to get canned over this, because both Buffy and I have been known to get messy. We'll get Raul and Machete for you, but I can't guarantee that we won't start a war with Mexico doing it. If you don't want to be associated with this, then you might want to get far away."

"Are you trying to get rid of us?" Sam asked, sounding hurt.

Angel shrugged. "Stay or go, that's up to you. Buffy has her Scooby Gang, and I have mine—so we like having help. But I'm a boss myself, and I don't like having my orders disobeyed."

After a moment of silence, Buffy added, "He's got a point. I don't think you should mess up your careers over two scummy vampires."

"¿Oyemé, tu hablas español?" Sam asked with hardly a trace of gringo accent.

Buffy nodded. "If you asked me, 'Do you want a taco,' the answer is yes."

Angel chuckled and replied in Spanish, "She doesn't, but I speak the language. It's very old-fashioned, since I learned it two hundred years ago, but I can get by."

From the driver's seat, Riley cleared his throat. "I

don't speak Spanish, but I have a hunch. I think this is bigger than two scummy vampires who killed their cargo to keep them quiet. We didn't come here by accident—there have been weird reports along this border for some time. It's like the last frontier, and who knows *what* comes across in the dead of night?"

Riley clenched his jaw and went on. "I once trusted my superiors without question, but I don't do that anymore. Our bosses are political animals who sometimes have their own agenda. I don't do this job to keep my bosses happy—I do it to protect people who are helpless in the face of these creatures."

Sam squeezed her man's arm with affection, then looked back at Angel. "That's your answer," she said.

"That's a good attitude," Angel said begrudgingly. "You can always come work for me, if you'll take a cut in pay." From the corner of his eye, he caught Buffy giving him a warm smile, but she quickly glanced away.

"On the other hand," added Riley, "if my superiors don't find out, that's all right with me."

"What is *that?*" asked Buffy, leaning over the seat and staring at bright lights looming in the distance.

Situated in the middle of dark, rolling hills, it looked like a Las Vegas casino—an oasis of light and civilization. As they drew close, Angel could also see a golf course stretching incongruously across the desert, plus several luxurious condominiums and a high-rise hotel.

"I guess that's not where we're staying," said Buffy.

"Afraid not," answered Sam. "As far as we can tell, it's some kind of new resort/retirement village. The signs say they're having a grand opening tomorrow. I hope the prices are good, because there's nothing else around here but a small town, a pecan farm, and a hospital. Plus a town across the border, also called Verdura."

As they drove by the ostentatious resort, Angel remarked, "Somebody around here has money. You don't build a thing like that with pecans."

Buffy glanced at him. "I told you that you should've brought your golf clubs."

"Oh, do you play golf?" Riley asked innocently. As soon as he said it, he realized it was the dumbest question anyone had asked the vampire in a long time.

"I'm more into hunting," said Angel, slumping back in his seat.

"Right!" Sam chirped cheerfully. "We're almost to the motel, and there's a little diner nearby. Honey, maybe we should think about getting something to eat."

"Absolutely!" agreed Riley.

Suddenly they were too square for Angel to hang around another second, and he stirred uneasily. "Uh, you can let me out here."

"Beside the road?" asked Sam.

"Yes," answered Angel. "I'll find my way back to your motel. Just get me a room adjoining Buffy's."

"Adjoining Buffy's?" asked Riley, sounding a bit protective. "Why do you—"

"So we can talk," answered Buffy, sounding as if she was also growing weary of the all-American couple. "And he can go back and forth without going outside during the day."

"Yes, of course," answered Riley with embarrassment as he guided the big car onto the shoulder. "Where are you going?"

Angel shrugged. "Across the border. You said that your survivor met Raul and Machete in Verdura, Mexico, so that's where I'll look. The night's still young, and I don't think I'll find them playing golf."

He patted Buffy fondly on the shoulder. "Make sure she gets something to eat. She looks too skinny to me." With that, the black-clad figure slipped out of the car and vanished into the night.

Leaping high over fences, walls, and rivers, Angel crossed the border between the United States and the Republic of Mexico, and he noted that the countryside, buildings, and people looked no different from one stretch of land to another. The border was purely artificial. If anything, the Mexican city of Verdura was bigger, brighter, and more vibrant than its American counterpart, with a bustling downtown and several sprawling suburbs. If this was desert, then it was a very green and lush desert, with many hills, trees, and riverbeds. He noted that dense clouds were creeping over the mountains that surrounded this part of the world, and he thought he smelled the coming of rain.

Angel paused in a dark alley in the most squalid part of town he could find: an area inhabited by strip joints, bars, souvenir stands, and tattoo parlors, most of them catering to wayward *gringos* slipping across the border for a little excitement. He heard loud, raucous laughter as a party of men and women staggered past the alley on the uneven sidewalk—the men speaking slurred English, and the women tittering in Spanish. This border town stirred his old hedonistic instincts and made him flash back on hundreds of similar towns he had visited throughout the ages.

Too many such thoughts gave him a headache, and Angel tried to concentrate on the task at hand: finding two sleazy vampires named Raul and Machete. Of course, few in this town would know they were vampires, although most would know they were in the people-moving business. For that, he would have to pretend to be Hispanic, not an easy task with his pale complexion.

So Angel's first stop was a *farmacia*, where he could purchase some dark makeup. To his relief, they accepted American dollars as readily as Mexican *pesos*, and he didn't even have to use his old-fashioned, proper Spanish. The sloe-eyed woman working in the pharmacy didn't seem to care why he needed makeup, so accustomed was she to the strange requests of *gringos*, and she offered to sell him quaaludes, morphine, and other prescription drugs that were illegal in the U.S. Never one to pass up an opportunity, Angel bought a bottle of potent tranquilizers.

He applied the makeup as best he could without looking into a mirror, which would have been impossible, anyway. When he was sure he was swarthy enough, Angel hit the street, trying to appear less like a tourist and more like a local in need. One strip joint named Cherie's had a bigger and gaudier neon sign than the others, and it was in an impressive three-story building with wrought-iron balconies that reminded him of New Orleans.

As he neared Cherie's, a hawker on the sidewalk called out, "Come on in!"

"Are you inviting me in?" Angel asked in Spanish.

"Yes, *amigo*, beautiful girls inside," the old man assured him. "There's one for you!"

"Thank you," Angel said as he slipped into the bawdy house and climbed the stairs, which shook from the powerful bass beat of loud rock music. At the top of the stairs stood a large, gray-haired *gringo* who was dressed like a cowboy, and he had the bearing of someone important. Two waiters were fawning over him, and he had his arms around two scantily clad girls. Angel wished to hear a little of their conversation, so he climbed the stairs slowly and didn't hurry past them. Even through the loud music, his acute hearing picked up their words in English.

"You haven't seen those two *bandidos*, have you, Felipe?" asked the big man.

"No, Sheriff, not since Tuesday," answered a waiter. "That's when they were last in here."

The big man squeezed one of the girls. "How about you, Lupe?"

She frowned. "I no like them. Bad men."

"Yeah, they'll be dead men if they don't show up soon," grumbled the man they called "Sheriff."

At that point, Angel was close enough that the group at the top of the stairs couldn't fail to notice him. The girls smiled beseechingly, and a waiter parted the curtain of beads and motioned him into the darkness beyond.

"Right this way, *amigo*," said the gold-toothed *camarero*. "We have a table waiting for you. Table dances are only seven dollars, and they're not like table dances in the States."

"That is for sure," one of the girls assured Angel as she took his arm. "I will show you to the table."

"*Muchas gracias*," replied the newcomer, sticking to his Spanish. If nothing else, Angel felt he needed the practice.

The big cowboy moved his stomach out of the way and gave Angel a fishy look as he slipped past. He sniffed the air, as if Angel smelled funny to him. Truth be told, the big man also smelled odd to the vampire—there was a musky animal scent about him that was hard to place.

The petite Mexican girl led Angel into a bar that was so dark, he wondered how mortals managed to see in here. He could make out a circular stage with the obligatory pole in the middle, but no one seemed to be dancing there at the moment. However, naked girls were dancing at tables along the back wall of the place, and their audience were copping many feels as they did. No, it wasn't like table-dancing in the U.S.

When they reached a vacant table, the girl ran her hand down Angel's chest, heading for lower extremities. "*Dios mío*, you have big muscles."

"I work hard," he answered.

"You want a dance?" she asked. "I will make it special for you."

"I've got seven dollars," he answered, "but I don't want a dance."

"More is more like . . . fifty dollars," she replied huskily, pressing close to him.

"I want information," answered Angel. "Do you know where I can find Raul and Machete?"

"*Por culo!*" she blurted. "Why is everyone looking for those two *hijos de puta?*"

He produced a ten-dollar bill. "I need to get to the States."

"You don't want to know them," she whispered. "They are bad news, *hombre*." With a suspicious look at him, the girl backed away. "Keep your money."

Angel was instantly surrounded by waiters who pestered him to buy a drink and try one of the other girls. Angel gave in and bought a beer, and he caught the big cowboy watching him from the doorway. One of the waiters went up to the sheriff and told him something, and the man eyed Angel with even more interest. The waiter brought him his beer while two more girls began to circle him like sharks.

This isn't working out, thought the vampire. *It's clear I'm not going to find them in here tonight, and neither is anybody else. After what they did, they must have enough sense to lie low.*

He saw no reason not to acknowledge his failure along with the sheriff's, since they were both looking in vain, so Angel lifted his bottle and toasted the big man. At that, the cowboy scowled and ducked through the beaded curtain, tromping down the stairs.

Without a stripper grinding away in his lap, Angel felt too conspicuous, so he quickly paid up and left his beer, minus a few sips. As he walked down the stairs, the vampire felt the hackles of danger rising on the back of his neck, and he wasn't too surprised when the big sheriff grabbed him by the collar, dragged him into an alley, and slammed him against the wall. Angel concentrated hard to maintain his temper and his human appearance. "Why are you looking for those two?" the sheriff growled. "What are you?"

That was a strange question, when "Who are you?" would have made more sense. "South American," Angel answered in English, with what he hoped was an acceptable accent. "From Argentina."

"Yeah right, and I'm an Eskimo," snapped the big man. "I can *smell* you buggers, you know. When you find your buddies, you tell them Clete is looking for them."

"What are *you*?" Angel asked calmly.

"You don't want to find out," answered Clete, letting go of Angel's lapels. "Let's just say I eat your kind for lunch. I don't care what you do over here, but you remember that *I'm* in charge on the other side. And we want to keep things peaceful over there. *¿Comprende?*"

"I think I can remember that," Angel said evenly. "If you really want to get a message to Machete and Raul, tell me one thing—"

"What?"

"Are there any cemeteries around here?"

"Yeah, south down the main street to the old ruined mission. That cemetery is three hundred years old. You'll like it there." The big man laughed as he walked away. "Just like a tourist, taking in the sights."

Angel straightened his leather jacket and released a pent-up sigh. If this Clete character was really in charge on the U.S. side of the border, then Riley was right: There *was* more to this business than a couple of ruthless vampires.

He strode to the end of the downtown section, where he left the garish neon behind to enter a dirt road that was dark and lined with hovels and shanties. Here, the sounds were babies crying and muted Mexican music from portable radios, and the smells were of cooking spices and poor sewage treatment. Silhouetted against the starlit sky was the outline of a ruined structure that looked like a miniature Alamo, with crumbling adobe walls and two weathered bell towers. Sprawling behind the old church was a gloomy cemetery full of tilted, wrought-iron headstones and aged wooden crosses decorated with withered flowers.

Feeling like Buffy on one of her solitary patrols, Angel meandered through the run-down cemetery. An owl hooted from a gnarled tree, and coyotes howled in the distant hills. Spanish missionaries and converted Indians had once inhabited this place, thought Angel, but their influence was long gone. It no longer felt like hallowed ground; to the contrary, he could feel cold eyes watching his every move, sizing him up as a *loco* or something more dangerous.

With a sigh, Angel sat on a stone sepulchre that had cracked down the middle and was overgrown with roots and vines. Here, the breeze was no longer warm as it had been farther north, but it felt surprisingly cool and refreshing. Dried mesquite pods blew across the dusty ground, where nothing grew except for scraggly weeds. Yes, it was the kind of place that would appeal to vampires, especially if they were lying low.

"I'm looking for somebody," Angel spoke aloud in Spanish. "Their names are Raul and Machete." No answer came, but he still felt someone watching him. In the distance, a coyote seemed to laugh at his plight.

"Your friend Clete is looking for you," he added.

Those words brought a stir to the night that wasn't simply the breeze, and the pods skittered more swiftly across the dry ground, as if they were being chased.

"We know what Clete wants," said a gruff voice that seemed to be behind him, then in front of him. "What about you?"

"I need passage across the border," answered Angel.

"You can make it on your own," hissed the voice.

Angel realized he would need some kind of bait to draw these two out of their shadows. "Not for me alone," he answered. "There is a girl who I want to sire . . . but not here."

The wind picked up a bit, and he caught a glimpse of a black figure moving among the tombstones on his left. If they were trying to surround him to attack, he might be in for a tough battle. Maybe he needed more bait.

"She is a beautiful girl," he added. "I have money."

"*We* have money," said a voice with a hoarse laugh, "and we have beautiful girls. We are out of the coyote business. *¡Vayase!*"

"*Hasta la proxima,*" Angel countered as he rose slowly to his feet and ambled through the decrepit graveyard. It briefly crossed his mind to try to kill them here, but they were too much on guard. He would be lucky to even catch them. Besides, then he wouldn't find out any more about Clete or the other businesses they were in. This was a dance, and he had made the first move. There would be other opportunities to get closer to them, and he knew that these vampires could not resist his bait.

After taking a few hearty breaths of the cool air, Angel took a mighty leap into the night.

CHAPTER FIVE

Buffy was sleeping lightly, as usual, when she heard the knock on the door of her motel room. At once, she was awake, hearing the hum of the decrepit air conditioner and the motel's neon sign crackling like an electric fence in the dry air. She slipped out of bed and wrapped a robe around her slender body. As Buffy hurried to the door, she glanced out a slit in the curtain of her window and saw the drab parking lot, illuminated by pale yellow flood lights. Although they were only six hundred miles from Los Angeles, it really seemed like the ends of the earth.

Pressing against the door, Buffy asked, "Angel, is that you?"

"It's me," he answered.

She opened the door, glanced past him, and said, "Come on in."

"Thanks," the vampire answered with a wry smile as he brushed past her. He looked around the small dingy room and said, "It's not exactly the Ritz-Carlton."

"It's not even Motel Six." Buffy shrugged and pulled her robe a bit tighter around her chest. "It's so cold, you could hang sides of beef in here, but I can't figure out how to turn down the air conditioner."

Angel found a frayed armchair and seated himself. "At least nobody has broken in while you're taking a shower, have they?"

"Just a couple of cockroaches." Buffy mustered a smile and sat on the bed across from him. "Any luck down there?"

"I think I talked to Raul and Machete in an old graveyard," said Angel, "but they were a bit shy. It won't be easy to get close to them, but I have a plan. I think I also ran into the sheriff that Sam and Riley were talking about. He's not so shy, and he knew I was a vampire."

Buffy blinked in surprise. "How could he tell?"

"I don't know. Maybe it was just a lucky guess." Angel turned to look at the door in the center of the wall. "Is my room on the other side?"

"Yes," Buffy said, jumping to her feet and fumbling on the nightstand for another key. "The connecting door is already unlocked, but here's your key."

"Thanks," Angel said as she dropped the fob into his hand.

"Are we going together to Mexico tomorrow night?" Buffy asked, bouncing on her toes.

Angel frowned thoughtfully before replying. "Some of us are going, but I'm not sure which contingent of our little Scooby Gang should go."

Buffy scoffed, "Sure, that would be hard to figure out, when one of us is the Slayer and has kicked more vampire booty than anyone in the known universe. Why would you pick me?"

Observing Angel's pained expression, she instantly regretted her outburst. "I didn't mean . . . all that."

"You have 'Made in America' written all over you," he answered somberly, "and you don't speak a word of Spanish."

"I took French in high school!" protested Buffy. "Yes, I got an incomplete, but I had a good excuse."

"In a fight, I'd rather have you than anyone," explained Angel, "but this is a fact-finding mission. Sam has more experience going undercover than you do, and her Spanish is excellent. You just couldn't pass for somebody having trouble getting into the United States."

Buffy pouted, but she understood. "Well, we're going to find out some facts tomorrow, while you sleep."

"I hope so," Angel answered, moving toward the connecting door. "Let's compare notes tomorrow evening. And it's good to see you, Buffy. I've missed you."

As her emotions rose, so did her self-defenses,

and Buffy couldn't do anything but nod. The idea of having Angel lying awake in bed on the other side of this paper-thin motel wall was having its effect on her, but she wasn't going to give in. At least, she didn't plan to give in. Although he could be an animal, he could also be a perfect gentleman, and that seemed to be his current mode.

"Good night, Buffy." Angel opened the door and slipped quickly into the next room.

The door was shut by the time Buffy said, "Sweet dreams, Angel."

By seven o'clock in the morning, the sun was already beating down with searing intensity when Riley and Sam finished their fitness run. Walking to cool down, Riley used his towel to mop the sweat off his face and neck. So far, he hadn't had a chance to talk to either Buffy or Angel, and he assumed both were still resting in their respective rooms. Of course, if Angel hadn't made it back to his room last night, then he probably wasn't going to return until darkness. But Angel was a big boy and could take care of himself; he had for several hundred years. Buffy was also self-sufficient, but she would need guidance and direction. This wasn't the Hellmouth, where vampires and demons just fell out of the trees.

Riley wasn't sure how they were going to proceed with the day's investigation, since most of their traditional channels had been cut off to them. Then he saw *them,* and he stopped dead in his tracks.

"Riley?" Sam said with concern. "What are you staring at?" She followed his gaze to a telephone pole near the two-lane highway that ran by the motel, but her quizzical expression told him that she still didn't notice them.

"Right there," he said excitedly. "Three crows sitting on the wire near the transformer."

She groaned. "Not with the crows again. Riley, you need a new hobby."

"This isn't a hobby," he explained. "It's processing the information that nature gives us."

"We saw two crows on our run," countered Sam.

"But they were dead. You may note that these crows are alive . . . and looking at us."

With a sigh, Sam crossed her arms. "Okay, I forget. . . . What do three crows mean?"

"Three crows a wedding," intoned Riley. Then he frowned, because going to a wedding seemed rather unlikely, given their present circumstances. "Where do weddings happen?" he asked rhetorically.

Sam shrugged. "Churches. Parks. Hotels. Country clubs—"

Riley snapped his fingers. "Right! We're going to the grand opening of that big resort today. Let's lay out our best clothes."

"The ones without camouflage?" asked Sam.

"Right. Let's shower, then wake up Buffy. I want to hear if Angel found out anything." Enthused by his new sense of purpose, Riley charged up the steps toward their room; fortunately, he didn't see his wife rolling her eyes, as only a wife can.

Over breakfast in the coffee shop, Buffy briefed them on what Angel had told her upon his return from Verdura, Mexico. The fact that he had conversed, however briefly and unsuccessfully, with Raul and Machete was encouraging. That he had run into Sheriff Clete Barton, who was pushing his weight around on the other side of the border as well, was discouraging. There seemed to be no end to the reach of Barton's long arms, Riley decided.

"Are you going back there with Angel tonight?" asked Sam.

Buffy scowled and lowered her head. "No, I think *you* are."

"Me?"

"Yes, he thinks that you're better typecasting for an illegal alien than I am." Buffy mock-pouted. "I'm too Valley Girl or something."

Riley wisely held his tongue, and Sam said, "Well, my Spanish is better than yours."

"Couldn't I be a deaf-mute or something?" asked Buffy.

"Don't worry," replied Riley, "we'll all go. I've got a special van parked up in Tucson, and we can put tracking devices on Sam and Angel and keep an eye on them."

Sam smiled. "You know Riley and his toys."

"Don't I, though," answered Buffy, sharing a moment of amusement with Sam.

Nothing like ragging on a guy to bring two women together, thought Riley. "We'll pretend to be tourists," he added. "I think Buffy and I can pull that off. We'll drive up to Tucson to get the van after the grand opening."

"Grand opening?" Buffy said warily. "Grand opening of what?"

The hotel and resort grounds were festooned with balloons and streamers, which seemed to belie the fact that the temperature was over one hundred at eleven o'clock in the morning. Huge banners in the parking lot proclaimed GRAND OPENING and LUXURY FAIRWAY HOMES, PHASE ONE. The ten-story, mauve-colored hotel sported signs that said DELUXE CONDOMINIUMS and SPECIAL SUMMER RATES, while the sprawling clubhouse on the edge of the golf course advertised LOW INTRODUCTORY MEMBERSHIPS and SUMMER GREENS FEES. Carved on a great slab of granite were the words RÍO CONCHAS, presumably the name of the resort. The only sign that looked out of place was a small one on the sidewalk that offered FREE HOT DOGS.

The parking lot was filled with cars with out-of-state license plates, and the clientele for the grand opening was decidedly older. As Riley, Sam, and Buffy walked toward the hotel, they were greeted by the sounds of a Jamaican kettledrum band pounding out lively island rhythms. That struck Riley as a bit odd, considering they were so close to Mexico and its wealth of music. But perhaps the owners didn't want to remind prospective customers just how close to Mexico they were. The tennis courts were tented over for the occasion, and that's where the band was playing. From a huge outdoor barbecue, the smell of sizzling hot dogs blended into the oppressive heat.

They strolled into the hotel lobby, and Sam elbowed him in the ribs. She pointed to a broad staircase rising behind an elaborate fountain, where a wedding party was gathering to have their pictures taken. She looked at him as if he had pulled off some minor miracle by predicting the wedding, and Riley just smiled. The handsome bride and groom looked young and prosperous, as if their parents owned this ostentatious palace in the middle of Nowhere Desert.

Sam and Buffy, both dressed in tight-fitting sundresses, began to attract some attention. Riley might as well have been invisible, which was all right with him. Waiters and salesmen descended upon them, trying to interest them in cheap margaritas and "very reasonable" condos and fairway homes. Río Conchas was a unique investment opportunity, they said, because this was the ground floor, "phase one," and all that. In one of the conference rooms, they could listen to a brief sales presentation that was scheduled to start in ten minutes. Riley wondered if they would explain why anyone would want to live in Verdura, Arizona, even if the country club lifestyle was dirt cheap.

Letting the girls absorb the brunt of the attention,

Riley wandered over to the ballroom, where scores of guests were assembling for the wedding. He was more interested in these people, because they were locals, the cream of the community. The men dressed like country-western singers, with Stetsons, alligator boots, and garish jackets, and the women wore fashionable gowns more befitting a Broadway opening than a morning wedding in a border town. Still, it was quite startling to think there was so much money around here. Of course, the region had vast tracts of land, cattle ranches, copper and silver mines, pecan orchards, golf courses, and tourists. The wealth wasn't in stocks, bonds, and factories—it was in the dirt. This fancy resort was just an attempt to make some more money off that dirt.

Suddenly a heavy hand landed on his shoulder, and he turned to see Sheriff Clete Barton, dressed in his Western finery for the wedding. "Boy, I thought you had blown out of town," he said in a folksy manner filled with venom.

"Hey, I wouldn't miss this grand opening," Riley answered, trying to sound friendly. "My wife and I kinda like this part of the country, and the salesman said there are some real deals to be had."

"Is that why you were poking around the coroner's office yesterday?" asked Barton.

Riley smiled. "Just doing my job. But now it's the weekend, and I'm off-duty. So who's getting married?"

"My daughter, Lisa," answered the sheriff, steely-eyed. "To Frederick Tatum's son, Josh."

"Tatum," Riley said with feigned interest. "Isn't that the name of the big pecan farm along the border?"

"That's his, along with the land you're standing on." Barton squeezed Riley's shoulder, letting him know he was more muscle than flab, despite his appearance. "Now you know everything, so you can leave."

"But we just got here!" chirped a cheery voice.

Both of them turned to see Buffy, flanked by Sam. With their unerring sense of danger, the women had come to his rescue.

Riley shook off the big man's paw and said, "Sheriff Barton, this is Buffy Summers. She's an old friend from California, just visiting us for the weekend."

Barton doffed his cowboy hat and eyed her appreciatively. "Pleased to meet you, Miss Summers. And, Sam, it's good to see you again. Of course, we saw each other yesterday, when you were in your little nurse's uniform. By the way, Paco has been moved, and you won't find him again. Your husband was just telling me that you decided to stay for a while, even though your work here is finished."

Sam met his steely gaze. "I know what your report says, but ours says something different."

"I didn't think you had to file a report on this case," Barton said pointedly. "I thought you were off it."

"You don't know everything, Sheriff," Sam answered, sticking to her guns. "For example, you said that the tree-huggers had been releasing wolves into this habitat, but I found out that wasn't true. The wolf reintroduction program is hundreds of miles from here. Even so, that was a wolf print we found."

The sheriff shrugged his beefy shoulders. "They don't call them Mexican gray wolves for nothin'. They come over from Mexico—happens all the time. The only thing you people will ever prove is your ignorance."

"Clete, you aren't being rude to our guests, are you?" boomed a deep voice.

They all turned around to see a tall, handsome man of late middle-age, dressed in an expensive Italian suit. Riley felt ignored as the newcomer's gaze traveled from Buffy to Sam, and back again. "Please introduce me to these delightful creatures."

"Yes, Mr. Tatum. This is Samantha and Riley Finn, the ones I told you about. And this is their friend, Miss Buffy Summers." The sheriff's bluster was gone now, replaced by the obsequious tone of an underling who knew his place. "Folks, this is Mr. Frederick Tatum, the man who owns Río Conchas."

"But I'm selling it little by little," Tatum said good-naturedly, "in case you'd like to buy a piece of paradise." He gazed approvingly at Buffy. "I'll make you a special deal."

"I don't know if it's paradise," said Buffy, "when people are dropping dead in the desert."

That froze the smile on the tycoon's face, and Riley almost burst out laughing. Sheriff Barton stepped away from the group and motioned to them to follow him to a remote corner of the ballroom. By the time the five of them reconvened, Clete Barton had composed himself, but Frederick Tatum looked as if he wanted to strangle them.

"Look here," whispered Tatum, "I've got millions of dollars invested in this place, and I'm not going to lose it over the death of a few wetbacks. That happens all the time out here. We don't need bad publicity or ridiculous rumors. The next thing you know, you'll be talking about giant Gila monsters with laser-beam eyes! My family homesteaded this territory in the eighteen fifties, and we fought off Apaches and Mexicans and rustlers . . . and everybody else. I've got plenty of juice in Washington, enough to get rid of the three of you. Go get your free hot dogs, then leave us the hell alone!"

"What about all the dead crows?" asked Riley. "What's causing that?"

Tatum whirled on him, scowling darkly. "I don't know, but more than crows and wetbacks can wind up dead in the desert. Don't you forget that."

The wealthy landowner stomped away, but the sheriff lingered for a moment, smiling like a rattlesnake. "If I were you, I'd think about what the man said. Frederick Tatum is not a good person to have as an enemy, and neither am I."

"Do we have until sundown to get out of town?" asked Buffy sweetly. "I've always wanted some dude in a cowboy hat to tell me that."

Clete Barton looked as if he was about to explode, and his meaty hands balled into fists. As much as

Riley would have enjoyed watching Buffy clean his clock, they were woefully outnumbered, and discretion was the better part of valor.

"Come on, let's go," Riley said, shepherding the women toward the door. "We're not going to watch their sales presentation either."

As they walked through the lobby, Riley frowned at Buffy. "I've forgotten how quickly you cut to the chase."

"Yeah," she agreed. "Tact 101—never my favorite subject. People also say I have a problem with authority, especially when it's rude authority."

"They'll be watching us now," Sam said with concern as she glanced over her shoulder at two uniformed deputies who were trailing them through the lobby.

"Then we watch them first," countered Buffy. "I think that sheriff deserves some heavy-duty recon. He hassled Angel last night too. Maybe we should put off going to Mexico in order to see what he's up to." She poked Riley in the arm. "So let's get your fancy van. And maybe some new cowboy boots . . . just so we'll fit in."

"Right," Riley answered, wondering how wise it had been to call in two free spirits like Buffy and Angel.

A vampire's sleep is never deep—it's more of a soothing rest, like the twilight between being asleep and fully awake. With all the drapes pulled tightly shut and the lights turned off, his motel

room was suitably dark, but his senses were alert—
alert enough to hear the door open into Buffy's
room next door.

Angel sat up, expecting to hear Buffy's voice or
her petite footsteps. It had been difficult to think of
her lying over there, alone, and not get aroused by
thoughts of what they could be doing. There was
always something about an anonymous motel room
that brought out the animal in him and, he supposed, most people. It would take all of his self-
discipline not to make a move on her, but he knew
he shouldn't.

The love and intimacy they had shared had been
special—fantastic—but it had also been tarnished by
distrust. Buffy's mission in life was to kill vampires,
and he was a vampire. Yes, he was unique in that he
had a soul, but he couldn't function properly unless
he maintained an edge of unhappiness. Happiness
would end the curse that made him almost human
and a servant to the downtrodden and helpless.
Buffy had made him too happy, and he had made her
too miserable.

He hoped he would hear her voice, but instead he
heard two unfamiliar men whispering to each other.
That was followed by drawers opening and suitcase
latches snapping. Someone was searching Buffy's
room.

Moving as quietly as the desert breeze, Angel
sprang from his bed and dashed toward the connecting door. It was still unlocked, and he knew he

couldn't lock it without making a telltale noise. He had left the DO NOT DISTURB sign on his outer door, but he doubted it would stop these intruders. They had probably gone through Riley and Sam's room, too, or were planning to do so. He could have escaped, but Angel wanted to meet these fellows who were diligently combing through Buffy's belongings, and he assumed they would try the connecting door before they left.

After a few more drawers and suitcases slammed shut, Angel heard whispers coming closer to the connecting door. The doorknob slowly began to turn, and he braced himself. Pressing against the wall, he hid himself behind the door as it swung open, and he watched the first hulking figure enter. Knowing there were two of them, he held perfectly still until the second one entered. Before they could turn on the light, he sprang from the shadows and grabbed both of them by their throats.

They screamed and choked and flailed their fists against him, but Angel was in vampire mode. He lifted their shuddering bodies into the air and demanded, "Who sent you? Who do you work for?"

Neither one of them would answer, and one tried to pull a gun. Before he got the weapon out of his shoulder holster, Angel cracked their heads together like two coconuts, and he dropped their twitching bodies to the floor. Swiftly, he dashed into Buffy's room, expecting to find a mess, but the intruders had neatly repacked and shut her luggage. That made

Angel suspicious, and he flung open her largest suit-case.

Lying right on top of Buffy's stylish clothes was a large bag of cocaine.

"Great," Angel muttered, his face still distorted by vampirism. "Not only a search job but a plant job."

Outside on the highway, a siren wailed, and it was definitely coming closer.

CHAPTER SIX

With the police car siren screaming ever nearer, Angel looked out the window of the cheesy motel room. It was bright daylight outside, probably mid-afternoon, and he was holding a bag of cocaine, with two thugs knocked unconscious in the other room. He couldn't do anything about those two being found, but he wouldn't let them find these illegal drugs in Buffy's room. The crooked sheriff wouldn't get his way that easily.

The vampire made sure the outer door was locked with the security chain in place, then he dashed into the bathroom, tore open the bag, and dumped the contents down the toilet. He was flushing away the planted evidence when the patrol car roared into the parking lot, its siren blaring. Angel stuffed the empty plastic bag in his pocket and looked around for an escape route. The bathroom had a small window that opened to the alley behind the motel, and he knew he could contort his body to fit through it. The problem was the blazing Arizona sun outside, and the fact that it would burn his pale skin like acid, turning him into dust if he got too much of it.

While heavy fists banged on the outside door and voices demanded, "Open up!" Angel looked around and found Buffy's bathrobe plus a couple of white bath towels. Since he had been resting fully clothed, he didn't have that much exposed skin to cover, and he was mainly concerned about his head, face, and hands. Avoiding the sunlight, he carefully opened the window as much as he could. Angel didn't want to break it, because he didn't want them to know how he had escaped. To his relief, he spotted a shady copse of cottonwood trees across the alley in the dry stream bed.

As the sheriff's deputies smashed down the door, the vampire swathed himself in terry cloth and squirmed headfirst out the window. He figured that he must look like a ghost as he dashed across the alley, down the riverbank, and into the welcome shade of the cottonwood trees. There he crouched and waited, still keeping himself covered as much as he could. A quick perusal of his surroundings told him that he had enough shade in the dry wash to run a few hundred yards in either direction, and he could move faster than any posse of mortal deputies.

Still, he was so angry, it took several moments for his face to return to human appearance. The worst part of all this was that they would find his supply of food. Of course, there were enough free-roaming cows on the range around him to supply him with his next meal, but he preferred to avoid hunting live prey. *Why didn't I stay in nice, peaceful Los Angeles?* wondered Angel.

He didn't know where Buffy, Sam, and Riley were, but he hoped they would stay away until darkness fell.

"How do these boots look on me?" Buffy asked, modeling the butterscotch ostrich-skin cowboy boots she had pulled off the rack of footwear. Sam nodded appreciatively, while Riley looked impatiently at his watch. Even though the Western-wear outlet store was on their way back to Verdura, he still felt as if they were wasting time. Although Sam was all-woman in every respect, the shopping gene was somewhat recessive in her, and he didn't usually have to put up with this, at least not while they were on the job.

Then again, Riley knew they were in no hurry. It wasn't as if they could stalk Sheriff Barton in broad daylight, and they couldn't exactly hunt vampires at four o'clock in the afternoon either. They had two vehicles outside in the parking lot—the rented sedan and his special van—so he could take off and leave the women to their shopping, if he wished. But that didn't seem a logical course of action, either, and he was worried the girls would get sidetracked.

Suddenly Buffy sat down and quickly pulled off the boots. "I like them because they make me look tall, but they'll make my bank account look small. Let's get out of here before I go totally cowgirl."

Feeling bored and slightly uneasy, Riley happened to glance out the store window into the parking lot. When he did, it was his turn to come to rapt attention. A sheriff's patrol car from Verdura was parked beside the silver rent-a-car, and two deputies were studying it. One of them produced a mobile phone and made a phone call. The deputies apparently didn't know that the white Chevy van parked a few spaces away was theirs too.

"Don't look now," whispered Riley, "but we've got company." He nodded to the scene in the parking lot, and Sam and Buffy slowly turned in that direction.

"Why, those cornpone cowboys!" snapped Buffy. "I'm going to deal with them." She started to march out of the store, but Riley stopped her.

"Wait," he cautioned. "I know we didn't do anything wrong, but they don't need much excuse to drag us in."

"Or drag us out into the desert," added Sam.

"If they know we're inside here, why don't they come in?" asked Buffy.

Riley looked around at the dozen or so customers and salesclerks in the outlet store. "They don't want any witnesses, or to make a scene. We'll have to abandon that car, but it can't be helped."

"How are we going to get out of here without making a scene?" asked Buffy.

Riley smiled and selected a broad-brimmed cowboy hat off the rack, then he grabbed a faded denim jacket and tried it on. Satisfied that these new articles of clothing fit, he said, "Have either one of you got an eyebrow pencil?"

"I do," Buffy answered, fishing in her purse and producing the item. "What are you going to do?"

"Grow myself a quick mustache," he answered, "to go with the rest of my disguise. When I go out the front door, you head out the back. As soon as you see the van, hop in."

The girls pretended to shop while Riley went to the cashier and paid for his hat and jacket. Then he ducked into the rest room and drew a quick mustache on his upper lip. It wouldn't undergo careful scrutiny, but he didn't intend to let anyone get that close to him. As he walked back through the store, he nodded to Sam and Buffy, put on his sunglasses, and pulled the cowboy hat low over his forehead. With his head bowed, very little of his face was visible.

He didn't even look at the deputies as he strode to the white van, because he didn't want to make eye contact. They weren't looking for a cowboy in a van but for three city slickers, two of whom were knockouts in sundresses. Without incident, he unlocked the van, climbed in, and started her up. In his rearview mirror he could see the deputies still lurking near the rental car, conversing with someone on their mobile phone.

Riley was sure he was out of their line of sight before he veered around the corner and headed toward the loading dock at the back of the store. Obeying his orders, Buffy and Sam scurried out the rear entrance, and he popped open the passenger door. By the time he had slowed down, they were in the van, squeezing into the passenger seat beside him.

As they roared away, Sam smiled admiringly at her husband and wiped the smudge off his upper lip. "You make a cute cowboy."

"Better duck down," he said. "We have to drive by them to get back on the highway."

As she ducked her head between her legs, Buffy grumbled, "I can't believe this—it's like something out of a Steven Seagal movie!"

"Now we'll have to go undercover for sure," said Riley. "We might be able to operate more freely on the Mexican side of the border."

"What about getting back to the motel?" Sam asked, her head under the dashboard. "And Angel."

"They probably went there first," Riley answered as he drove past the two deputies and the car they were keeping under close scrutiny. "To return to the motel is going to take some planning, because we have to disappear."

As the blue shadows of night crept across the craggy desert, Riley checked his watch; it was almost 9:00.

He was grateful that Arizona didn't observe daylight saving time, or the long day would have been even longer. They were parked in back of a feed store about a quarter of a mile from the Bates Motel, where one or more squad cars had been stationed all afternoon, waiting for their return. In the seat beside him, Buffy ate a microwave burrito while Sam manned the communications console in the back of the specially equipped van. It was configured to look like a commercial vehicle, with panels instead of windows to discourage prying eyes. The crackling voices of police-band radio echoed throughout the vehicle, as they had for hours. A second stream of voices came from captured mobile phone conversations as the local lawmen carelessly spilled their plans.

He rapped on the partition separating the passenger compartment from the rear section. "Any change?"

A small window opened, and Sam's face appeared. She was wearing headphones and glasses, which made her look like a high school student. "No, they're still on duty," she answered. "And Sheriff Barton is still yelling at all his deputies for letting us get away. I think I've got enough samples of his voice to generate just about anything we want. The computer is compiling it."

"Good," Riley said, glancing at the slate-gray skies swept with salmon-colored clouds. A couple drops of rain struck his dusty windshield. "Have you got a fix on Sheriff Barton?"

"I'm working on it," answered Sam. "I'm going to

activate the remote receiver and triangulate his signal. And I just sent our message about the crows to Dr. Genzo. Being the weekend, I'm not sure when I'll get an answer." She shut the window and returned to her equipment and the stream of disembodied voices.

"Who's Dr. Genzo?" asked Buffy.

"He's a biologist in our organization," answered Riley. "We've asked him about the dead crows—what they could mean."

"You're still on about the crows?" Buffy asked with amusement.

Riley shrugged. "They haven't failed me yet."

The Slayer peered at the darkening skies. "You know, I'm pretty sure I could outrun a few doughnut-stuffed deputies."

"I'm sure you could too," answered Riley, "but they have squad cars, and maybe helicopters. Once they see you, they'll know we haven't left the area, and we want them to think we're gone. There's a safe way to get rid of them, and I'd like to try that first. Do you think it's dark enough for Angel to move around?"

"I'd say so," answered Buffy. From the jagged mountains to the north came a brilliant flash of lightning, ripping static through the voices in the air. A rumble of thunder followed a few seconds later. "Whoa! It looks like they might have some other kind of weather here besides blast furnace."

"Believe it or not, they have monsoons," answered Riley. "Those are ocean storms that come up the Gulf of California and get slowed down by the mountains. Did you know that southern Arizona leads the nation in per capita deaths from lightning strikes?"

"I didn't know that," answered Buffy. "I bet most of them are golfers."

Riley smiled. "That's true. Good deduction."

Buffy returned the smile and looked at the empty burrito wrapper in her lap. "You never did think much of my brain, Riley. But I depend on it more now than when you and I . . . were together."

"Back then, you were like a raw nerve," he answered wistfully. "All action and reaction, a bundle of energy and physicality. I remember the first time I saw you fight—it was like looking at that lightning bolt, a force of nature. I didn't think you could possibly be controlled."

"You came close," she whispered.

Riley shifted uneasily in his seat. "I got lucky."

Rain began to fall upon the twilit desert, beating a gentle rhythm on the roof of the van. Riley opened his mouth, but didn't trust himself to say anything, because the woman beside him in the skimpy sundress was still a primal force of nature, the strongest yet most vulnerable being he had ever known. She was beautiful and ethereal, and seemed no more real than the creatures of the night they had hunted side by side. She could break his arm or break his heart with the slightest motion.

"You were my 'normal' boyfriend," she said softly.

"Normal? *Me?*"

She shrugged her delicate shoulders. "In comparison. Sure, you were living a double life and all that . . . but for a while there, I almost felt like a regular student. Thanks for that."

"You're welcome," he said hoarsely, gazing into her huge green eyes.

Suddenly the partition window opened, and Sam's voice broke into their reverie. "I've got the sheriff's position!" she announced. "It's only about two miles from here."

"Good job," Riley said, clearing his throat and snapping back into business mode. "Can you send a fake call to that unit at the motel?"

Sam produced a pen and a pad of paper. "Sure, sweetie. The computer can do Barton's voice better than he can. What do you want to tell them?"

"Just tell them to return to the station," said Riley, "and that another unit will replace them."

"Got it," replied Sam. "Hey, did I see lightning out there?"

"In the mountains," answered Riley.

Sam looked pointedly at Buffy. "They say it never strikes twice in the same place."

"Lightning's not stupid," Buffy answered, returning Sam's gaze. Riley wasn't sure, but he thought that some silent pact had been settled between the two women.

"I'll send them their orders," Sam replied, disappearing into the electronics-filled rear compartment.

With a sigh, Riley started the van's engine, and

they slowly pulled out of the parking lot of the feed store.

As the long shadows crept across the parking lot, so did Angel. He had left his hiding place in the arroyo in order to count the number of enemies arrayed against him. The two thugs who had tried to plant the drugs on Buffy had apparently recovered and slunk away, but the deputies remained. Fortunately, Buffy, Sam, and Riley hadn't returned yet, but that might mean they had been captured elsewhere. Angel couldn't shake the feeling that his friends had done something to bring all this unwelcome attention upon them. Buffy was impulsive like that. As a gentle rain pelted him and lightning briefly lit the thick clouds over the mountains, Angel scurried behind a Dumpster and crouched down to watch the watchers.

To his surprise, the deputies got into their squad car and drove away from the motel. Angel was about to make a move toward their abandoned rooms when a suspicious-looking white van pulled into the parking lot. The van stopped, and another thug—this one in a ten-gallon cowboy hat—jumped from the van and dashed through the rain into Riley's room. Angel got a glimpse of him in a flash of lightning, and he covered the same ground in about one tenth the time.

Just as the new arrival opened the door, Angel tackled him, and his weight propelled both of them into the dark motel room. The cowboy landed on the floor with an oomph that drove the wind out of him, and he barely put up a fight as Angel hurled him onto his back.

"Angel! It's me!" gasped his quarry between labored breaths.

The vampire took a closer look at the stricken cowboy. It was dark, but his vision didn't need much light. "Riley?"

"Yes . . . aaghh. I guess . . . you're all right."

Angel let his fierce vampire visage fade from his face, and he helped his comrade to his feet. "Where are the girls?"

"Out . . . in the van." Riley coughed and looked around the overturned room. "What happened here?"

"They tried to plant drugs on us. These are not nice people," he added dryly.

"They're hiding something," Riley rasped, the color returning to his face. "Let's go on the offensive."

"I agree," Angel said, scooping a dark object off the floor. "Here's your cowboy hat."

"It's my disguise." Riley put on his hat, moved to the open door, and peered into the rainy parking lot. "Let's get our stuff out of these rooms before they get back, then we're going to do some spying on the sheriff."

"Is that where he *lives?*" Angel asked, peering over the top of some thick hedges that buttressed a stone wall topped by cut glass. Only by standing on the top of the van were he and Riley able to get a view of the palatial ranch house south of the pecan orchard. The mansion sprawled across a most unusual ground covering for this part of the world—a grassy lawn—and was surrounded by horse corrals to the east and a complex of large buildings to the west. The sheriff's patrol car was parked in front of this impressive abode, and a fleet of delivery trucks lined a driveway near the buildings. The rain had turned into an erratic drizzle, and the desert smelled as if it had been washed with disinfectants, thanks to the pungent scent of the creosote. A distant flash of lightning and a low roll of thunder reminded them that the storm was still lurking over the mountains.

Riley lowered his binoculars and answered, "That's not the sheriff's place. It's Frederick Tatum's house, the guy who owns the pecan orchard and the new resort."

"Oh, yeah," Angel answered, "the guy you pissed off while I was asleep, minding my own business."

"We only went to a public place," Riley answered defensively. "You'd think he'd be in a good mood at his daughter's wedding, but he seemed worried that we would find out something."

"So let's find out something," Angel concluded, leaping down from the van.

Buffy was waiting for him on the ground, and she was dressed in one of Sam's camouflage fatigues, wearing a helmet and communications headgear. "I'm ready," she said.

Suppressing a laugh at the sight of Commando Buffy, Angel answered gravely, "I think I can handle this one by myself."

Before she had time to protest, he gathered himself into a crouch and leaped over the ten-foot wall and hedge with a single bound. Angel hurried across the expanse of lawn, keeping his ears open for any sound of an alarm, but he heard nothing except for some laughter coming from the grand house. It sounded as if the wedding reception was still going on. He paused near the corrals and some covered stalls, where a skittish black horse snorted in alarm and banged against its metal enclosure. Angel quickly moved away from the animal before it could make too much noise.

Using the delivery trucks as cover, Angel dashed past the house and headed to the complex of buildings on the other side of the property. A golden pecan logo with the words TATUM PECANS emblazoned the panels of every truck and every building, and he could smell the old husks in the Dumpster. Outside the structure were tall, yellow tree-shakers, huge mechanical rakes, and various bins and conveyer belts. He peered into a window of the processing plant and saw more conveyer belts, a forklift, cracking and shelling machines, choppers, and roasters— the kind of stuff he would expect to see in a pecan-harvesting operation.

As he cowered in the shadows, Angel had the sinking feeling there was nothing amiss here. They were taking extreme risks only to spy on a wealthy man who was doing nothing more than enjoying his abundance. The fact that Sheriff Clete Barton was visiting Frederick Tatum didn't strike him as unusual, either, considering their offspring had just wed each other. With any luck, the kids would take a long honeymoon.

Angel heard a porch door squeak open, then slam shut, and he tensed for a moment. The laughter inside the house had stilled, but that didn't mean the party was over. He heard footsteps crunching through the gravel of the driveway, accompanied by a low rumble of thunder in the distance. He sensed the walker was coming closer, but the footsteps suddenly stopped, and a guttural voice began to mutter. It almost sounded like an incantation in some forgotten language—or perhaps a drunk talking to himself—it was hard to tell, because the words seem to blend with the rolls of thunder. Angel moved forward cautiously in a crouch to see what he could make out in the driveway.

What he saw was a hulking figure near the sheriff's patrol car—probably Barton himself. Still muttering under his breath, the big man opened the trunk and took out what looked like a large rug or tarpaulin. Angel wanted to move closer, but there was nothing but open ground between his position and the sheriff's car. The hulking figure tilted his head back, as if he was smelling the air, then he turned and seemed to look directly at Angel. He remembered Barton's words from the night before: "I can smell you buggers." Barton's eyes glowed eerily in his dark face, but he quickly turned away and slammed his trunk door shut. Then he threw the rug over his shoulders like a cape, hunched his back, and began to stomp around. After a few moments of this drunken dance, accompanied by howls and guttural singing, the clouds opened up, and the rain began to pour down. As Angel got drenched, he began to wish that he, too, had an old rug to use as a cape.

He wiped the rain out of his eyes and looked around, but the dancing lunatic was gone. Thunder rumbled across the desert, and lightning flashed in the cloudy sky, briefly illuminating the drenched vehicles and machinery on the grounds of the estate. Angel had the feeling that the moment to discover anything had passed, and it would be best to escape before he was spotted by someone sober.

On his way back to Riley's van, Angel skirted along the side of the house, thinking he might catch a glimpse through a window. He looked for one that cast a bit of light, and found a multipaned dormer decorated with bits of stained glass, spilling tiny rainbows into the gloom. He carefully maneuvered around a prickly cholla plant and looked through a lower corner of the window, finding himself staring into a breakfast nook. At the table, his back to Angel, sat a broad-shouldered man in a blue bathrobe who was going over lined pages that might have been accounting statements. Country-western music twanged on a small radio, and the whole scene looked so normal on this rainy night that Angel felt momentarily guilty for harassing these people.

So they didn't want outsiders poking into their business, and they had whitewashed a tragic incident to avoid unpleasant publicity. That made them no worse than lots of other businessmen. If given a preference, they probably didn't want illegal aliens expiring on their doorsteps. The sheriff was obnoxious, but he had gone across the border to look for Raul and Machete, the same as Angel had done. Who's to say he wasn't just doing his job, trying to bring them to justice? Sure, planting drugs was going overboard, but these weren't the first lawmen to have done that. And lots of people found Riley annoying, Angel among them.

He decided it was best to go back to Mexico, where they knew the bad guys were at large. As he watched Tatum at his desk, the vampire smelled something musky and animal-like, and he heard the almost imperceptible squishing of footsteps in the mud. He whirled around just as a huge, hairy beast hurtled toward him.

Angel caught the monster's immense jaws on his arm rather than his neck, but the weight of the thing still propelled him against the house. He crashed into it with a thud and slid to the ground.

Before the vampire could even muster his strength, he was fighting the long fangs and deadly claws of the monster. Its breath was as hot as a blast furnace and as rank as vomit, and its savagery was primeval. The animal was intent upon tearing him apart, and he cringed with pain as it tore gashes in his flesh. Angel punched the bushy head with all his strength, but his blows had almost no effect. All four of its mighty legs continued to dig in the mud, forcing its weight upon him. Lightning briefly illuminated the area, and he got his first good look at the beast's head. Canine snout, canine teeth, long pointed ears, thick haunches, and the glowing eyes of the devil . . .

It was a huge silver wolf.

Angel staggered to his feet, but the creature leaped again for his throat. He went down under the weight of slashing claws and teeth, with every ounce of its being intent upon killing him. When Angel forced the jaws away from his neck, the jagged teeth sunk into his shoulder instead. The searing pain almost plunged him into blackness, and he had to fight to keep his wits. The bite burned like venom . . . *like fire*.

This was no ordinary wolf, and Angel feared the beast would kill him. He knew it wouldn't quit until it did.

CHAPTER SEVEN

Pinned down in the mud by a monstrous wolf, Angel hardly had time for his lengthy life to pass before his eyes. He couldn't even go on the offensive, because his defense was too busy failing. Angel couldn't move the brute—it took all his might just to fend off the ripping teeth and slashing claws. In the struggle, it was hard to tell which creature growled louder: the wolf or the vampire.

From nowhere, a shape flashed through the rain, plowing feet first into the shaggy wolf and knocking the beast off Angel. His savior bounced lithely to her feet, her fists and eyes pointed toward the stunned animal, and Angel managed to scramble to his feet.

His panting breath came in heaves, and he realized that he was covered in blood—his own.

"I know you don't need any help," breathed Buffy. "You had him right where you wanted him."

"Thanks," Angel rasped, moving a few steps toward her right so the wolf's attention was more divided. The beast snarled and growled at them, his huge silvery mane of fur standing at attention, and saliva and blood dripping from his massive jaws.

"Bad doggie!" scolded Buffy.

"That's not a dog," panted Angel. "It's a wolf—a big one."

"Sam said there was—"

Before Buffy could finish her thought, the wolf leaped again toward Angel, hoping to finish the prey it had already wounded. The vampire wasn't taken by surprise this time, and he sidestepped the attack while plunging a fist into the animal's gut. At the same moment, Buffy whirled with a deadly leg-kick and smashed the beast in the snout. The one-two punch drew blood, and the stunned brute backed away, its whimpers quickly turning to snarls.

A second later a door banged open, and a voice demanded, "Who's out there? What's going on?" The light from the doorway cast a long shadow across the lawn, and the man seemed to be holding a weapon, like a rifle or shotgun.

Angel pulled Buffy back against the house, hoping the wolf would distract the angry gunman. Sure enough, the animal bolted into the gloomy rain, and the man fired a wild shot over its head. Buffy and Angel immediately escaped by skirting along the side of the house, their movements aided by rumbles of thunder.

Buffy spoke into the microphone on her helmet. "Echo One to base: Use alternate pickup B. Repeat, use alternate pickup B." She evidently got an acknowledgment, because she nodded and said, "Out."

"You've been hanging around Riley and Sam too much," Angel observed when they stopped for a second behind a delivery truck.

Buffy surveyed his bloody wounds, which would have killed a mortal man. "I don't think you've been hanging around them enough. We're a team, Angel. None of this lone-wolf stuff, if you'll pardon the expression."

"Noted," he said, dabbing his shredded clothing to an oozing slash. "He tore up my best jacket."

"We're not going to go over the wall," said Buffy. "Riley found a service road in the orchard and will pick us up there. Ready to go."

He gave her a pained smile. "Yes, and I promise not to go alone next time."

With Buffy leading the way, they dashed across the lawn, jumped a low wooden fence, and vanished into neat rows of tall, bushy trees. Both the greenery and the geometric symmetry of the orchard seemed at odds with the surrounding desert. As they jogged through the rows of stately pecan trees, the canopy of leaves caught most of the rain—it was as if they were in another world. Angel kept the pace up, even though every step brought a jab of pain from his wounds. He knew he would recover quickly, but he didn't want to take any more damage.

He kept glancing back over his shoulder, worried that the wolf was trailing them. In fact, he did see a low shape stalking them, moving at their own speed. When he tried to point it out to Buffy, the shape was gone.

"There's the van!" she said, pointing toward a boxy shape parked among the trees. She turned on her headphones and said, "Echo one to base: Give me confirmation."

The van blinked its headlights at them, and Angel turned around in that instant of light. He could see a monstrous shape bearing down on them. "Hurry!" urged the vampire. "It's right behind us!"

"You go!" Buffy said, whirling around. "I'll give you time."

"No!" Angel insisted, grabbing her arm. "This is not a normal wolf. We can make it—run flat out!"

So they did run flat out, even as the four-legged apparition gained ground on them. The side door of the van flew open, and Sam motioned to them with a flashlight. At the same time, Riley jumped out of the passenger door and tossed something over their heads. Twenty feet behind them a gas bomb exploded, and the wolf ran wide to get around the greenish cloud, giving Buffy and Angel another precious few seconds. Except for the detour, the monstrous beast never slowed down.

They dove into the side door of the van, and Sam hurled the door shut just as a powerful force slammed into the vehicle, rocking them like an auto collision. Riley gunned the engine, and the van bounced down the dirt road, jarring the passengers in the back.

Angel had ridden over to the orchard in the front seat with Riley. Now he looked around and saw that he was surrounded by beeping electronics equipment and two camo-garbed women staring at his wounds with concern. Sam produced a first-aid kit and began ripping off his shredded shirt.

"I'll be okay," Angel said, brushing her hands away. He was angry and embarrassed that he had been beaten by a lone animal, no matter how powerful it was. He was also abashed that he had put himself in a position to need rescuing.

"Let me treat you," insisted Sam. "I'm a certified EMT."

"He's not a good patient," said Buffy. "Never has been."

"Okay," Angel conceded, pulling away the remains of his shirt to reveal his muscular chest covered with bloody gashes.

"What was that thing?" Sam asked, dousing a gauze pad with antiseptic and beginning her ministrations.

"Angel found your wolf," said Buffy. "It was as big as a pony, with silver fur."

"Are you sure it was a wolf?" asked Sam. "The Mexican gray wolf isn't nearly that big."

"This wasn't a normal wolf," Angel answered,

grimacing from the pain. "It was like a dire wolf—
something from the old forests of Europe."

"Yes, these are impressive claw marks," answered
Sam. "And those bites in your shoulder—more like a
bear than a wolf. You should be dead, Angel. No
more talking—just hold still and try to rest."

Sam's skillful hands applied a large dressing to the
worst of his wounds. They moved him onto a blanket, which also made him more comfortable, and
Angel closed his eyes and allowed his head to loll
back into Buffy's lap. There were worse fates than
having two lovely women fawning over him, and the
gentle rocking of the vehicle lulled him to sleep.

A little before midnight, they pulled off the road and
parked behind an abandoned gas station, and Angel
stirred fitfully from his sleep. Sam opened the side
door, and she and Buffy got out and gratefully
stretched their legs. The rain had stopped, and the
freshly doused desert smelled clean and cool. The
driver's door opened, and Riley approached them,
still wearing his cowboy hat, of which he had apparently grown very fond.

"Okay," he said, "the border crossing is only about
a mile up the road. I took back roads to get here, to
make sure no one was following us. We seem to be in
the clear. With Americans entering Mexico, the
chances of the van being searched are slim, but we
can get into a lot of trouble for bringing guns there.
Sam, you'll have to hide all the weapons in the false

bottom, and we'll do our camouflage thing to the interior. Remember, we're just four goofy kids off on a wild weekend in Puerto Peñasco, also known as Rocky Point. That's the closest beach to us, on the upper part of the Gulf of California."

He pointed to the women, who were still wearing fatigues. "So you two had better change your clothes. Angel, I'm sorry, but you'll have to get some clean clothes on."

"No problem." Angel groaned as he staggered out of the rear compartment. Although still banged up, he was already feeling much better, and Sam shook her head with amazement.

"I think I've got an Hawaiian shirt in my bag, for disguise." Holding the bandages to his bare chest, he reached into the van and grabbed his small suitcase.

The girls retrieved their sundresses, and everyone retired to the shadows of the empty parking lot to change. When Sam finished dressing, she pulled up the rug on the floor of the van's rear compartment, opened a secret panel, and carefully stashed their small but impressive collection of firearms. With some perfectly fitted Formica panels, Sam and Riley turned their tracking and communications consoles into tables, shelves, cup holders, and an entertainment center. Along with the two captain's chairs, the van now looked like a typical camper conversion.

Impressed, Buffy said, "If James Bond had a van, this would be it."

"That's the general idea," said Sam. "When we get

some time, I'd like to check in with headquarters."

"Why?" Riley asked with a scowl. "They're not going to be too happy with us. When they hear about that abandoned rent-a-car, they'll know we're still around here."

"To hell with them," snapped Buffy. "You're on vacation!"

"I could use a little rest," said Angel. With a grunt, he crawled back into the van and sat down in a captain's chair.

Sam stepped close to the door and said, "You never did tell us what you found back there, except for the wolf."

Angel shrugged. "I saw a big man who looked drunk—it might have been the sheriff. He got something out of his car, then started dancing and singing in the rain. I saw a man in the kitchen who might have been Frederick Tatum. It was raining hard, and the wolf attacked me before I could get a clear look."

"Would he keep a wolf for a guard dog?" asked Riley.

"Doubtful. He shot at it," answered Buffy, "but missed."

Angel went on: "I couldn't get into the buildings, but I saw plenty of stuff for harvesting and processing pecans. Sorry there's not more to report."

Sam clapped her hands enthusiastically. "I think a change of scene would do us all good! So it's back to looking for Raul and Machete. But not tonight . . . tomorrow night."

"Tomorrow night," agreed Angel.

"Pretty girls up front with me," Riley said, heading back to the driver's seat of the van. "That should speed us through the border checkpoint."

As she shut the rear door, Sam gave Angel a sympathetic smile. "You rest, okay? Doctor's orders."

"Thanks, Doc," Angel answered wearily, thinking back over the last few months and welcoming the chance to catch up on some rest. "I'll be a good patient."

At midnight, there were few vehicles passing through the border entry point, and the two girls in the front seat definitely charmed the Mexican *federales*. They were waved through with the most cursory inspection, with no show of I.D. Rocky Point sounded like a logical destination for the beautiful young Americans, and it was close enough to the border that they didn't need any additional paperwork for the van.

Soon they were cruising over another dark highway, and Angel allowed himself to be lulled to sleep by the gentle rocking of the road.

The soothing sound of ocean waves breaking against the shore greeted Angel as he slowly returned to consciousness. He stirred on the bed in the darkened room and found his bleary eyes directed toward the slit of light coming through the curtains on the French doors. Like a moth drawn to the flame, Angel slipped out of bed and padded across the cool saltillo tiles to the edge of the light beam. He could go no farther, but he could peer out the slit in the curtain to see a patio, a low brick wall, and the white sands and blue sky beyond. The ocean itself was like a turquoise ribbon that expanded and contracted with every sigh of the waves.

A door clicked open, and Angel whirled around to see Sam looking at him from the doorway. "I see the patient is better," she said cheerfully. Sam was dressed in a sparkling blue bikini that concealed very little of her trim, athletic figure.

Seeing his shirt on a chair, Angel grabbed it and pulled it over his almost-healed wounds.

"Feeling better?" asked Sam. "Do you need anything?"

"An explanation," he said, moving back toward the bed. He sat down, then took a moment to look around. Apparently they were in a large suite, with a living room beyond this nicely appointed bedroom.

"We upgraded," Sam said with a smile. "Riley took a look at the fleabag hotels in Verdura, Mexico, and decided that we might as well actually go to Rocky Point, where the hotels are nice, as you can see. We found this two-bedroom bungalow on a secluded beach. You were dead to the world, so we carried you in. Fortunately, it was so late that nobody was around to pay much attention to us. We're only an hour away from Verdura."

Sam adjusted the back of her bikini bottom and laughed. "Apparently we're going to shoot our wad of expense money on this case, because we don't know if we'll have a job after this."

"Why not," Angel answered, mustering a smile.

"I would like to have a look at your wounds," Sam said, stepping closer.

Angel pulled back his shirt, and they both looked at his scars for a moment. "Almost healed," he reported. "I heal quickly."

"That's quite an advantage," Sam said thoughtfully. "If only we could clone you—"

"A race of good vampires with souls?" Angel asked with a trace of sarcasm. "Now *that's* scary."

"And impractical," Sam replied, sitting at the foot of his bed. "You need vampires to make more vampires, and then they wouldn't be good anymore. But the idea of immortality—that's the real attraction, isn't it?"

"Never fails," Angel said grimly, feeling a bit uncomfortable about the subject matter, Sam's proximity, and her skimpy bikini. "Where are Buffy and Riley?"

She shrugged. "The beach, looking around, getting a bite to eat. I volunteered to stay with you. It feels so good to just relax, get away from it all."

"I came here for a job," said Angel. "Sunbathing doesn't hold much attraction."

Sam laughed uneasily. "No, I guess not. Don't worry, we'll get back to business tonight. What's our plan to find Raul and Machete?"

"I know two places in Verdura where they hang out," answered Angel. "They weren't eager to deal with me before, but they were busy hiding out from

Sheriff Barton. I think if I have the right bait—"

"Me," Sam said frankly.

He nodded. "Yes, you. With you along, posing as a girlfriend, I want to sneak into the U.S. I think I can get their attention. But I warn you, this may be dangerous. I would take Buffy instead, but she's too—"

"All-American cheerleader," concluded Sam. "Yes, I agree. And Buffy's upfront, in your face, not good at hiding her feelings."

"She's also the Slayer," Angel added. "Vampires can sense that she's trouble. Some are attracted to the challenge, but I think Raul and Machete are the type to run from real trouble."

Sam abruptly stood up and said, "You get some rest, Angel, and so will I. We'll get back to work tonight. *Hasta luego.*"

He couldn't help but watch her saunter out of the room, her backfield in motion. *What have I gotten myself into?* the vampire wondered. *In this business, no paycheck ever comes easily.*

Buffy stood on some ancient stone steps that led down to the beach from a walkway that looked as if it had been there since the days of the Aztecs. She watched several amazing sights: One hippie couple was camped out on the beach in a pup tent with four dogs; two people were riding horses through the surf; another was riding a noisy ATV through the sand; and a group of six people were setting off fireworks, which were plentiful down here. Out in the water, people were tearing it up on Jet Skis. Nobody seemed to mind or find any of this activity unusual, when all of it would have gotten a person busted in California. The walkway connected several bungalows and small hotels, and it was lined with vendors in makeshift booths, selling sunglasses, cheap jewelry, trinkets, and food. None of this mattered as much to Buffy as the sun, which beat down with glorious warmth, drying her out from the wet night before.

She looked back and saw Riley ambling toward her along the walkway. He was still wearing his cowboy hat, looking like a tourist from Phoenix, and carrying two enormous plates full of Indian fry bread. As he walked, he scanned the cerulean sky as if searching for the meaning of life among the wispy clouds and blazing sun.

He finally reached her and handed her a paper plate with a disc of doughy deep-fried bread covered with honey, as she had ordered. His own fry bread had onions and melted cheese on top. He craned his head to look at the roof of the closest hotel.

"What are you looking for?" asked Buffy.

"Crows," Riley answered with a sheepish smile. "I know you think I'm crazy, but I'm still looking for black birds. I guess there aren't any at the beach."

"We've got seagulls," Buffy said, pointing to the sand, where several large gray birds were searching a strand of kelp that had washed ashore. "And a pelican or two. Plus we've got people breaking fourteen laws in California."

"Only this is Mexico," Riley answered with a smile. "It almost makes you wonder why we're breaking our necks fighting bad guys when all anybody wants to do is ride a horse on the beach."

Buffy tore off a piece of bread, popped it in her mouth, and chewed thoughtfully. The hot, crunchy dough began to warm her inside as much as the sun warmed her skin. "They're innocent," she said. "We're not. They don't know what we know."

"Oh, they know there's danger in the world. Unlike us, they just choose to ignore it." Riley stuffed a chunk of bread in his mouth and chewed.

"You've gotten a lot more cynical since I first met you," said Buffy. "Back then, you were going to save the world. What's changed? Is it that you don't think it's worth it, or you don't think you can?"

Riley frowned as he pondered the question. "At times, I feel like I'm fighting a war that I can't win. But then I think of monsters like Raul and Machete, and what they did to those people in the desert, and I know I can make a difference, however small. What about you, Buffy? What keeps you going?"

"I'm the Chosen One, remember? I'm not the one who does the choosing."

"You can't ever quit?"

She shrugged. "I've tried quitting. I've tried dying. Nothing ever seems to work."

"And your . . . personal life?" Riley asked hesitantly. "You don't think you'll ever settle down?"

"With a guy?" Buffy responded incredulously.

"The guys I like are not the settling-down type." She quickly added, "Present company excepted."

He answered softly, "I got lucky. Sam is one in a million."

"So if you ever lose her, it'll be rough." When Buffy realized how gloomy that remark was, she mustered a smile and said, "Don't worry. G.I. Jane can take care of herself."

"I hope so," he answered with a heavy sigh. "Sometimes I put her in a lot of danger. Like tonight."

"We'll back them up," Buffy said with determination. "We don't want to lose either one of those two."

"No," Riley agreed gravely. "That won't happen."

CHAPTER EIGHT

Samantha Finn took a deep breath and adjusted her pink sundress so that even more cleavage showed, if that was possible. She was more comfortable in camouflage fatigues, but she could look plenty slutty when given a chance, and the high heels, tight-fitting dress, heavy eye-makeup, and spiky hair did the job. She knew she had the shapely muscular legs to complete the package. Angel could hardly look at her without grinning, which was a good sign; Buffy and Riley both scowled whenever they looked at her, which was another good sign. To heck with crows—these were the best omens she could imagine, even if running at any rate of speed would be a problem in that outfit.

The van was parked on a side street in Verdura, Mexico, not far from the red-light district of bars and strip joints that was their target. They had already checked the old cemetery south of town, and Angel and Buffy had pronounced it clean of vampires. That meant Raul and Machete were back at their old haunts, if they were still in the border town at all.

"I'm ready!" Sam said, hefting a garish sequined purse that contained a tracking device. As long as she carried that purse, Riley and Buffy would always know where she was, and she would always be armed with a nine-millimeter Glock, plus a fat wooden stake.

Angel straightened his denim jacket, which Riley had loaned him to replace his shredded leather one. It also contained a tracking device and a stake hidden in the interior pocket. "You look great," he said, giving Sam an appreciative once-over. "If I know vampires, they won't turn us down this time."

"No kidding," Riley grumbled, his scowl growing deeper. "If there's trouble, you know how to alter the signal to alert us. You've also got an extra bug to plant on somebody. Hey, how far are we going with this? Are we going to nail these guys at the first opportunity?"

"I think we want to find out about their operation," answered Angel. "There may be more vampires working this scam, or they may have other scams. If there are more vampires here, we should find out soon enough, because they don't stray far from each other."

"I agree," Buffy said somberly. "There could be a

huge nest of them, or it could just be Raul and Machete. We won't know unless Angel gets close to them."

"Are you going across the border with these two coyotes?" Riley asked with concern. "We won't be able to follow you or be much help out there in the desert."

"I don't think we need to go that far," Sam interjected. She cast a worried glance at Angel. "At least I hope not."

"Okay," said Angel, "we won't go that far. The important thing is to prevent any more innocent people from going into the desert with vampires as guides—agreed?"

"Agreed," said Riley and Buffy together, and an uneasy pact was formed on that dark street corner.

Angel held out his arm to Sam. "Okay, let's go turn some heads."

"Sounds good." With a smile, she took his brawny arm and sauntered with the dashing vampire down the uneven sidewalk. With a glance over her shoulder, she saw Riley and Buffy rolling their eyes as they hurried into the van. One thing was certain: They would be keeping a close eye on their delectable piece of bait, which was just what she wanted.

Sam and Angel rounded the corner and found themselves cruising the tenderloin of Verdura, just east of the more respectable parts of town. This was definitely the honky-tonk street, with lots of garish neon, seedy bars, loud music, strip joints, fleabag hotels, and drunk Americans weaving down the sidewalk. Some of them looked shockingly young, although Sam was no old lady. She felt bad that all she was getting to see was the seamy underbelly of Verdura. There were palatial homes in the hills, and they had driven through modern suburbs and shopping areas on the western side of the city. All of this contrasted sharply with the Arizona city of the same name, which was nothing but a rural township with a collection of feed stores, gas stations, motels, old diners, and Tatum's incongruous new resort.

Sam sighed, because she wasn't here to ponder the economies of these two places that shared a name, a desert, and a border but were otherwise as different as night and day. Americans could come and go freely across the border, turning the Mexican side into their playground, but Mexicans had to risk their lives to enter Verdura, Arizona, which existed in some kind of Old West time warp. It wasn't fair or even very natural, but it wasn't in their power to correct; the best they could do was kill the bloodsuckers who profited from the inequities.

She and Angel ambled past a wizened Indian woman sitting in the doorway of an abandoned store. She looked as old as Methuselah, yet she held a very tiny baby in one hand and a plastic cup in the other. She held out the cup, looking for an offering. Sam didn't intend to stop and stare, but she did, forcing Angel to stop as well.

"Alms for the poor," said Angel. "This is a sight I've seen for hundreds of years."

Ignoring their conversation, the woman jiggled her cup insistently, and Angel dug in his pocket for a dollar bill, which he handed over. The old woman gave him a toothless grin and held up her baby for them to take a closer look.

"*Muy bonita,*" said Angel. Then he looked closer at the child, and a look of disgust came over his face.

"What is it?" asked Sam.

"Look at her neck," said Angel.

Sam peered more intently at the child, and her eyes widened at the sight of vampire fang marks on the emaciated child's neck. "She's trying to sell you the child," Sam whispered in horror.

"Yes," Angel agreed, looking troubled. "Is there a sign around my neck?" He held out a few more dollars and asked, "*¿Dónde está Raul y Machete?*"

The old woman grinned toothlessly and nodded, quickly grabbing the proffered bills. Then she pointed across the street toward a bar called La Bandera, according to the garish neon sign. "*Estan allí.*"

Angel nodded and grabbed Sam's hand. They carefully wound their way through slow-moving traffic to get to the other side, and Sam asked, "Do you suppose vampires are common here?"

"I'm beginning to think so," muttered Angel. "Let's hope she's right—it would save us some time."

"What about the baby?" Sam asked, glancing back over her shoulder.

Angel scowled. "Maybe I gave her enough money to take care of it for one night. We can't save everyone."

"I know."

Angel pushed open a heavy metal door, and they entered a dark bar with lots of wrought-iron fixtures, heavy wooden furniture, and bullfighting posters on every wall. The posters weren't so bad, but mummified bulls' ears, tails, and testicles hung from the ceiling and the posters, representing victories in *la corrida de toros*. The bar looked ancient and somber, as if it might have been a hangout for workers from the Spanish Inquisition. Nevertheless, it was filled with well-heeled tourists, hardened young men, and young women wearing even less than Sam. The smell of good brandy and cigar smoke filled the air, and their feet scraped through aged sawdust. Tasteful flamenco music played in the background, not loud rock, and there was no stage in sight.

"Blood sport," Angel said, glancing at a large bullfight poster. "That one's from Madrid in nineteen thirty-one."

"How can you tell?" asked Sam, who was unable to make out a date on the faded but still vivid work of art.

Angel shrugged. "I was there. I saw Machillo cut off that ear."

"Lucky you," replied Sam with distaste.

"Yes," Angel said wistfully, not noticing her sarcasm. "It was a wonderful season. Back then, the bulls were like the wolf I met last night—nothing like what passes for a bull now. One *toro* disemboweled El Guapo."

"Good for him," answered Sam. She was feeling disemboweled by several of the stares coming from the men and some of the women in the place. She teetered on one foot and tried to look half-drunk as she flirted in a slatternly fashion with the nearest dark-haired gigolo. She pulled Angel closer and whispered, "What kind of place is this?"

Her experienced escort gave the clientele a once-over. "I'd say this is a bar for hookers and their pimps."

"No kidding," Sam replied as a fat American tourist in shorts and T-shirt ambled up to them.

"Hey buddy," the tourist said to Angel, "what will it take for a couple of hours with Barbie doll here?"

"She's with me," Angel said, putting his hand around Sam's waist.

"Yeah, I know that, but what will it take for you to get lost?" the man asked insistently.

"Not tonight." Angel brushed past the man, hauling Sam with him. He headed for a row of booths in the back, but that scene was little better. Most of the bloodred enclosures were filled with people who were making out. Angel quickly steered Sam into an empty booth and sat protectively on the outside.

She didn't need much coaxing to get close to him, because the men were still eyeing her—an unfamiliar and exotic piece of fresh meat. "Are we going to ask about Raul and Machete?" she whispered.

He shook his head. "No, I made that mistake last time and got identified as a vampire. I think we'll just hang here and watch. I don't see anyone yet who fits the profile."

A Latin lounge lizard strolled by and stood staring at Sam while twirling the gold chains around his neck. She flirted drunkenly, hoping he wouldn't take it too seriously, and he winked. Angel tried to remain patient, but the man was obviously not going to go away.

"Can I help you?" Angel asked in Spanish.

"Yes, *amigo,* you can tell me what you're doing here," the man said with a sneer. He leaned over the table, letting his open jacket reveal a hunting knife stuck in his belt. "I know everyone. I must *approve* everyone, and you have not been approved."

The old shakedown, thought Sam. *They think Angel's a pimp, horning in on their territory. Maybe I've overdone the slutty party-girl look.*

While Angel slowly stewed, she decided to defuse the situation. "I approve of my *ángelito,*" she said in Spanish. To prove it, she gave him a big sloppy kiss on the mouth. To make it look good, the vampire was forced to return the kiss as passionately as possible.

Sam was unprepared for the mild rush along her central nervous system brought on by Angel's kiss. He tasted intoxicating, like the smell of brandy, tobacco, and perfume that permeated the place. He was a good kisser, and she indulged herself. After all, she had to make it look good.

He slowly pulled away, leaving her breathless. "It's okay," breathed Angel, "he's gone."

Feeling a bit guilty at the fun she was having, Sam let go of his muscular shoulders. She had killed vampires before, but had never kissed one. "Has he gone away?" she asked.

"Yeah," agreed Angel, "I think you convinced him you're not for sale."

A gargoyle of a waiter limped over to the couple and looked quizzically at them. *"¿Bebidas?"*

"Margarita," answered Sam. *"Sin sal."*

"Dos," added Angel, and the old man limped away, leaving them alone again.

Now Sam was beginning to feel sheepish over her reaction. "I, uh . . . I hope you didn't mind the kiss."

"Not at all," Angel answered with a smile. "Did I seem as if I minded?"

"No!" she said too quickly. "You . . . played along very well."

"It's a good idea to look like we're together," he said, scanning the dimly lit bar as he slipped one arm around her. "Even if we don't see our quarry, it may get back to them that we're here. I have a feeling that news of fresh blood travels fast in this town."

"Yeah," answered Sam.

The old waiter returned quickly with their drinks, and Angel paid him. She took a sip of the margarita and was nearly knocked head over heels again, because it tasted like pure tequila with a garnish of lime juice. "Whoa! They don't cheat you on the drinks."

"Cheap, too," Angel said with a smile. He lifted his triangular glass and toasted, *"Salud."*

She didn't mean to drink half the margarita, but she was suddenly thirsty. And it tasted so good. She wiped her mouth, and her forehead seemed clammy. "Oh," she breathed, "I must have been thirsty."

But Angel's attention was elsewhere, as he surveyed every person who came or went from the bar. He was also watching a staircase at the back of the joint that led upward into some very dark shadows. A velvet rope stretched across the bottom of the stairs, connoting that it was off-limits except to certain people.

Suddenly a fat American tourist was at her side, having slipped into the other side of the booth. "Are you sure you don't want to party, baby?" he asked. "I've got lots of money."

Angel's short fuse was burning, but Sam knew how to put it out. At once she planted another deep, passionate kiss on his full lips. Angel was all too willing to make the kiss look real, and she was soon lost in his embrace. The tourist muttered something and slid away.

Finally they parted, and Angel's eyes were once again scanning the clientele. Sam felt oddly miffed, as if he should be watching her, and she realized she was developing a mild crush on him. "Why don't you take a quick look around?" she said. "I'll be okay sitting here."

"Are you sure?" he asked. "I thought I saw someone—"

"Check it out," she whispered.

With a nod, Angel rose from the table and eased

into the crowd. She could see him moving among the cheap women, hard men, and soft tourists. She took a sip of his drink, which wasn't nearly as potent as her own. Somebody was trying to take advantage of her, and she was sure glad it wasn't Angel.

Outside, Riley and Buffy were stuck in traffic, having a hard time maneuvering the big van through the narrow, choked streets. Looking frustrated, Riley finally pulled over into the first available parking spot he saw and slammed the vehicle into park. On a handheld device, Buffy continued to track Angel and Sam's signal, which hadn't moved since they entered the bar called La Bandera. Everyone around them seemed to be having a jolly time, and all they were doing was driving in circles, literally spinning their wheels.

"What do you suppose they're doing in there?" Buffy asked rhetorically.

Riley shrugged. "Probably not much. Just sitting around, looking for our two vampires. At least they haven't gotten thrown out."

"That's good," she agreed. "What kind of place is it, do you suppose?"

"I don't know," he answered. "It looks nicer than most of these joints. At least it's not a strip club."

"Yeah," Buffy said with an uneasy laugh. "You know, I feel like a jilted wife spying on my slimebag husband."

Riley chuckled. "You pegged the feeling exactly. Sam has been undercover before, lots of times, while I've been on surveillance. But somehow this is different."

Buffy nodded. "Yes, because there's always the possibility *they're* having fun."

"You got it," he answered, giving her a smile. "We really drew the short end of the straw, didn't we?"

"The only thing that bothers me is that they may be having dinner, and we're not." Buffy craned her neck out the window to look at the offending bar. Well-dressed people were coming and going, people who looked as if they could be eating dinner in there.

Riley reached under the seat to draw out an olive-green packet. "I've got some K rations."

"No kidding," Buffy said dryly. "K rations?"

"They're not too bad, if you kind of close your eyes. And hold your nose."

"We're living it up now," Buffy said, taking a package of crackers from him. "Riley, do you think you're ever going to live a normal life?"

He shrugged. "Depends what you mean by 'normal.' I am happily married."

"And your wife is on a date with a vampire," countered Buffy. "And we're sitting in a van, eating K rations. Normal people are not on surveillance in weird border towns. They're at home, watching undercover cops and FBI hotties on TV."

Riley glanced worriedly out the window. "Some people are watching us. Why don't you pretend to look at the map."

"I've looked at this map until it almost makes sense." With a sigh, Buffy unfolded the road map again and pretended to be studying it. "You're avoiding my question, Riley."

He pointed out the window at the milling merrymakers. "Are you telling me you want to be like *them*? That you want to party and drink and screw around, oblivious to all the danger? I don't know if I can sit at home and read a book when I know what's out there. It's a never-ending battle, and there are not too many of us fighting it."

Buffy nodded glumly. "So you don't think we'll ever live normal lives?"

"I didn't say that," Riley answered, his tone softening. He gazed sympathetically at her. "Every soldier lays down his weapons someday, and our day has to come too. I just hope the war is over by then, and the good guys have won. It will take a lot to make me quit before then."

"That's fair," answered Buffy. "But I've thought the world was going to end before—that everything would be lost—and somehow it has survived. The Watchers are always looking for the next Slayer, in case I fail. We're not irreplaceable. Even if we get out, the world will go on."

"But you said you've tried to quit, and couldn't."

"And that's what makes it scary." She looked down worriedly.

Riley smiled and took her hand. "Maybe the omens will be there someday, and you'll realize you can quit. If that's what you want, I hope so."

Suddenly someone banged on their windshield,

jarring them out of the moment. Buffy looked up to see a brutish-looking Mexican with a hawk nose, long black mustache, and a fringed leather jacket. He grinned, and she could see a scar cutting across his angular face. She rolled down the window to see what he wanted.

"That's a nice van you've got there," he said in English. "Do you want to sell it? I'll give you top dollar—cash."

"No thanks," Riley said in a friendly tone. "It's not even paid off yet."

"You'll be able to pay it off with what I'll give you," the man assured them. "And buy some pretty jewelry for your girlfriend."

"No, we've got a whole camping trip planned," Riley said more forcefully.

"Too bad." The lanky Mexican twisted his mustache and stepped away from them. *"Vaya con diablo."*

Buffy quickly rolled up the window. "I think we'd better keep moving."

"What did he say at the end?" Riley asked, starting up the engine.

Buffy shook her head. "I took French, remember?" She looked down at the tracking device in her lap and saw that the blips had remained stationary. "They're still in that same bar."

"I'm sure they're spending their time wisely," Riley said as he nudged the big vehicle back into traffic.

* * *

Sam was on full alert by the time Angel returned to her booth in the back of La Bandera, although the heavy smooching and sighs from surrounding booths did little to calm her. She sat primly as he slid into the booth beside her, still paying more attention to the customers of the bullfighting bar than he did to her.

"Your drink's not as strong as mine," she told him, switching drinks with him.

"Why, that's sexual discrimination," Angel said with a smile. He lowered his voice to add, "I did ask around. Raul and Machete were in here earlier this evening, but they left suddenly. I also got a description of them from the old waiter, thanks to a very generous tip. Machete is tall and lean, with a drooping black mustache, and he wears an old fringed leather jacket. Raul is short and dapper, wears trendy clothes, and speaks with a raspy voice."

Sam shrugged nonchalantly. "We haven't seen anybody who looked like that."

"No," Angel agreed, glancing around the room. "Next we'll try another hangout of theirs, a strip joint down the street. But before we go, I'd like to see what's upstairs."

"Let me go," suggested Sam, who felt the need to get on her feet and do something useful. "If you go after having asked around, it will look like you're spying. If I go, I'm just a ditzy tourist who got lost."

"Okay, it's back there." Angel pointed to the old mahogany staircase at the rear of the bar, which was guarded by nothing more than a velvet rope. He moved to his feet to let her out. "After you go up, I'll wander over that way, like I'm looking at the posters. I'll hear you if you shout my name."

"Roger," Sam said, grabbing her sequined purse and sliding out of the booth. Angel smiled at the military term as he watched her leave.

Once again, Sam was aware of several lascivious stares as she sauntered along the back wall of the dimly lit bar. As a tipsy, beautiful foreigner, such things were second nature, to be acknowledged by a slight smile and cock of the head. In due time, she reached the velvet rope and looked around to see if anyone would physically stop her from going up the stairs, but it appeared that no one would. So she lifted the rope's hook from its slot, mounted the first step, and replaced the rope. Sam carefully climbed the stairs in her high heels and tight-fitting sundress, acting as if no harm could befall a ditzy girl on vacation.

Upon reaching the landing, she was confronted by two doors, both enforced with iron bands. She tried the one to her left and found it locked, and then she heard male laughter coming from the right-hand door. Sam nonchalantly twisted the doorknob and opened the heavy wooden door.

The voices stopped. In fact, all time seemed to stop as she intruded upon a particularly vulgar scene. Two American men, their shirttails hanging out and pants unzipped, stood poised over a young woman who was bound and gagged in a chair. It was clear that their intentions weren't honorable, but what was less clear was how willing the young redhead in the chair was. This being a hooker bar, Sam might have intruded upon a consensual business deal. The girl's dress was ripped, revealing her underwear, and her ankles were bound as tightly as her wrists, making it impossible for her to move.

"Hey!" one man snapped angrily. "This is private!"

"Wait a minute," said the other tourist, taking a good look at Sam. "Come on in, baby—"

Weaving drunkenly, she waved them off. "Maybe I do have the wrong room. Just one question—"

"Yeah, baby?" asked the friendlier man, moving closer.

But Sam was looking past him at the young redhead in the chair. "Sweetie, do you want to be tied up like that?"

She shook her head fervently.

"I didn't think so." Before the men could blink, Sam drew her nine-millimeter Glock from her purse and pointed it at them. "Untie her."

"Wait a minute," said the first, angrier man. "You don't know what you're doing, lady."

The other one didn't wait to argue with her—he dashed out a side door into the next room, and she heard him bolt the door shut behind him. "Hey, Carl!" his compatriot angrily shouted. "Don't leave me here with these crazy bitches!"

With her gun, she motioned toward the door. "Get out."

Fastening his pants around his belly, he gratefully

ran past her. "You're gonna pay for this!" he warned.

"I don't pay for it," countered Sam. She slipped the gun back into her purse and drew a commando knife, which she opened with a snap of her wrist.

"How did you get into this mess?" she asked the girl as she cut the cords that bound her hands, feet, and waist. More carefully, she untied the gag in the redhead's mouth.

The freckled girl, who looked to be about nineteen, spit the foul rag out of her mouth and stretched her sore limbs. "Wow, thank you! You really saved me."

"You're American?" asked Sam.

She nodded and staggered to her feet, looking much the worse for wear. She tried to piece together her torn clothing, without much luck. "I was here with my sorority," she explained. "It was kind of a dare . . . you know, go to Mexico and get drunk. But I . . . I don't know what happened. I think somebody put something in my drink, and I got separated from my friends. These guys offered to take me back to the States in their car. Like . . . what a trip."

Now Sam frowned, wondering what she was going to do with this damsel she had rescued. She couldn't abandon her, and she couldn't let her tag along. Not only that, but she had blown her cover for no good reason and let three complete strangers know she was carrying a firearm, which was one of the few laws that would get an American seriously busted down here. "What's your name?" she asked, for lack of anything better to say.

"Megan!" answered the girl cheerfully. "What's yours?"

"Samantha. Have you got any money, any way to get home?"

The girl shook her head glumly. "No, I lost all my money and I.D. All I've got is you."

Sam tried not to roll her eyes in disgust. "Listen, I'll give you enough money to take a taxicab to the pedestrian border crossing. From there, you can call somebody, or maybe hitch a ride—" The words sounded rather cold and brutal after what Megan had been through, but it was important that Sam and Angel get out of there before the two men she had run off tried to cause trouble.

"I'm sorry, it's the best I can do." Sam started moving toward the door, but Megan grabbed her arm. Her grip was surprisingly strong. "What's your hurry?" asked the redhead, sounding more sultry than injured. "I've always like girls with guns. I owe you one, and I like to pay my debts."

Like a gaucho dancer, Megan pulled Sam toward her in a forceful embrace, and she planted a kiss on Sam's protesting lips. Sam was a little drunk, but not that drunk; she realized this waif was a lot stronger and more determined than she looked. Sam had already kissed a vampire that night, so she forced herself to kiss the coed while she wriggled a hand between their heaving chests.

When Megan's lips brushed across her cheek and down her neck, all the alarms went off in Sam's head.

With all her strength, she pushed the girl off just as Megan's innocent face contorted into the loathsome visage of a vampire.

"Oh, crap!" Sam exclaimed, suddenly fighting with all her might as the bloodsucker drew her closer to the protruding fangs in her wide-open mouth.

CHAPTER NINE

Sam kept her wits even as the redheaded vampire tried to plunge her fangs into her neck, and she kneed her attacker in the crotch. That didn't have much effect on the supernatural predator, but it opened up enough space between them for Sam to bring her purse into play. She shoved a hand into the bag, fumbling among her various weapons.

The vampire thought Sam was reaching for her gun, and she gave a low, sultry laugh as she stalked the supposed tourist across the empty bedroom. "That won't do you any damn good."

In a movement so quick that Sam could barely see it, Megan cut off her retreat to the door. In another blink, the monster was on top of her again, trying to sink her teeth into her white neck, left so vulnerable by the skimpy sundress. Sam struggled and pushed with her free hand until she finally drew the weapon she had been seeking. While the vampire's fangs scraped her flesh, Sam shoved a fat wooden crucifix against Megan's freckled cheek.

A flash of fire lit the room, and the acrid smell of burnt flesh filled Sam's nostrils while she pushed the crucifix deeper into Megan's flesh. The vampire shrieked in horror and tumbled backward, giving Sam a chance to draw her second weapon, the wooden stake. Wielding both weapons and moving like a quarter horse cutting out a calf, Sam herded the vampire into a corner and had her cowering there when the door burst open.

Sam glanced over her shoulder to see that it was only Angel. "Shut the door," she ordered.

Thinking her nemesis was distracted, Megan tried to move toward the window, but Sam lunged and seared her back with the crucifix. As the acrid smoke wafted in the air, the vampire turned into a quivering lump cowering on the floor.

"I heard some bumping around, saw two men run out, and thought you were in trouble," explained Angel. "My mistake."

"She played me like a fool," Sam said angrily. "I thought I was rescuing *her* when I was really rescuing those two idiots."

From the floor, Megan hissed at her. "Leave me

alone! I didn't hurt you. Help me, mister . . . she's crazy!"

Angel didn't move any closer whatsoever, and he acted like an innocent bystander. "Oh, I know she's crazy. Likes to kill vampires—weird hobby, huh?"

Sam smiled at Angel, deciding to play along. "Yeah, and there are two vamps down here who are really on my hit list. Their names are Raul and Machete. Maybe you can tell me where they are?"

"You'll let me go if I tell?" Megan asked hopefully. Faced with the crucifix and stake, she was unable to shed her vampiric face, but her tone of voice sounded almost human again.

Sam's mind worked frantically, trying to decide how she could arrange the logistics of this encounter to make it work in their favor. She couldn't let this creature leave the room, or they would never see her again. No matter how tempting it was, they couldn't trust Megan, because she would say anything to save her singed hide.

"You tell my friend where they are," said Sam, "and he'll check it out. If they're where you say, I'll let you go."

The vampire hissed, not liking those terms. "Why don't I tell them where *you* are, and I'll arrange a meeting?"

"Is that your real hair color?" asked Sam. "Never mind, because every inch of you is going to be flaming red in a second." She loomed over the creature, threatening her with the crucifix and looking anxious to use it.

"All right, all right!" Megan screeched, cringing in fear. "I'm not their keeper—I don't know for sure where they are. But I can tell you the places where they hang out. This is one of them."

"Tell me something I don't know," snapped Sam.

"Cherie's is another—it's a strip joint up the street. Or they could be at the Club Monterey."

"Club Monterey?" asked Angel. "Where is that?"

"It's a crummy dance hall favored by the locals," said Megan. "They make connections there—for their business. It's on a side street three blocks north of here, Calle Carroza."

Sam snorted a laugh. "*Carroza.* Appropriate name. Isn't that the word for 'hearse'?"

Angel moved quickly for the door. "I'll check out both places. Are you sure you'll be all right?"

"We'll be fine," answered Sam, faking a worried glance at her partner. "Take care of yourself, darling. Remember, killing vampires is *my* hobby."

"Yes dear," Angel said submissively. He opened the door a crack, looked down the stairs, then slipped away.

Sam stared at her captive, realizing there was no way she could turn this creature loose. Megan was a threat to humanity and stupid tourists, and an even bigger threat to their mission now that she knew Sam was armed and not so dumb. Whether Megan was honest or deceptive, she would have to die. However, it was strange to spend this much time *talking* to a vampire.

What would Buffy do? she wondered. Sam already knew what Riley would do with the red-headed vamp: There would be a pile of red dust on the floor right now. The thought of Riley brought conflicting emotions because of the rush she felt with Angel.

"You look sick," said Megan.

"What?" Sam asked, snapped out of her reverie.

"I said, you don't look too well. Are you sick or something?" The vampire's gnarled face suddenly reverted to sweet teenaged freckles, mixed with third-degree burns in the shape of a cross.

"Stay on the floor!" warned Sam. "I'd stake you as soon as look at you."

"I believe you would," Megan replied, gingerly touching her burns. "I'm just saying you don't look well."

Sam frowned in thought, because she did have an upset stomach. Of course, she hardly ever drank alcohol or kissed vampires, and she had done too much of both that night.

"You know, you can't bring down Raul and Machete," Megan said matter-of-factly. "Both are old, powerful vampires, with lots of friends. Raul sired me."

"He did, did he?"

Megan sighed wistfully. "Yes, I thought he was a cute college boy. Shows you how wrong you can be about people."

"I think it's time to shut up now," ordered Sam.

Never taking her eyes off the vampire, she maneuvered the chair so that she could sit down while facing Megan. If the vampire thought she was going to get out of this mess semi-alive, she had also misjudged her captor.

"They've split up," Buffy said from the front seat of the van. She had checked her readings twice before reporting this, but now it was certain. "Angel is on the move, going north, while Sam has stayed behind in that Bandera place."

Easing out into the weekend traffic, Riley leaned over to check the handheld device. "That's weird," he said with a frown. "I didn't expect them to do that."

"Do you think they're all right?" Buffy asked with concern.

"Yeah, they can alter the signal if they need help," answered Riley. "Sam knows how to do it."

The traffic began inching ahead, and he had to do likewise in the van. "Buffy, did you ever learn to drive?"

She nodded proudly. "Yes, in fact, I've got an SUV now."

"Good," said Riley, "then you can drive this van. If they're split up, then we're going to lose one of them from the range of your little monitor. I need to fire up the screens in the back, while you drive."

"Now?" she asked in horror.

"Now." He slowed the vehicle. Buffy had no choice but to slide across him even as he maneuvered under her, heading for the small window that opened into the back area. A moment later she heard the flicking of switches and knew he was in the back, manning his sophisticated console. A horn honked at her, and she sped up the big vehicle, wondering which way to go. Her initial instincts told her to follow Angel, but logic told her to return to La Bandera and see what Sam was doing. She knew Angel could take care of himself, even if he did occasionally have lapses of macho over-confidence.

She turned right, since that was the easiest thing to do, and used residential streets to circle around. From the back, Riley's voice called out, "I've got them both. Angel has stopped moving—I think he's in that strip joint."

"Just like a guy," grumbled Buffy, "to ditch his date and go to a boob bar. But when we get back to the main drag, I want to park in front of the place where Sam is."

"That's okay with me," answered Riley.

Fending off predatory strippers and waiters, Angel made a quick pass through the fleshy environs of Cherie's. He was beginning to feel guilty for leaving Sam with a vampire, although this side trip had been her idea. Plus she seemed to be in charge of the situation upstairs at La Bandera. One fact remained: The freckle-faced vampire had given them a lead, and it had to be checked out.

As Angel wormed his way back to the exit, he saw

a short man duck through the beaded curtains and head down the stairs. The vampire gave chase and was about to catch him, until a half-naked woman darted in front of him, pulling at his shirt. He brushed her insistent hands aside, slipped past her, and rushed down the stairs; but the man was gone. Even with the delay, Angel moved fast, but his quarry moved faster.

Muttering to himself, Angel stepped onto the dirty sidewalk of Verdura's tenderloin district, glancing in both directions. Among the *gringos* moving in and out of bars and souvenir stands, no one looked suspicious enough to concern him. But weirdness was crackling along this street like the aged neon above his head, and he felt an urgency to head immediately to the Club Monterey.

He also felt an urgency to take Sam with him, so he reversed his steps and headed back to La Bandera.

Sam rose from her wooden chair and paced a few steps, still keeping an eye on the redheaded teenager cowering in the corner of the empty room upstairs at La Bandera—only Megan wasn't a teenager, she was an enlistee in the cadre of the undead: a vampire. Sam had to keep telling herself that, because the girl's plaintive, hound-dog expression tugged at the natural pity in her heart. *I'll be doing her a favor when I send her to her eternal rest,* thought Sam. *I'll be doing the world a favor too.*

"I'd love a cigarette," Megan said wistfully.

"Me too," muttered Sam. "But it's not good for you."

The redhead snorted a laugh. "Oh, I think it's a little late for me to worry about that. Come on, you don't need me. Let me go."

"So you can warn Raul and Machete?" Sam asked, hefting her crucifix in one hand and the wooden stake in the other. "You already told me that Raul sired you."

The girl glowered in anger. "So what do I owe him for *that*? I had a good life—it was kind of wasteful and foolish, but good. Now I've got an eternal life full of blood, darkness, and death. I wander the night, looking for prey and some moments of fun and challenge. Those men who had me tied up—they knew who I was, you know. That's why they told you that you were making a mistake letting me go. This is a kinky town, not a place where you should be. You should let me go before those men come back, bringing their friends."

Sam stopped pacing, assessing the possible truth to her words. She couldn't let the vampire go; that would be insane. But they couldn't stay trapped in this room indefinitely, because somebody was bound to want in. The door was locked, but she could hear the din of voices, tinkling glasses, and flamenco music rising from the bullfight tavern below. Suddenly Sam longed for Riley's straightforward morality or Angel's street smarts, or even Buffy's wisecracking sense of purpose. This limbo of indecision was far worse.

Sam turned around, knowing she had to kill the vampire. Something in her eyes must have warned the monster, because Megan rose to her feet and assumed a defensive crouch. Her innocent, freckled face distorted into a loathsome, stony mask of death, and she hissed, showing jagged fangs. Just then, a loud knock sounded on the door, jarring both of them out of their caution. Megan leaped for the window, but Sam sprang just as quickly, dragging her to the floor in a football tackle. The two women fought with all their might, and Megan tore her fingernails into Sam's back, while the mortal planted the cross on the vampire's chest in a searing blast of flame and smoke.

The undead howled in fury, while a man yelled in Spanish on the other side of the door. Sam had thrown the deadbolt, and it was a heavy oaken door with iron bars. Whoever wanted to get in, he wouldn't be a factor in the life-and-death struggle on the floor. When Sam tried to drive the stake into Megan's chest, the vampire caught her wrist in both hands. The crush of her grip was excruciating, but Sam was a body builder with a decathlete's physique. With all her strength, she dug the cross into the monster's forearm, and the air reeked with burnt flesh. As Megan shrieked, Sam pressed forward with her advantage until the singed vampire had to release her arm.

Now Sam wielded the wooden stake like a dagger, plunging it repeatedly into the creature's torso, trying to find her shriveled heart. Megan's wild flailing made the task difficult, but Sam imagined herself as one of the *toreadors* in the old bullfight posters downstairs, going for a killing blow against an animal five times her size. When Megan caught her right hand, Sam switched to her left, and she persevered until she found the mark. With a gasp and a look of surprise, the vampire turned into dust, and Sam collapsed onto the floor where Megan had lain a second before.

Sam heard voices yelling and shoulders crashing against the door, and she looked around in desperation. First she found her purse and stuffed the stake and crucifix into it. Then she spotted the ropes and old rags the men had used to tie Megan to the chair. Sam scurried to scoop them up, and she wrapped the gag around her mouth and the remnants of rope around her wrists. Rubbing her eyes to simulate tears, she staggered to the door and threw open the bolt.

Two pimps and a tourist crashed in like the Three Stooges, landing in a pile on the floor. Her breath coming in genuine pants and her eyes filled with almost-real tears, Sam showed them the bindings even as she cast them off. She pulled off her gag and said in Spanish, "Oh, thank you! Thank you for saving me!"

Before her rescuers could think too clearly, she pointed out the window. "He went that way! The man who tied me up went that way!"

Since there was no one else in the room, and they had heard a struggle, the men were forced to believe that someone had escaped. Two of them went to stare out the second-story window, while Sam collapsed into the arms of the third. Then another figure darkened the doorway, and she looked up to see Angel. With great relief, she rushed across the room and hurled herself into his arms.

"Oh, *mi amor!* Take me away from here. *¡Rápido!*" Angel quickly complied, dragging the shaken woman down the stairs while the three strangers were left to ponder what had happened. Sam figured that such dramatic scenes were not altogether unknown in La Bandera.

They stumbled onto the street, where they got another stroke of good fortune, because there sat Riley's high-tech van. Seeing them, Buffy called out something, and the side door flew open. Riley took his wife's hands and pulled her inside, while Angel jumped in after her. It was clear from their demeanor that a quick escape was warranted, and Buffy threw the van into gear and pulled into traffic, causing a screech of tires and several honks behind them.

Sam collapsed onto the floor of the van, and Angel took the second chair. "What happened?" Riley asked with concern.

"Yeah," seconded Angel, "what happened?"

"I had to stake her," breathed Sam. "The three men were trying to rescue me, I think. But I'm glad you came along, Angel, because there would have been a lot of questions."

"Stake her?" asked Riley. "A female vampire?"

"Yes, a friend of Raul's," answered Sam. "She gave us a tip on where they might be, and Angel went to check it out."

His eyes flaring with anger, Riley glared at Angel. "You left her alone with a hostile vampire?"

"It was her idea," he explained. "Actually I wasn't real happy about it, so I came back."

"That was real stupid . . . and dangerous!" Riley snapped, not assuaged one bit by this explanation. He moved toward Angel, his jaw clenched and his hands balled into fists.

Sam leaned forward and grabbed her husband before he did something rash. "No, no, honey, it's all right. I captured her before he got there, and I had her under control. It was *my* idea to send Angel off, and *my* idea to kill her. I had made a deal with her, but I realized that wouldn't work. It's done, but we got what we wanted."

"Your back is scratched," Riley said, noticing her minor wounds. "You'll need some first aid."

"Okay," Sam replied with a thankful glance at Angel. "And I'll need something to hide the scratches."

"You're not going back out there," Riley said, aghast.

Sam nodded forcefully. "Sure we are. Why not? Now that we know where they are."

"Or know where they aren't," muttered Angel. "They aren't at Cherie's, but I didn't make it to the Club Monterey yet. At least now we know that Raul and Machete aren't the only vampires in town."

Riley still looked suspiciously at their unusual colleague. "Why don't you go up front and tell Buffy what happened, and how to get to this place. I'll patch up Sam."

"Okay," Angel said, looking grateful. He eyed the small window in the connecting partition, shook his head, then tapped on it. "Buffy, pull over. I'm coming up front."

"Okay," she answered, and they could feel the van veering to the right. As soon as the van came to a stop, Angel opened the door and jumped out, leaving Sam alone with her husband.

He pulled out the first-aid kit, the same one she had used to treat Angel the night before. As Riley cleaned and dressed the scratches on her back, he asked, "So what were you two doing in that bar for an hour?"

Sam shifted uncomfortably, and not only because the antiseptic stung. "We were making inquiries," she answered. "We got some information from an old Indian woman outside the place, and a waiter inside. Really, we didn't get very far until I discovered the female vampire and took her prisoner."

Riley nodded appreciatively. "That was brave of you, but I still don't like the fact that Angel left you there. Did you get a description of Raul and Machete?"

"Yes," Sam answered eagerly, glad to be on a different topic. She described them the same way they had been described to her.

Her husband suddenly stopped his healing ministrations and stared at her. "You say one was tall and lean, with a black mustache, facial scar, and a fringed jacket?"

"Yes, that's Machete," she answered. "Did you see him?"

"Damn," muttered Riley. "He, or his twin, came right up to the van and tried to buy it from us. We were a little put off by him, but we didn't think—"

She shrugged. "Well, we know they need a new van."

"Let me finish with your scratches," Riley said, gently applying ointment to the skin of her back. As he did, Sam grabbed her suitcase, opened it, and fished out a lightweight wrap.

"You seem awfully worried about me tonight," she said with mild irritation, both at herself and him. "You know, I've done this before, and we've got primo backup in Buffy and Angel."

"I know," Riley said with a sigh. "Bear with me, okay? I think I'm on edge because we're cut off from our support base, maybe permanently. Instead, we've got two loose cannons. I'll admit, I'm not real good at being Clint Eastwood and telling my superiors to go screw themselves."

"But they're dead wrong," insisted Sam, "and you know it. There's no way we should have been called off this case, just because those yahoos in Arizona have some pull. We can nail these vampires without upsetting anyone's apple cart. And they tried to plant drugs on us too. Remember that."

"I haven't forgotten anything," Riley said through clenched teeth. "We're here to save innocent lives, and we're going to do that. Now stop talking and let me finish with your scratches."

"Okay, Doc," answered Sam tensely. She tried to relax, but all she could think about was being alone with Angel in another dark, smoky bar. Feeling a chill from the van's air-conditioning, she was happy to pull her wrap around her.

Minutes later, the van rolled to a stop a block away from their destination, the Club Monterey, and Sam and Angel got out. If Sam was worried about being stuck alone with the handsome vampire in another dingy bar, she quickly put that out of her mind, because the place was like a carnival. The front half of the club was a large courtyard full of street musicians, food vendors, and Mexican youths in their club finery. Girls were congregated in large groups, and the boys hung around the open-air bar in the back, ordering soft drinks. Pulsating salsa music boomed from the actual club behind the bar, and a shoulder-to-shoulder crowd was packed in there. This was a dance hall—a place to see and be seen. It was no place to find a dark, secluded booth.

Angel took her hand and led her through the throng of dancers, revelers, and vendors. They tried to look as if they were blissfully intent upon each other, even while they scanned every face and body they passed. If anyone wanted to conduct nefarious business out in the open, this would be the place. There were clutches of people everywhere, and the overlapping music was loud and insistent. Sam and Angel did their best to circulate throughout the courtyard, but the crowd kept ebbing and flowing, making surveillance difficult.

By mutual consent, they finally ducked into the

dance hall proper, where the salsa was as hot as the steamy air. There were a few tiny tables pushed against the walls, but almost everyone was dancing under an old-fashioned mirrored ball and shifting colored lights. This place wasn't sophisticated, just jumping. The only oasis of relative calm was two old pool tables in a far corner, and Sam and Angel found themselves headed in that direction, if only to regroup. It was clear that they could spend a week in this place and not get a good look at everyone. In order to conduct business, Raul and Machete would have to have a station, someplace where would-be clients could find them. Sam figured they could find it, if they were persistent.

Then again, it was possible that the redheaded vampire, Megan, had been lying to them. If she wanted to send them looking for a needle in a haystack, the Club Monterey was a good haystack.

As they reached the pool tables, Angel finally let go of her hand, and the electricity seemed to go out of the air. He was all business as he surveyed their immediate neighbors. Two young men were playing pool at one table, and three girls were sitting on the other pool table, laughing and talking. Sam could feel the heat of all the bodies and the poor air circulation, and she longed to take off her shawl and relax. But vacation was their cover, not their reality.

Angel planted himself in the corner and folded his arms, surveying the club as if he owned it. Sam burrowed under his arm, trying to look as if she belonged to him, and she felt his body tense. "What's the matter?" she asked in Spanish.

"Look on the dance floor, coming this way," whispered Angel.

Nonchalantly, Sam shifted her gaze to the chaos under the glittering lights, and she saw the dancers parting slightly to let two men stride through. The one in front was short and clean-cut, dressed in a black silk shirt and dapper cream-colored pants. Behind him walked a lean figure in a fringed leather jacket, which made him look like a latter-day Apache. They stopped to greet a handful of women, and a man came up to them, bowing as if they were royalty.

Angel reached into his jacket pocket and brought out a small black disc about the size of a button. "I don't know how this will go," he said, "so I'd like to plant this bug on them."

"Good idea," Sam answered, although it also sounded risky. *Then again, what isn't?* "Do you think they'll remember you?"

"They got a good look at me in the cemetery," said Angel.

A moment later, Raul turned and peered at them through the gyrating bodies, his gaze languorous and heavy-lidded yet oddly chilling. Sam could see a look of recognition pass between the vampires, but she wanted to appear blissfully unaware of it. So she craned her head upward and kissed Angel on the lips again. His lips responded, but she could tell he was only feigning interest. Upon ending the kiss, he clutched her shoulders possessively, and she melted into his chest.

I'm the bait, Sam told herself, *and I look like I've already been caught.*

CHAPTER TEN

Angel held on tightly to Sam's trim body, thinking that she was either a great actress or was enjoying this romantic interlude. It didn't really matter, because reality was about to rear its ugly head, in the form of two tough-looking *hombres* who weren't really men. Raul and Machete finally broke off from their admirers on the dance floor of the Club Monterey and walked unhurriedly toward the pool tables in the corner. Angel held his ground, while Sam closed her eyes and dreamily ignored their approach; but the young people around them were suddenly alert. The pool players worked quickly to finish their game, and the girls sitting on the second table jumped down and slipped away, with sidelong glances at the ominous pair of vampires. By the time Raul and Machete reached the remote corner of the dance hall, only Angel and Sam remained to greet them.

"Hola," Angel said in a low-key but friendly manner.

Raul looked directly at Sam, while Machete picked up a discarded pool cue. From the way he handled the long wooden stick, it was clear that he knew it could be used as a stake to kill a vampire. To Angel's relief, he began to plink at the balls left on the table, leaving his shorter *compadre* to do the talking.

"I hear you've been looking for us," Raul said in a raspy voice. "You persist, even though we told you we cannot help you."

"Who am I to trust?" asked Angel. "Strangers?" He gave Sam a very familiar caress. "This is a precious package, and I want it delivered safely to the other side."

"¿No es gringa?" Raul asked, reaching out to lift Sam's delicate chin with his long, manicured fingers.

Like someone drugged, the girl took his hand and kissed it. "I'm German, from Argentina," Sam said in perfect Spanish. "Please help me enter U.S.A." The name of the country to the north she pronounced "Ooosa."

Raul smiled with appreciation and looked at Angel with a newfound respect. "I would like to help you, but the border is very tight now. Stupid terrorists. We are not making any more crossings."

"Why not?" Angel asked, trying to sound patient and

nonconfrontational, "Everyone says you are the best."

With that, Machete snorted a laugh as he sank a difficult bank shot. "Our canaries are never captured by *la migra*," he claimed. "They either make it to Tucson . . . or disappear."

Angel realized he needed an edge in this negotiation, so he gambled with a mild threat. "It sounds as if you are leaving a good business unattended. Perhaps I should step in."

Anger flashed in Raul's dark eyes, and Machete snapped to attention, holding the pool stick like a lance. "That would not be advisable," said the lean, hawk-faced man.

"I don't want to do it, but you leave me no choice," Angel said, holding Sam protectively. "If I have to make the crossing myself, then I might as well make some money from it."

Raul stepped toward Machete, and the two of them conversed in low whispers for a moment. Meanwhile, Angel readied the bug in the palm of his hand, not knowing when he would have a chance to plant it.

Sam looked up at him and whispered. "Let me do it. It will be easier for me." Angel nodded and handed the button-sized device to her, and she peeled off its adhesive backing. After that, Sam fell back into her dreamy, compliant state.

When Raul returned to the couple, he had a thoughtful look on his face. "We're not afraid of you."

"No, of course not," said Angel. "This is your town. We're just passing through, and you can determine how much time we spend here."

"Right now we have business to do," said Raul. "Come back here tomorrow night, and we'll see."

"Oh, thank you," Sam cooed, breaking away from Angel and giving the dapper vampire a heartfelt hug and kiss. The kiss lingered a bit longer than Angel felt comfortable with, and Sam languorously pulled away and did the same thing to Machete, who took the opportunity to run his hands up and down her body. However, Angel saw her own active hands reached under his fringed jacket and leave something behind. That was smart thinking, because Machete obviously never went anywhere without that jacket.

Reluctantly, the tall vampire let her go, and Sam returned to Angel, a look of bliss on her beautiful face. With this helpless act, Sam had worked her charm on the pair, making sure they would see them again.

Raul straightened his silk shirt and cleared his throat. *"Muy bien. Hasta mañana."*

"Mañana," Angel echoed, gripping Sam, who seemed unsteady on her feet.

Machete playfully poked the cue stick at Angel, then slapped it on the table. He and Raul sliced back through the crowd of locals, who were gyrating to the pounding salsa music, oblivious to the monsters in their midst.

Looking woozy, Sam touched her forehead. "I think I need to sit down."

"No kidding," Angel said, guiding her to the pool table. He lifted her onto the felt-covered slate and held her upright until she seemed to recover her senses.

"Man," she breathed, "that is four vampires I've kissed tonight. Must be a record . . . without getting bitten."

Nice company she's lumped me with, Angel thought, mustering a smile. "You did great. Just the right attitude."

"Thanks," she replied uneasily.

He offered her his hand. "Come on, let's find the back door and slip away. I want to get back to the van and find out what business Raul and Machete are up to."

Wiping her eyes, she jumped off the pool table and took his hand, and he used his unerring instincts to find a rear exit from the dance hall. Ten minutes later, the two of them casually strolled toward a white van parked at almost the exact place where they had left it. As they approached the vehicle, Angel dropped Sam's hand. A moment later, the side door slipped open, and Riley bounded out. "Everything okay?" he asked, staring pointedly at Sam, who still looked a bit disheveled.

"Yeah," she answered with a game smile. "We planted the bug on Machete and have another date with them tomorrow night."

The driver's door opened, and Buffy joined them on the dark residential sidewalk. "Are the boys going to take you on Mr. Toad's Wild Ride?"

"We'll know tomorrow," said Angel. "Let's see what we can pick up from that tracer."

They all piled into the back of the van, where Riley

sat at his console and adjusted the receiver. He had no problem locating the combination tracking device and bug, and he reported, "It looks like they're headed back to La Bandera. Buffy, can you drive us there so we can pick up the audio?"

She saluted. "Chauffeur Buffy at your service." The Slayer rushed back to the driver's seat, and Angel joined her in the passenger seat.

"Are you okay?" he asked.

"Sure," she answered as she started up the engine. "I came all this way to drive this big honkin' van, while you two have all the fun."

"Don't you and Riley have . . . stuff to talk about?"

She gave Angel a sidelong glance. "There's only so much you can talk about with a married man." Buffy jammed the van into gear, and they were on the move again, careening dramatically in and out of traffic.

To Angel, Buffy's driving was the scariest part of the evening, and he tried to relax. "Sam's a brave girl," he said conversationally. "She throws herself into it."

"Yeah, I know," answered Buffy. "You've got her Barbie lipstick all over your cheek."

Angel touched his cheek and tried to find the smear, although that was impossible. There was no sense looking in the mirror on the visor either. In truth, Buffy's flare of jealousy meant more to him than all the kisses in the world from Sam, and he sat back, quite enjoying the harrowing drive through the chaotic streets of Verdura, Mexico.

In due time, they passed La Bandera and pulled

around the corner onto a side street, where Buffy parked. She opened the window in the partition and asked, "Can you hear them from here?"

"Yes," answered Riley. "They're not saying much, and it's all in Spanish."

"Not really," came Sam's voice, correcting her husband. "Actually I think it's Portuguese . . . and an obscure dialect."

"No telling how old those two are," remarked Angel, "or where they're from originally. Can you make it loud enough for me to hear?"

"Sure," answered Riley. He made an adjustment, and the husky, slurred voices of Raul and Machete filled the van. From the cacophony of background noise and flamenco music, it sounded as if they had just entered the bullfight tavern. Even if their voices had been perfectly clear, Angel wasn't sure he'd be able to translate the ancient tongue they were speaking, although he had to agree with Sam that it sounded like a romance language.

"Raul!" came a third voice, booming over their incomprehensible mutterings. "I've been waiting for you."

"English!" said Buffy, suddenly alert. "That's English."

"We had business elsewhere," answered Raul's insolent, raspy voice. "What's so urgent?"

"We have a new shipment ready to go," said the third party, whose voice didn't sound familiar, although it was clearly American. "Thursday."

"So soon," interjected Machete, his voice louder than the others, because the bug was on him. "We need a vacation."

"Yeah, you do," agreed the American. "No more border runs with those damn illegals. *¿Comprende?*"

"Hey man, you don't tell us what to do!" snapped Machete.

"Oh yes, we do. That cargo never makes it alive, which invites suspicion. If you work for us, you don't freelance . . . or take stupid chances to make a quick buck! That's why we use your people—and pay you well—because you can keep a secret."

Machete cut loose in Spanish—swear words that Angel didn't bother to translate. After his burst of anger, Raul said something to him, and Machete muttered, "Okay, man. We'll kiss your ass, but we want a good payday."

"Oh, you'll get that," said the mystery man. "You have to look out for some U.S. agents over here too. You got careless, so they got suspicious."

"U.S. agents down here in Mexico?" Raul asked in disbelief. "If they are, we'll take care of them."

"Not regular agents," came the reply. "The monster squad."

"*¡Mierda!*" exclaimed Raul. "Okay, thanks." That last bit of information seemed to have put a damper on the conversation, and no words were exchanged for several moments.

"Okay, Thursday," said the unknown American. "Usual setup."

"Gotcha," replied Machete. "Later, man."

After that, the two vampires went back to speaking in archaic gibberish, and Riley turned down the audio. "What do you suppose that was all about?" he asked.

"I doubt if it's something good," said Buffy. "With that bug, we could locate them during the day, couldn't we?"

"Yes," answered Riley.

Buffy added, "And take care of them while they sleep."

"Then we'll never find out what they're up to," countered Angel. "We should meet them tomorrow night as planned, and try to earn their trust. Tomorrow is only Monday, so we've got time to find out what this is all about."

"Sam is done in," said Riley. "She's asleep back here. I've never seen her like this."

"A lightweight," remarked Buffy.

Riley ignored her and said, "Why don't we go back to the hotel to plan our next move? I'll drive."

He jumped out the back door, circled around to the driver's side, and stopped in mid-stride, staring glumly at the street. "There's another one," muttered Riley.

"Another what?" asked Buffy, poking her head out the window.

Riley pointed into the gutter, where their headlights illuminated a dead crow, its glistening feathers half-eaten by vermin. "That's the third one I've seen tonight. Whatever is killing them, it's down here, too."

"Don't crows die of old age?" asked Buffy.

"Sure they do, but not in numbers like this." He sighed and shook his head. "I don't know if I'll get a response from my expert or not, but I can't worry about it now." Riley glanced expectantly at Buffy. "I'm driving, remember?"

She looked at him and pouted. "Do you really have to? You're taking away my only job."

He mustered a smile. "I'm sorry. Maybe you should look at this as a paid vacation."

"I'll go in the back," Angel offered, realizing there were only two seats up front and one of them would have to move.

"No, I will," Buffy said, quickly jumping out. "But I warn you two, I may just take care of Raul and Machete, collect my paycheck, and go home."

A moment later she was gone, leaving the two men alone to deal with each other. "Maybe we should just let her stake them," Riley said thoughtfully. "I've got a bad feeling about all of this."

"You called us in for a reason," answered Angel. "Something bad stretches from here across that border, and we won't end it with a quick fix. Your wife is putting it all on the line for this operation, and we should equal her effort. Besides, there are more vampires in this town than just Raul and Machete— we know that now—and powerful people don't want us to be here. That's enough reason for *me* to stay."

"Okay," Riley muttered, putting the van into gear. "We'll hang in there until the end." His jaw clenched tightly, Riley drove off into the warm Sonoran night.

CHAPTER ELEVEN

Buffy paced the white sands of the beach outside their bungalow in Puerto Peñasco, wondering what the heck she was doing on this beautiful strand. Neither Riley nor Angel needed her to fight the baddies—they were both seasoned pros. They didn't even need her to be sexy window dressing, because they had the lovely Samantha Finn to do that. Sam could be either hard as nails or insufferably sweet and vulnerable in the same crazy night. It had been years since Buffy could muster that last commodity: innocence. She had seen too much, done too much, killed too much.

Still, the sun felt good on her bare shoulders, and

the sand was squishy under her bare toes, although the whole place felt unreal. Here they were, fighting ruthless vampires while sunbathing at the beach; it was as weird as the differences between Mexico and the U.S., even though the border was just an invisible line in the desert, drawn by long-dead politicians. The haves and the have-nots were so evident here, and they created opportunities for monsters like Raul and Machete. Of course, these same divisions existed in any large city, such as Los Angeles, and even between the dead and the undead. One group had light and love, and the other had darkness and death.

Despite the sunshine, such thoughts weighed heavily on Buffy's mind as she strolled through the sand, kicking the broken shells and lumps of seaweed. Although there were four of them on the case, she felt like the fifth wheel. Angel was the gun-for-hire, and he was the one with the best fix on Raul and Machete. Riley and Sam were perfect as his sidekicks, while she felt like that wolf they had encountered: a lone hunter, no matter how many people tried to help her. Most of the time, her helpers got in her way, or she got in their way. As the odd girl out, it was hard not to feel as if she should just pick up and leave this sun-drenched resort and return to a place where the vampires at least spoke English.

As she paused to knead the hot sand with her toes, a large shadow darkened her path. Buffy looked up to see a big man with white hair, a ruddy face, and a straw cowboy hat that did not match his Bermuda shorts and polo shirt. Upon recognizing Sheriff Clete Barton, she instantly fell into a defensive stance.

"Whoa, little girl," said the big man, holding up his open palms. "Don't get your piggies in a polk. This is Mexico—neutral territory—and I don't mean you any harm."

"Yeah, right," Buffy said with a sniff. "You didn't exactly drive the Welcome Wagon across the border."

He smiled like a congenial Buddha. "Buffy Summers. You have quite a rap sheet, lots of scrapes with authority."

"And you tried to make it longer, didn't you?" she said. "If you had half a brain, you'd see that we're trying to help you."

That brought a scowl to the big man's face. "There's a fine line between helpin' and buttin' in. But I'm not here to rehash our differences—I'm here to offer you the olive branch of peace. As far as I'm concerned, you can butt in all you want on this side of the border, where you couldn't screw things up any more than they already are."

"But you don't want us coming back to Verdura, Arizona," Buffy replied darkly.

"Now we understand each other," the sheriff said with a grin. "You can go back through California, where they're a lot more tolerant of your kind of troublemaker. It might be hard to pin anything on those people you're with, because they're all special cases. But you—you're just a regular person."

Buffy couldn't help but smile at that comment. "You're right. So why are you so afraid of me?"

That brought the scowl back to his face. "I'm not. I'm just trying to see if you're smart enough to back off."

She shrugged. "I'm on vacation. You're the one with the unsolved murders, not me."

It was Barton's turn to shrug. "Wetbacks dying in the desert—it's like crabs dying on the beach. It's to be expected."

Both her stomach and her jaw tightened at that heartless remark, and Buffy's green eyes bore into the big man. "How did you get your job?" she demanded.

"I've had it a long time," he answered. "And I'll be in office a long time after you're gone. I would say, 'I'll see you around,' but I'm hoping I won't. *Adiós*, Miss Summers." With a tip of his cowboy hat, the sheriff turned gracefully for a big man and ambled toward the hotel walkway.

Still simmering, Buffy was tempted to follow him. She knew that would be difficult to do in this bright sunlight without being spotted, but there was nothing wrong with seeing where he went. Even among a throng of tourists, the big sheriff stood out like a totem pole as he made his way through a white gate onto the grounds of an older hotel. It helped that he wasn't walking very fast and that she could blend in with the tourists as she kept pace from a distance. Young women in bathing suits were plentiful along the shore, but rangy cowboys were not.

He ducked into the hotel, and she wondered if he was staying there. Buffy had to hurry her pace in order not to lose sight of him, and she expected to see him enter an elevator to return to his room. Instead, Sheriff Barton strode right through the lobby, past a tour group newly arrived by bus, and out the front door. She reached the door and was able to watch him through the glass window as he walked to a large Lincoln sedan in the parking lot. So he was just going to drive away, she thought.

Barton surprised her again by not going to the driver's door of his car. Instead, he went to the trunk and opened it with his key. *Is he going to get his suitcase?* she wondered. No, he didn't pull anything out of the trunk, but he carefully handled something that she couldn't see. After fiddling in his trunk for several moments, he shut the lid without taking anything out. Satisfied, he strode back toward the front door of the hotel.

He's got something of value in there, thought Buffy, *and he wants to make sure it's safe. But why wouldn't he bring it up to his room?*

As the sheriff entered the front door of the hotel, Buffy joined a party of other women in bathing suits headed toward the beach. From the corner of her eye, she saw Barton turn toward the bank of elevators and disappear into one of them.

I could search his room, she decided, *but it would be more interesting to search the trunk of his car. Safer, too.*

Filled with purpose, Buffy hurried back to the bungalow she shared with Sam, Riley, and Angel. Only the men were on view, because Sam had been sleeping most of the day. Angel sat in the living room with the blinds drawn, shaving his face, and Riley sat at the kitchen table, hunched over a laptop computer. The vampire shaved like a blind man, running his fingers over his cheeks and chin to find the stubble and following the tactile search with his razor. After a few centuries of doing this, he was pretty good at it. Riley also looked to be pretty good at the computer, as his fingers flew across the cramped keyboard.

"I hope you're wearing sunscreen," Angel said as Buffy walked in and closed the door behind her.

"Sunscreen with bug repellent," she answered. "Listen guys, I just talked to our old friend Sheriff Barton."

Angel put down his razor, and Riley looked up from his computer. "What?" they said in unison.

She gave them the condensed version of their tortured conversation, ending with Barton's threat. "He doesn't want us to go back to his little kingdom, or he'll cause trouble for me, personally. That's because he thinks I'm the only regular one among us."

Riley laughed. "He doesn't know you very well, does he?"

She crossed to the couch where the vampire was sitting. "Listen Angel, didn't you say you saw him in the rain at Frederick Tatum's house? And that he got something out of his car?"

"It might have been him," answered Angel. "I couldn't tell for sure. Whoever it was, he was acting crazy."

Buffy frowned thoughtfully. "He doesn't have his squad car, but he has a big Lincoln. And he still has something important he's keeping in his trunk."

Now both men looked at her with interest. "You want us to search it?" asked Riley.

"You can pick a trunk lock, can't you?"

"Sure," answered Riley. "I've got four different gadgets that will do it. You can be the lookout."

"No problem." Buffy left the couch and went to Riley's side at the kitchen table. "He also said he's been sheriff in Verdura for a long time, and I believe him. In fact, I'd like to know just how long."

"I've got a wireless Internet connection," the young commando said, pointing to his laptop. "Why don't I see what I can find out?"

Buffy smiled. "I love computer geeks." She pointed toward the closed bedroom door. "How's Sam?"

Riley shook his head with a mixture of concern and amazement. "She's been sleeping around the clock. She was also complaining about an upset stomach, but that was hours ago."

"I'll go check on her," offered Buffy, "while you Google and Yahoo."

"Go easy on her," suggested Angel. "She had an action-packed night."

Buffy tried not to roll her eyes too noticeably as she headed into Sam's bedroom. The blinds were drawn, and it was even darker in this room than in the living room beyond. The only sound was the constant whispering of the surf as it rolled across the beach, and the figure in bed was curled in a fetal position and covered by sheets. Still, Sam stirred at Buffy's approach, as if her sleep were not as deep and untroubled as it appeared. "Buffy," she said drowsily.

"Hey, Sleeping Beauty, how are you?" Buffy sat at the edge of the bed. "You're missing the shuffleboard tournament."

"Just saving up my strength for tonight," Sam answered with a yawn. She managed to sit up and give Buffy a wan smile. "Just between you and me, kissing vampires takes a lot out of you."

Just what I want to hear, Buffy thought. "Don't I know it," she replied. "Are you sure you're up to this? I've had more practice than you."

"That's okay," said Sam. "I think I've got Raul's and Machete's attention. What are the guys up to?"

"Angel's doing personal grooming, and Riley's checking something on the Internet." She told Sam about running into Sheriff Barton on the beach.

"Geez, that guy never gives up," Sam muttered, running a hand through her tousled hair. "Do you think he'll cause us more trouble?"

Buffy shook her head. "He thinks there's a truce between us, as long as we stay in Mexico. But I don't plan to leave *him* alone. He's got something valuable in his car, although it may just be a white robe with a pointy hood. But I'm gonna find out."

Sam yawned again, but she swung her legs over the side of the bed. "I think I'll take a shower and join the living."

"Good idea," Buffy said, rising from the bed. "I'll be happy to eat a late lunch with you. See you out there."

"Thanks, Buffy," Sam said warmly. "For everything."

"For what?" Buffy asked, confused.

"You know . . . for sharing your two old loves with me."

I'm not sharing *Angel with you,* Buffy thought before she could stop herself. Buffy sighed loudly. "I never really had that much control over them . . . even back then. See you in a bit."

She returned to the living room, where she found Angel reading the laptop screen over Riley's shoulder. "Buffy, look at this," said the vampire, motioning her over.

"You found our favorite sheriff?" Buffy joined them, but she couldn't see much with the two males hogging the small screen.

"He has been sheriff an awfully long time," reported Riley. "He was first elected in nineteen fifty-four."

"What?" said Buffy. "That's like fifty years ago. He's old, but he's not *that* old. Did he become sheriff when he was in grade school?"

"No, look at this," Riley said, pointing to an old photograph on his screen. "That's him, making an arrest in nineteen sixty."

The men moved aside to allow her a good look at

the grainy black-and-white photograph. Naturally, Clete Barton was hassling a Mexican who was hogtied on the ground, but he hardly looked any different in the old news photo, which was over forty years ago. Yes, his hair was darker and his waistline a bit thinner, but he appeared to be a man in his thirties or forties, not in his teens or twenties. "Could that be his father?" asked Buffy, not wanting to think about the former Sunnydale mayor, Richard Wilkins—and knowing Angel was thinking the same thing.

"There's no mention of his father in his biography," answered Riley. "You would think if there was a dynasty of sheriffs, they would mention it. They do mention that Frederick Tatum's father, Arthur, was a judge and a big landowner back then. They don't mention what Barton was doing or where he came from before being elected sheriff."

"I'd help you look in that trunk," said Angel, "but I can't go out for a few hours."

"How is Sam?" Riley asked, suddenly remembering his wife.

"Oh, she's fine," Buffy answered, although in truth she wasn't too sure of that. "Do you want to check out his trunk now?"

"No time like the present," Riley agreed, rising from his seat. "Let me get my locksmith tools. Angel, do you want to keep looking on the Web?"

"I prefer real searches to virtual ones," answered the vampire, "but I'll try."

Ten minutes later, Buffy and Riley were strolling

through a half-empty parking lot sandwiched between a pothole filled road and an older Mexican hotel on the beach. She and Riley looked like a typical young American couple, of which there were many in the vicinity. Almost every car was from Arizona, with a few odd ones from California, and Buffy had no trouble pointing out Barton's big silver Lincoln. Riley jiggled an electronic lockpick in his hand, as if it were a key, and approached the car as if it were his own.

"Let's see if there's an audio alarm," whispered Riley. "I doubt it, because cops usually don't like shrieking noises that get them called out in the middle of the night." Gingerly he touched the trunk lid, and nothing happened.

Buffy, meanwhile, hovered nearby, but her eyes never left the front door of the hotel. She hoped that Barton didn't have a room that overlooked the parking lot, or if he did, that he wasn't gazing out his window at the moment. The few tourists who could see them weren't paying much attention.

"Okay, here goes," said Riley. He turned on the slender device and began to probe the trunk lock. "There might still be a silent alarm," he warned, "so keep on the lookout."

"Don't worry, I am," answered Buffy.

"Chances are good he's got a GPS and a tracer built in," said Riley, "but since we aren't stealing it, that shouldn't matter."

"Just get on with it," Buffy snapped, suddenly nervous. She could stand up to a roomful of demons or vampires, but petty thievery made her sweat. Plus, Clete Barton would like nothing better than to pin her with an actual crime.

"It's coming," Riley reported, working hard. "Almost there."

With a click, the lock gave up its secrets, and Riley nonchalantly lifted the trunk lid. Buffy was anxious to peer inside, but she didn't dare take her eyes off the hotel door and the tourists coming and going. "What do you see?" she asked impatiently.

"I don't get it," muttered Riley. "There's just a spare tire, a few tools, and an old animal skin."

"Animal skin?" Despite her caution, Buffy had to take her eyes off the hotel in order to peer over Riley's shoulder. What she saw in the spacious trunk made her shudder. It was a huge animal skin, aged yet dense with luxuriant black-and-silver fur, and a monstrous head still attached. The deadly teeth seemed ready to rip and tear, and the amber eyes glittered with an eerie vitality. "It's a wolf skin," she rasped.

"He must be breaking the law with that," Riley said with a chuckle. "It's an endangered species."

"You don't get it," she said. "Have you ever heard of skinwalkers? The wolf we fought—"

"Hey!" bellowed a loud voice coming from the direction of the hotel.

Buffy looked up to see Sheriff Clete Barton running toward them at an impressive rate of speed for a big man. As he charged, he drew a pistol from his waistband and fired at them.

CHAPTER TWELVE

The bullet whizzed through the parking lot, streaked inches away from Buffy chest, and slammed into the open trunk lid of the silver Lincoln. Riley was already running for his life in one direction, and Buffy hurriedly went the other. Sheriff Barton would also have to pick one or the other of them to pursue. Buffy had thought momentarily about grabbing his wolf skin, but that would have invited a chase and battle to the death, she was sure.

Both of them used the other cars in the parking lot as cover, running in a crouch and presenting poor targets. But that didn't keep the enraged sheriff from firing at them, and other tourists screamed as bullets ricocheted from car to car, shattering windshields and the sun-kissed calm. As Buffy had hoped, Barton ran to his car to check the precious skin, and he took the time to slam the trunk lid shut. He must have realized that shooting up a Mexican parking lot was not a good idea, especially when gun-toting Americans were frowned upon.

She didn't hear any more shots, and she ran until she reached a row of beachside establishments and finally ducked into a funky bar. Driftwood, decrepit bamboo furniture, and puffer fish hanging from the ceiling were the main elements of the bar's decor. Buffy moved to the shadows in the rear of the place and sat at a table with her back to a wall and her eyes fixed on the door. The only customers were six loud tourists who appeared half-looped. If Barton knew where they were staying, he might go to the bungalow, but Angel could handle him without worrying about the gun.

A waiter came up to her, and she ordered a Coke, knowing she had a few dollars stuck in her shoe. After several minutes, Buffy figured she had escaped from the pistol-toting sheriff, and she spied a pay phone. Keeping her eyes on the door, she went to the pay phone, deposited a few pesos, and dialed the bungalow.

"Yeah?," answered Angel.

"It's me," she said. "We got into Barton's trunk, but he went ballistic on us. Literally."

"Yes, I know. I've got Riley on the walkie-talkie. Tell me where you are, and I'll send him over to you."

She looked at a sign that read SEX ON THE BEACH, then remembered that that was a drink. A matchbook cover lay by an ashtray, and it said THE BLUE SQUID. "I'm at The Blue Squid," she answered. "A dive on the walkway just north of Barton's hotel. I'll wait here for Riley."

"Fine," said Angel. "Wish I could be more help."

"No problem," she said. "Bye."

It was only a couple of minutes before Riley showed up, looking preppy as usual. No matter how casual his clothes, it was impossible for him not to look preppy. She finished her Coke and walked across the bar to meet him. "Is Billy Bob still chasing us?" she asked.

He shook his head. "I'm not sure, but I think I saw his car pull out of the parking lot. Why don't we circle back and check?"

"Why not?" She shrugged. "It's our funeral."

Going through the hotel lobby for protection from errant gunshots, Buffy and Riley stopped at the front door and stared into the parking lot. A Mexican patrol car was now parked there, and *la policia* were interviewing two tourists; but Barton's Lincoln was gone. He had either moved it or had beat a hasty retreat to the border.

"Do you want to ask if he's still registered in the hotel?" asked Riley.

Buffy shook her head. "If he was, I don't think he'd be here under his own name. Besides, I don't really want to see him again."

Riley nodded, and they strolled through the hotel

lobby, out the back door, and into the sunshine. Out of earshot of tourists, he said, "You were going to tell me about skinwalkers."

"Yes, I ran into them once before," answered Buffy. "It's a Southwestern Native American belief—that an evil sorcerer can become an animal by wearing its skin and performing the right ritual. I know some white folks have learned this trick, too, and it keeps a person young. So, add two and two together: We've got a sheriff who looks fifty and must be eighty. We've got a big wolf running around where there aren't any wolves, and the sheriff carries a full wolf skin in his trunk. Angel remembers him putting it on and dancing around just before that silver wolf attacked us on Tatum's property. What does this add up to?"

"A werewolf with a badge," Riley answered gravely. Suddenly he held out his hand and stopped her. "Hey, look at that."

"What?" Buffy followed his gaze but couldn't see anything until he pointed. On a phone wire overlooking the beach sat four crows; they seemed to be looking right at the two humans. "What does your grandma's poem say about four crows?"

Gazing solemnly at the birds, Riley replied, "One crow sorrow, two crows mirth, three crows a wedding . . . four crows a birth."

"A birth?" Buffy snorted. "I'm not holding my breath for that."

"I don't think we can afford to waste any more

time," Riley said with urgency. "I want to be back at the border as soon as it gets dark . . . to meet with Raul and Machete. We'll bring the car around to protect Angel from the sunlight."

"Back to driving," Buffy said glumly.

"I think we've been stood up," Samantha Finn said, staring across the pool table at Angel. She leveled her cue stick and took a shot, deftly sinking the fourteen ball in the side pocket. For the last two hours they had actually been playing pool in the Club Monterey, and she had beaten him six games out of ten.

Angel nodded grimly and surveyed the crowd, which was smaller than the night before, although the music was just as loud. He could swear that he'd heard the same songs starting to repeat, although maybe that was just his frustration. He knew that Raul and Machete hadn't been eager to help him in his phony quest to get Sam across the border, but he didn't think they would just blow him off. *Is there no honor among vampires?*

Of course, a mysterious stranger—an employer— had warned them not to take any more groups across the border just the night before. Maybe Sheriff Barton had also gotten word to them, or arrested them, or killed them. Buffy's encounter with Barton that afternoon had boded poorly for their success, especially after finding out that the cornpone sheriff might be a skinwalker. To Angel, that explained a lot: such as why Barton had pegged Angel as a vampire upon taking one whiff of him, and how a wolf had attacked him out of nowhere.

He heard the crack of billiard balls and looked up to see that Sam had nearly run the table. She was about to go for the eight ball while he still had five solid balls to sink. "You're beating me again," he muttered.

She smiled and leaned over the rail, looking very fetching in her skimpy halter top, revealing shorts, dog-collar choker, and spiky hair. "Nothing like getting twelve hours of sleep," she said. "Eight ball in the corner pocket."

Angel watched disgruntledly as she sunk the black ball, polishing him off for the seventh game.

"Rack them up again?" she asked.

"No," he said with a scowl. "I'm going to check in with the roach coach and go to plan B."

"What's plan B?"

"I don't know. Anything but this." Angel stepped into the corner, turned his back to prying eyes, and took out the small walkie-talkie that Riley had given him. "Echo one to base, come in," he said, feeling as if he were playing soldier.

"Base here," responded Riley. "What's up?"

"I can't stand to lose any more pool games," grumbled Angel. "And I know when I've been stood up. Any sign of them from your end?"

"No," answered Riley, "but the range is only a couple of miles. If they're here in Verdura, we need to drive around and look for them. That is, if our friend hasn't spotted the souvenir we gave him."

"We won't know until we've tried," said Angel. "We're coming back to you now. Echo one out."

"Aw," Sam said with a sly smile. "I was just getting warmed up." She held her hand out to him, and he took it with some hesitation.

"No more vampire kisses?" he asked.

"No, I think I'm over that," answered Sam. "It was fun while it lasted, but the hangover . . . whew!"

Looking like a vaguely foreign—if not exactly American—couple, Angel and Sam strode out the front door of the Club Monterey. To their left was the garish neon of the main drag of Verdura, and to their right was a dark residential street, where a humble white van was parked. It had been left purposely dirty from their travels, so as to conceal how new it was. They strode leisurely in that direction while Angel kept his eyes open for onlookers. Except for a few club goers and an old Indian woman who seemed to be sleeping at the side of a Dumpster, no one was around. And none of them seemed to care about the handsome couple.

The side door of the van slipped open at their approach, and Sam and Angel slipped inside. Immediately, Buffy started up the engine and drove off into the sultry night. Riley was seated at his console, studying blips on his screen. "I've got the bullfight place and their other hangout in our range," he reported, "and they're not at either one."

"Where should we go?" Buffy called from the front seat.

"Get on the main street," Angel answered, "and head south. Even after you hit a dirt road, keep going."

Riley looked at him with interest. "You want us to go to that old cemetery down there?"

"Yes," answered Angel. "They were hiding out there before, and they might be hiding out there again."

With Buffy driving and Riley searching electronically for Machete's tracer, they drove south until the garish neon and drunk tourists faded far behind, along with the paved road. Soon the jagged outline of the old mission appeared silhouetted against the silvery clouds, and they could see the aged crosses, tombstones, and decrepit wrought iron of the graveyard. The old graves stretched into the black hills beyond, and this countryside looked as if it hadn't changed since the Aztecs had confronted the conquistadors five hundred years ago.

"Bingo," Riley said as his screen lit up. "Machete is here—or at least his jacket is."

"Buffy, don't stop here," ordered Angel. "Keep driving until we get out of sight, then park."

"Gotcha," answered the Slayer chauffeur. "Who's going up there?"

"Just me," answered Angel.

"No way," argued Sam. "We're a pair. They'll think there's something odd if I'm not with you."

Riley gave Angel a worried glance, as if he wanted the vampire to talk his wife out of this plan. But Sam crossed her arms and glowered at both of them,

179

standing firm. "In my purse I've got a gun, a stake, a cross, and holy water—and I've done this before. I'll be okay," she insisted.

"I'm not going to park far away!" Buffy called from the front. "We'll be ready to back you up."

Angel scowled. "We won't need it, because if they don't cooperate, we're going to stake them and be done with it."

"That's fine with me," Riley said, sounding relieved.

A few moments later, Buffy pulled off the dirt road into the weeds and soft sand of the shoulder. There wasn't even the hint of light on the lonely road, except for the three-quarter moon hiding among wispy clouds in the night sky. Angel patted his jacket pocket to make sure he had his own wooden stake, then he threw open the van door and stepped out. He reached behind him to help Sam jump out, and she teetered on her clunky heels. The summer breeze was unusually cool in this forgotten place, as if the ancient mission and cemetery existed in another time and space. Somewhere nearby, an owl hooted an eerie welcome, and far-off in the hills the coyotes yipped at their puny plans.

Angel took Sam's hand and helped her walk across the uneven terrain. Her usual bravado was missing, and she gaped in awe at the crumbling adobe walls in the shape and style of a miniature Alamo. It didn't look as if these weathered walls could stand for another week, let alone the hundreds of years they had already guarded the empty fields and crowded cemetery. An owl hooted over their heads, making both of them jump, and the wind twisted into dust devils full of leaves and old mesquite pods.

Sam and Angel moved slowly through the aged cemetery, with its rusty iron markers, wind-beaten wooden crosses, crumbling mausoleums, and dead bouquets. If possible, it was even cooler here, and the breeze was alive with strange currents of heat and cold and the reek of decay. Angel glanced from side to side, wondering how deeply they should tread into this ancient burial ground. He already felt unfriendly eyes upon him, and heard the padding of feet along the dead ground. Angel gripped the walkie-talkie in his hand and fought the temptation to summon Buffy for help.

With a tug on her hand, he stopped Sam in midstride and held her protectively to his chest. "Raul! Machete!" he called. "You stood me up—I don't appreciate that. I have only asked you for what you have given others. Why won't you help me?"

The only answer was the beating of wings in the night, probably the owl that had greeted them. Growing with anger, Angel shouted, "Have you ignored me because you're *cowards?* You have to hide like rabbits in this cemetery. I would be better off to find street urchins to guide me than two old women like you!"

"*¡Callate!*" a voice growled, telling him to shut up. He whirled around to see a stocky figure rise from behind a tombstone. Raul shook a fist at him. "We told you we couldn't help you, and that is all we need to say. We don't trust you, or your woman. If you are still in Verdura tomorrow night, we will *kill* you."

Angel laughed. "You couldn't kill a hiccup! You are two old women who are afraid of the border patrol."

"Aarrrgh!" screamed a voice attached to a wiry figure that sprang from the top of a mausoleum. It was Machete, wielding his namesake blade, and Angel barely had time to catch his weapon hand and avoid a beheading. The two vampires wrestled each other into the dust and grappled ineffectively, their strength equal. That left Sam to fight Raul by herself, and the monster was instantly upon her. Prepared with her stake and crucifix, she nearly dusted him, but missed by centimeters. Summoning her courage and wielding the wooden weapons, Sam drove the suave vampire back against his crumbling mausoleum, where she held him at bay.

Relieved to see she was holding her own, Angel turned all his attention to fighting his foe, who was every bit as strong as he. Plus he was enraged by the insults and had already turned into a fearsome beast. It was all Angel could do to keep the sharp blade from his throat, until he got a foot under Machete and kicked him head over heels into a patch of weeds. As he leaped to his feet and charged his opponent, Angel felt his own face and body changing into something inhuman that only wanted to tear and mutilate. Any thought of using the walkie-talkie to summon help flew from his primitive mind.

Angel caught Machete's wrist and snapped it,

causing the long blade to clatter to the ground. Then he gripped Machete by the throat while he fumbled for the wooden stake in his jacket. The vampire squirmed in his grasp, trying to escape, until Angel was frozen by a low growl behind them. It was a sound he instantly recognized, because he had heard it only two nights earlier. With a right cross and a kick, Angel sent Machete flying, and he was able to spin around as the silver wolf leaped upon him.

With a desperate lunge, Angel was able to ram the stake deep into the wolf's chest, but that didn't slow the monster down for one second. It would have torn him apart if Sam hadn't leaped upon its back, digging her own wooden stake into the enormous animal. The wolf howled in pain and turned upon the brave woman, raking her chest with a claw and chomping on her arm. With a scream and a whimper, Sam collapsed to the ground, and the wolf began to maul her. Their eyes gleaming with bloodlust, Raul and Machete closed in for the kill.

Then a bright flare popped overhead, showering them with sparks and drenching the area with a sickening gray gas. Angel heard Sam fall into a coughing fit, and he couldn't see his own hand in front of his face. It was mass pandemonium as the combatants collided with one another, trying to make their escape. Angel thought he saw Buffy slice through the fog to deliver a firm kick to one of them, but it might have been a hallucination. He dropped to the ground and began to crawl out of the fog, finally making his way to a stretch of clear air over the rocks of a sunken grave.

When Angel could finally see again, he almost wished he were still blinded. There stood Buffy with a flashlight in her hand, training the beam on Riley, who held his wife in his trembling arms. Sam was covered in a mass of blood that seemed to ooze from every pore of her body, and she wasn't moving.

"She's dying!" croaked Riley. "She's bleeding to death."

CHAPTER THIRTEEN

Because Angel was stronger, and because he felt shaky, Riley allowed the vampire to pick up his wife and carry her into the emergency room of the Mexican hospital—Immaculate Heart, it was called. He followed closely on Angel's heels with Buffy right behind him. To his surprise, the triage room was packed with patients late on this Monday night, and two thirds of them appeared to be young pregnant women, ready to give birth any moment. All the rest were husbands and family in attendance to the expectant mothers. Riley and Buffy shared a glance, and he knew that both of them were thinking about the four crows they had seen that afternoon.

Riley tried to stay calm as Angel dealt in his fluent Spanish with the medical staff. Little explanation was needed, because it was clear that Sam had been attacked by a wild animal; Riley heard Angel say *"lobo"* several times. Even though Sam was a bloody mess and would need more stitches than one of Grandma's quilts, Riley's initial fear that she would die was unfounded. She was young and strong, and most of her wounds were superficial bites and scratches. The worst injury was to her upper left arm, which was where most of the bleeding occurred. Still, his beloved was clearly in shock and badly hurt, although her face and head had mercifully been spared. A bite to the head from that monster might have proven fatal.

He felt somebody touch his arm, and he turned to see Buffy staring helplessly at him. Riley put his arm around his friend, and they held each other for support until the moment that Sam was placed on a gurney and wheeled into the depths of the hospital.

Looking glum and disheveled, Angel returned to them. "You know," he said, "she sacrificed herself to save me from that wolf."

"That doesn't surprise me," Riley said softly.

"It wasn't a normal wolf," Buffy rasped through clenched teeth. "I know the sheriff has something to do with this, and he might have tipped off the other two. They were waiting for you."

Riley nodded somberly. "It's a good thing we heard the struggle over Machete's bug. Did all three of them get away?"

"I was about to finish Machete when . . ." Angel didn't have to complete his sentence. "Yeah, they got away."

"Then whatever they're planning for Thursday is still on," concluded Riley. "We have to stop them, without Sam."

An uneasy silence followed for several minutes, although the pregnant ladies interjected an occasional groan. One by one, the expectant mothers were admitted and put into wheelchairs for a much happier trip down the corridor than Sam had taken. Somewhere off in the bowels of the hospital, a newborn baby cried.

"Looks like the crows were right," said Buffy.

"Crows?" asked Angel.

"Yeah, four crows a birth," she answered. "Or, in this case, a dozen births."

"I hope they can spare a doctor for Sam," muttered Riley, his arm still around his former girlfriend.

"I think they know something about birthin' babies around here," Buffy said encouragingly. "And also plenty about stitching up animal bites. Why don't the two of you go out to the van and get yourselves some clean clothes? Maybe you should even rent a room nearby—morning is going to come before long. I'll stay here and call you on the walkie-talkie if there's any news. Chances are good that you'll be back before I hear anything."

Riley looked down at his clothing, then at Angel, and he had to admit that they were both bloody messes. He was also still trembling from worry, and he knew that pacing up and down that drab waiting room wasn't going to accomplish anything. It was best to make sure that Angel was protected from the approaching sunlight. "Thank you, Buffy," he said. "Come on, Angel."

The vampire gave Riley a nod. "It doesn't seem like it now, but you're a lucky man. That girl's a fighter, and full of life. She'll be okay."

Riley nodded hopefully, unable to muster any words in response. He didn't want to say anything to Angel and Buffy, who were condemned to their fates, but he was reconsidering the whole idea of staying in this insane profession.

It was Tuesday, mid-morning, and Riley and Buffy were still lounging in the waiting room of Immaculate Heart Hospital, watching sick people come and go, along with women having babies. Via the one nurse who spoke English, they had received a few cryptic bits of information on Sam's condition: She was in surgery, she was in the recovery room, and she was unconscious but stable. Waiting in a hospital was something that Buffy had endured before, but this time all the old magazines were all in Spanish.

She and Riley had very little to say to each other, and he seemed to be immersed in his own thoughts. She wondered if he blamed Angel for what had happened to Sam, but she couldn't bring herself to ask him. If he did, that was unfair, because Sam had insisted upon going with Angel to the decrepit old cemetery in back of the mission. He had wanted to go alone, although it seemed now that nobody should do anything alone on this crazy case.

Finally a doctor who was so young that he looked like a high school student walked into the waiting room. He didn't need to look hard to find the only Anglos, and he approached them and said in accented English, "Are you Mr. Finn?"

"Yes!" Riley answered, springing to his feet. "And this is our friend Buffy."

"Pleased to meet you," said the youthful doctor with an old-fashioned bow. "I am Dr. Armando Salvatore. You would like to know what has happened to Samantha, yes?"

"Yes," agreed Riley.

The doctor nodded and consulted his chart. "We repaired twenty-six lacerations with over two hundred stitches. She has received a blood transfusion and antibiotics to protect from infection. We didn't know if she has had a recent tetanus vaccination, so we gave her one, anyway. She is receiving intravenous fluids and more antibiotics. Samantha is stable, but still very weak, and I think she will sleep a long time."

"But she'll be all right?" Riley asked nervously.

"Yes, she is young and strong . . . in good health." Then Dr. Salvatore's smile turned into a mild frown. "Her left arm has torn muscles and ligaments—it is likely she will need physical therapy. When she leaves here, she will wear a sling."

"And when will she leave here?" asked Buffy.

The doctor frowned again. "Yes, I was meaning to discuss that. Normally I would keep her here for three days at least. But she is healthy otherwise, and we are short of beds. Also there is a mysterious fever in this town, and it might be better for you to return to the United States, if you can."

"Of course," said Riley with determination. "Today?"

"No, she needs another night of rest. Tomorrow morning we will release her. One thing more—"

"Yes?" Riley asked expectantly.

The young doctor smiled. "Did you know your wife is pregnant?"

Riley staggered backward, and Buffy feared she would have to catch him. "No," he croaked. "I didn't know that."

Salvatore shrugged. "Perhaps she also did not know it. She has not complained of feeling sick? Tired?"

Riley ran his fingers through his reddish hair, still looking stunned. "Well, come to think of it, she has."

"Congratulations," Buffy said with a hint of envy. "Doc, can we see her?"

"She's asleep. But if you want to sit with her, please come," answered Salvatore. "It is a small room with three patients—only one of you at a time, please."

"You go with her," Buffy said instantly, giving Riley a nudge. "I'll go back and see how Angel is."

"Are you sure?"

"Yes, go ahead." She gave him a smile and added,

"Angel will be glad to hear she's all right, and that there will be little Finns."

"I'll see you later," Riley promised as he followed the doctor into the corridor. "Maybe I can find out something about the mystery illness too. Keep looking for crows!"

"I will," answered Buffy, watching him go. For a moment, she wondered if she would ever see Riley again.

Angel stood by the window, looking forlornly at the bright sunlight playing across the black rooftops of downtown Verdura. They had gotten a room on the top floor of one of the fleabag hotels Riley had rejected earlier. Angel listened without comment to Buffy's report, although a smile crept across his face when she told him Sam was pregnant. "Good for them," he said.

"And that mystery illness is down here too," added Buffy, reminding him of the epidemic Sam mentioned, in the Arizona town across the border. "The hospital is packed."

"All the more reason to get her out of there quickly," answered Angel. "But I'm not leaving Mexico until I finish those two . . . and the wolf."

Buffy nodded somberly. "As long as we've got Riley's van and his James Bond stuff, we've got a way to find them. We know they'll be doing something on Thursday night."

He turned to face her. "You're with me, aren't you?"

"As long as I get to do something else besides drive the van."

"Don't worry, your days of sitting on the sidelines are over. Now it's time to do what you do best."

"A-slaying we will go," said Buffy, forcing down the memories of previous hunts with Angel by her side. "I'm tempted to go look for them now."

"No, nobody is going alone against those three. You need full backup." He smiled grimly. "And maybe a silver bullet or two."

"Yeah, silver," she replied thoughtfully. "That's the fifth line of the poem: 'Five crows silver.' What caliber is Sam's gun?"

"Nine-millimeter," answered Angel. He motioned out the window at the old buildings baking in the hot sun. "If you go to find silver bullets, be careful. This isn't the U.S., where even the kids carry guns."

"I know," she answered, grabbing her purse and heading for the door. "But we passed lots of jewelry makers and silver artisans, and they all seem to like American dollars. Something tells me it won't be that hard. What's Spanish for 'silver bullet'?"

"*Bala de plata,*" Angel answered with a smile. "Getting them to make a silver bullet might be hard, but they could fill one of our hollow-points with silver. Let me get you a few."

"Thanks," she answered, waiting patiently for him to bring her a sample of their munitions. "See you later!" Buffy called as she hurried out the door and down the stairs of the aged hotel. Upon reaching the street, she paused to look up at the high wires, where the birds tended to congregate.

Sure enough, five black birds sat on a telephone wire, gazing down at her. There was no doubt in Buffy's mind that she would return to the hotel with some modern-day silver bullets.

"I look like Frankenstein," Sam muttered unhappily as Riley guided her wheelchair out of the hospital into the bright sunlight of Wednesday morning.

"Really, Frankenstein's daughter," Buffy said with a grin.

"I think you look more like the Mummy," suggested Riley. It was true, because she was swathed neck-to-toe in bandages, and her left arm was in a sling, just like the Mummy's useless left arm. But Sam still looked radiant, thought Buffy, owing to the fact that she was always beautiful and was now carrying another human being inside her banged-up body.

"I don't want to leave you guys," said Sam. "I can still be useful."

Buffy brushed aside her comments. "Forget that, it's already been decided. You're going back to the U.S. for some rest and recuperation. Riley's going to leave us the van and most of his toys. Isn't that right?"

"Yes," agreed the happy husband. "I've already rented another car. We're taking some of the portable devices and gas grenades with us, but we'll leave the big stuff with Buffy and Angel. Oh, and I've got something else for you two." He reached into his jacket pocket and pulled out two sealed envelopes, which he handed to Buffy. "Your pay."

"Pay?" she said with a smile. "This is a novelty. Money will definitely lift Angel's spirits. He's been kind of down ever since . . ." She didn't finish her sentence.

"I know," replied Riley. "I hope it helps."

"And I've got something for you," Buffy said, reaching into her purse. She pulled out five silver bullets wrapped in a rubber band and handed them to Riley.

He looked at them for a moment, then quickly stuffed them into his pocket. "Are these what I think they are?"

Buffy nodded. "Yes, but you'll have to find your own nine-millimeter gun, because we're keeping Sam's. I've got five too."

"You saw five crows?" asked Riley.

"I saw them."

Sam shook her head with amazement. "You two have been spending too much time together."

"We've all been spending too much time together," said Buffy, "but we're going to wrap things up by tomorrow night."

"I hope so." Riley reached out for Buffy and gave her a warm hug. "You've got my cell-phone number—keep in touch."

She nodded. "Where will you be?"

"I'm going to stay near Verdura, Arizona," answered Riley, "because there's been another development."

"What's that?"

He glanced worriedly at his wife before saying, "I

finally got word from my expert. All those dead crows—they could indicate an outbreak of West Nile Virus. It's been moving west, and large birds are usually the first ones to come down with it. I want to contact the CDC and have them send a team to investigate. That will no doubt drive Frederick Tatum and Sheriff Barton crazy."

Sam peered thoughtfully at her husband. "So the crows really have been trying to tell us something."

"Yep," answered Riley, "so you're not the only one who needs to watch her health. We'd better get going. Do you think you can stand, sweetheart?"

"I'm sliced-and-dice, but not dead," she answered. With a grimace, Sam rose to her feet and gripped her husband's arm. He guided her carefully into the parking lot, toward their waiting car.

Buffy's lips thinned, and her jaw took on a determined set. *Now it's up to me,* she decided.

Armed with wooden stakes and a Glock pistol loaded with silver bullets, Buffy and Angel strolled through the ancient cemetery behind the mission ruins south of Verdura. The place was still eerie in its quiet desolation and decrepit condition, but on this Wednesday evening, only the dead were present. Buffy already suspected as much, having found no blips on their tracking devices, but Angel still wanted to check with his eyeballs. Buffy had driven them all over the Mexican city—twice—and no signals had shown up. Wherever Machete was tonight, he was either far from Verdura, or he had destroyed the tracer they had planted on him.

"Why do I get the idea that we aren't going to find them?" Angel asked, his voice seeming to boom across the deserted cemetery.

"Because we aren't," answered Buffy. "They've got a big deal going tomorrow night, and they don't want anything to mess it up. We're their biggest headache, and they're not going anyplace we know about."

Angel shrugged. "So what do you want to do?"

"Go dancing!" Buffy said cheerfully.

"Are you kidding?"

"No. I've been sitting in a van on stake-out for two nights while you and Sam partied, and now it's my turn." She grabbed his arm. "Come on, we used to shake a tailfeather at the old Bronze. We've even got money to spend!"

The vampire shrugged. "I guess nothing else is going to happen tonight."

"That's the grim spirit," she replied. "Come on, all vengeance and no play makes Angel a dull boy."

He laughed in spite of himself. "Buffy, you can really be fun."

"I keep trying to tell boys that, but they can't get past the slaying bit." She steered him away from the crumbling tombstones and crooked crosses back to the van they had left at the side of the road.

In their new room back at the Bates Motel, Riley Finn sat in a chair facing the door and hefting the nine-millimeter Beretta 92F he had bought that afternoon. One good thing about rural Arizona, it wasn't difficult to buy a gun under the table, and he had loaded the clip with the five silver bullets Buffy had given him. The hot wind howled outside, whipping dust and tumbleweeds past the window, but little else moved in the nearly empty parking lot. At least he'd had the sense to get a local doctor to check Sam out and make sure she was healing all right.

If I had any sense, I'd be on my way back to Washington, D.C., he told himself. *We're crazy to stay here.* He shifted in his seat, switching his attention back and forth between the window and the door.

"That's pointless, you know," a soothing voice said from behind him. He turned to see his wife, curled up in bed and looking remarkably fit for a woman who'd been mauled by a wolf two nights ago. "They're not going to bother us tonight."

"How do you know that?"

Sam shrugged. "Because they're getting ready for their big shipment tomorrow night . . . whatever it is. And no, I don't think it's going to come across the desert. They've been warned to stay far away from the desert."

"I suppose," said Riley. Unable to refute her logic, he slipped the pistol back into his jacket pocket. "Maybe the crows will tell us what's going to happen next."

"The crows?" she asked doubtfully.

He nodded and said, "We've had the 'five crows silver.' Now it's 'six crows gold' and 'seven crows a secret which must never be told.'"

"Well, I was pregnant," suggested Sam. "That's a secret *nobody* knew."

"But it's not 'a secret which must never be told,'" he answered. "That would have to be a real serious secret."

She laughed at him. "*You're* real serious. Why don't you come to bed? My bandages need changing, and I've got nothing on underneath them."

Riley turned to her and smiled. "You're pregnant, and you're sewed up like a football."

"But I'm not dead," Sam replied seductively. "Come on, we'll be careful."

Shaking his head with amusement, Riley left his chair and crawled into bed with his wife. He gave her a tender, loving kiss while he held her body as if she were made from the most fragile crystal. He was especially watchful of her left arm, and he finally broke away from her insistent lips. "How long are we going to keep hunting monsters?" he asked.

"Until they're all gone," she whispered, pulling him closer and resuming their passionate kiss.

"That was fun," Buffy said as she and Angel returned to their drab hotel room in Verdura, Mexico. They had listened to salsa music for a couple of hours, shot some pool, walked, and talked; it had almost seemed like old times back in Sunnydale. *Well, except that it's not—and can never be,* she thought. Angel shut the door behind them and stood gazing expectantly at her. A window air conditioner gurgled in the background, but it had little effect. Buffy was hot and sweaty. For a moment, she thought—and hoped—that he would kiss her, but he looked away.

"We only have one room now," he pointed out. "And one bed."

"I know," she answered hoarsely. "I guess we didn't plan ahead very well."

"We never do," he answered with a boyish smile. "But I'm worried."

"I won't hurt you," said Buffy. "I mean, I killed you once and sent you to Hell, but I'm really harmless."

"I'm not worried about you," he replied, moving closer. "I'm worried about the van."

"The van?" she repeated in disbelief.

"Yes, if anything happens to that van and Riley's equipment, we're out of luck. We'd have no way to locate Machete and Raul. So I'm going to spend the rest of the night in the van, maybe turn on the screen and do some scanning. Who knows, I might get lucky. Just before dawn I'll come back, and we'll switch off."

"Sure, we'll switch off," Buffy answered, trying to hide her disappointment—or was it relief? She knew that neither of them would ever really get lucky.

"Good night, Buffy," he said just before making a quick escape out the door.

"Good night, sweet prince," she answered softly.

CHAPTER FOURTEEN

"Mr. Tatum will see you now, Mr. Finn," said the middle-aged secretary sitting outside the plain executive offices of Tatum Pecans.

Riley rose from a threadbare chair in the waiting room and approached the desk, and the receptionist motioned him toward a metal security door. He gave her a grateful smile, even though he'd been waiting over an hour, but the secretary was finished with him. On his way into the inner sanctum, Riley glanced out the window at the complex of machinery and buildings just behind Tatum's mansion. Seen by daylight, the spread was more impressive than it had appeared by night in the rain. The surrounding orchard of stately pecan trees made him feel as if he were in the Old South rather than directly on the Arizona-Mexico border.

He opened the door and stepped into an office that was paneled appropriately enough in pecan wood. A variety of Tatum Pecan logos decorated the walls, as if to remind a visitor that the family had been in this business for 150 years. There were also photos of Frederick Tatum with prominent politicians and celebrities, some taken on hunting and fishing trips. On a display table sat an architect's model of the Río Conchas Resort, where Riley, Sam, and Buffy had gotten into trouble several days ago. The great man himself was not present in his office, but Riley heard a toilet flushing in an adjacent bathroom.

That door opened, and Frederick Tatum stepped into his office, looking dapper as usual. Riley thought that he must dye his hair black. The rancher didn't offer Riley a handshake, and he barely glanced at him as he strode behind his desk.

"Mr. Finn," he muttered, "I have no clue why you wanted to see me. I don't think we have anything to say to each other."

Riley tried to muster a smile. "How are the newly-weds doing?" he asked. "Still on their honeymoon?"

That won a polite expression from the pecan tycoon. "They're on a world cruise, having a great time," he answered. "Did you really come here to ask me about the children?"

"No," admitted Riley, "this is a courtesy call

before I alert the federal government about a serious problem here in Verdura."

Tatum gave him a grim smile. "Oh, you came here to threaten me. Well, I'm afraid there's very little you can do to me, Mr. Finn. Please see yourself out."

"I'm about to call in the Centers for Disease Control," said Riley quickly. "You have a serious outbreak of West Nile Virus."

"What!" Tatum roared, suddenly giving the young man his full attention. "What on earth makes you think that?"

"The dead crows, the bulging hospitals on both sides of the border, and the mosquito problem in all those new lakes and ponds you built on your resort." He pointed to the model on the table. "I think they're the source of the disease."

Now Tatum's lips thinned, and he gulped back his first response. After considering the problem for a moment, the rancher summoned a wan smile. "You haven't called the CDC yet, have you?"

"No," answered Riley. "I thought you had better be prepared for the publicity onslaught. The CDC will come in force—taking samples, testing everyone, taking over the hospitals, and draining your lakes. It will be a PR disaster." He held back a smile.

Tatum breathed a sigh of relief. "If you haven't called them yet, then we can reach some kind of . . . understanding. I underestimated you, Mr. Finn, and I don't usually get caught by surprise. To keep you from calling in the dogs, what is it you really want?"

Calmly, Riley took the seat he had not been offered, and he perused the photos on the wall before answering. "That man," he said, pointing to a picture, "Sheriff Clete Barton, is a dangerous menace, and you know it. He has a terrible secret too. I don't know if you're aware of that, but you *do* know that he covered up the deaths of those illegal aliens in the desert. In fact, I think he's working with the people who killed them, and I use the term 'people' loosely. He's got to be removed from office and arrested."

Tatum was aghast. "You're talking about the man who's my in-law! Clete Barton was sheriff when my *father* ran this company—he's a fixture in this county. Why, I could no more run Clete Barton out of this town than I could turn back time or erase the border! You've asked the one thing that I can't deliver."

"You're afraid of him," said Riley.

"You're damn right!" snapped Tatum.

"But he works for you—I've seen the way you two interact."

Frederick Tatum stepped around his desk and tried to appeal to Riley with open palms and a snake-oil smile. "Listen, let's work together. There are things I can do to help. I'll take care of the mosquitoes in the lakes—I'll spare no expense. And maybe I can rein in Sheriff Barton. We'll reopen the investigation into those deaths, if you like. I'll, uh . . . I'll even tell your superiors that you're doing a great job and should be put back on the case. We'll start off on a new foot, like these bad feelings between us never happened."

Riley pursed his lips, trying to look as if he were mulling over the offer. In truth, he had gotten what he wanted: to throw some fear into Frederick Tatum and make him admit that Clete Barton was bad news. If what they suspected about Barton was true, then Tatum had good reason to fear him. The tycoon was the wealthiest, most powerful man in the region, and they couldn't hope to clean it up without his help.

"I'll think about it," Riley said, rising to his feet. "If Barton or his deputies get within a hundred yards of me or my wife, I'm calling in the CDC. If I don't check in hourly, my report will be sent automatically. Do I make myself clear?"

"Yes, you make yourself clear," Tatum answered, clearly gritting his teeth to keep from ripping into Riley.

"And start getting rid of those mosquitoes," the young man said on his way out the door. No matter what Tatum and Barton did, Riley intended to call in the CDC as soon as the vampires were eliminated.

Sundown was still an hour away, but Buffy drove leisurely around the border town of Verdura, Mexico, listening to the scanner in the back. It was turned up loudly so she could hear it, because Angel was still holed up in their hotel room. She had almost given up hope of finding Machete again, so thoroughly had the vampire disappeared from their radar screens. Still, this was Thursday, and something was going down tonight along the schizoid border. Even if she hadn't heard the threat with her own ears, she could feel it.

Something prickly was charging through the hot, humid air. Rain clouds had returned to hover above the desert, and there were ominous flashes of lightning over the mountains both to the north and the south.

It seemed incredible that she and Angel had arrived in this part of the world only a week ago, when it felt as if they had been there a month. She had actually picked up about a dozen words and phrases in Spanish, which was way more than she had learned in two years of studying French in high school. Of course, this might be called "Spanish immersion." Leisurely, Buffy tooled down a side street that ran parallel to a twenty-foot-tall sheet-metal fence. Only that ribbon of metal differentiated the United States from Mexico.

Suddenly the beeper in the back of the van sounded, and Buffy nearly slammed on the brakes. Unless she had screwed up the frequency or set the equipment wrong, this meant that Machete's tracer had been detected.

Buffy pulled the van off to the side of the road and took a good look at her surroundings. South of the road was a depressing array of overgrown fields, and clapboard shanties that looked as if a strong wind would blow them over. Somehow she didn't think Machete was hiding among these impoverished Mexicans, so she looked toward the metal fence that marked the border.

The wall wasn't the only thing in the area: There was also an old drainage ditch that appeared to conduct rain run-off into a wash that snaked along the border. Farther up the street, the drainage ditch disappeared into a circular culvert that ran under the border fence. The culvert's opening was blocked by a metal grate clogged with debris, but this rusty barrier didn't appear very formidable. She had no idea what was on the other side of the border fence, but she could see treetops.

Was Machete hanging out in a drainage ditch? That also seemed a bit unlikely, and Buffy had driven by there last night without getting a blip. Maybe he had just thrown his jacket, or the bug, into the ditch. She opened her door and jumped out, fighting the temptation to crawl into the ditch to investigate. Instead, Buffy went around to the back door of the van, opened it, and sat down at the console. She intended to make sure the reading was legitimate, but it quickly grew fainter. A moment later, the pointer faded away entirely.

A phantom blip? she wondered.

Whatever it was, this was the first sign that Machete hadn't fallen off the face of the earth, and it was enough to warrant a trip back to the hotel to pick up Angel. By the time they returned, the sun would have set completely, and he would be free to move around.

Buffy jumped out of the back, ran to the driver's door, and got behind the wheel. *Finally!* Her mind racing with excitement, she made a ragged U-turn and headed back toward downtown Verdura.

* * *

Samantha Finn looked at the array of pills she had to take and wanted to throw them all into the toilet. She was kind of a health nut, and the last few days she'd spent either in a hospital or in smoky bars, drinking and kissing vampires. All the while, she'd been pregnant! Now she felt like a very poor excuse for a would-be mom, and she didn't want to take any more drugs. Even though Sam understood the necessity for the antibiotics and painkillers, all of which came from Mexico and had unfamiliar names, she would rather have the pain. The threat of West Nile Virus also lay heavily on her mind, especially since she had spent two nights in a hospital rife with it. Although Sam tried to maintain a brave and carefree front for Riley, the number of things to worry about had quadrupled.

She decided to take the antibiotics but not the painkillers, even though her body was like a pincushion of aches, sores, bruises, and stitches. If she didn't come down with an infection, it would be a miracle, and there was no position of sitting, lying, or standing that was comfortable.

Ah well, it was better than the alternative. Scarier now was the thought that her death would have meant the death of another—an innocent, unborn child. Of course, Sam had been pregnant without knowing it when she had thrown herself at Angel. So that infatuation now had something of an explanation: Her hormones were in an uproar. Everything in her body was changing. *Even before a supernatural wolf had rearranged my skin.*

Now night was coming, and Riley hadn't returned to their dingy motel room. Sam knew he was buying stuff for her, including esoteric food that she didn't really need, but he had fallen into a protective anything-you-want mode, and who wouldn't take advantage of that? Considering the lack of real stores out there, she realized she had sent him on a wild goose chase. All because she had to be selfish.

I'll call him, Sam told herself. *I don't need onion bagels, or carrot cake, or hair conditioner. I don't need anything but my husband.*

Leaning painfully across her bed, Sam picked up her mobile phone and dialed Riley's phone. After six rings he didn't answer; instead came the female voice of his generic impersonal voice mail, which she hated so much.

"Riley," she said testily, "why aren't you answering? Listen, you don't need to bring me all that stuff. Just quit where you are now, and come home. I mean, come back to the Bates. Love ya, Sam."

She hung up, thinking her message sounded so mundane and helpless. In the span of two days she had ceased being a vibrant, independent woman with an adventurous marriage and had become her own mother. And she had always thought she could avoid that.

Just then the lights in the parking lot flickered as big globs of rain hit the picture window. The wind, which had been gusty, shifted into overdrive, making the timbers groan, the shutters bang, and a stoplight swing desperately above the dusty road. A crash of lightning shook the room and Sam's spine, and she curled painfully off the bed. A second later, the lights went out in her place and all along the length of the L-shaped motel. Sam could still see—it wasn't dark outside, but was an eerie phase of twilight, turned violent by the storm. The parking lot was suddenly alive with shapes, like ghosts, moving through the shifting rays of light.

She retreated from the window and looked for her weapons—the crucifix and the stake. Riley carried the new gun with the silver bullets, but most of their armaments were down south with Buffy and Angel. The figures loped on two legs across the parking lot, like a mob of runners at the start of a marathon. Considering the crash of wind, rain, and lightning, she couldn't blame them for running. Plus, darkness was crushing the sky, driven by the rain. *But where did these apparitions come from? Who are they?*

One of the shamblers suddenly bounced face-first into the picture window and made her jump in surprise. To her embarrassment, she even screamed. The creature clinging to her window had a horrid face: dark and subhuman, although the rain might have distorted it. He looked longingly at her, then dashed away, his long black hair gleaming in the half-light.

Sam pounced on the phone again and dialed Riley. This time she got him.

"Hello," he answered simply.

"Riley!" she responded with a gasp. "You didn't answer your phone before, and—"

"Oh, I was just letting the shopkeeper borrow my phone," answered Riley. "We were looking for that conditioner you wanted."

"It doesn't matter," insisted Sam. "Just get back here, please!"

"What's the matter?" he asked with growing alarm.

Sam peered back out the window, but the stampede of ghostly figures was gone. The parking lot was still buffeted by wind and rain, but it was empty, except for old trash and tumbleweeds skipping across the concrete. "The lights have gone out," she answered. "And there are some weird people—"

"On my way," he replied without hesitation. "Bye."

"Bye." Sam ended the call and set down the phone, feeling like a wimp. Had she really seen anything out there, or was it just her nerves, hormones, and raw emotions? She crossed to the door and made sure it was locked with both the bolt and the security chain.

"Is this it?" Angel asked doubtfully as he peered into the gloom of the dirt road along the Mexican side of the border. There was no electricity in the shanty town to the left, so that was just a foreboding outline of clapboard ruins, which shook and groaned in the strong wind. On the driver's side, Buffy's window was open, and she survived a variety of smells, including something that was as rank as a sewer in the Hellmouth.

As soon as the Slayer stepped out and shut the door, a flock of crows bolted from the top of a rusty old water tank. Buffy tried to count the black phantoms as they sped into the slate-gray sky, and a flash of lightning made it easier. In the strobe light, she glimpsed at least six great birds before they vanished into the quickening clouds.

"It might have been six or seven," said Angel. "How does it go? 'Six crows gold. Seven crows a secret which must never be told.'"

Buffy looked amused. "You're with us crow people now?"

"They were dying in order to warn us about the Nile fever," he answered. "That got my attention."

As he talked, Angel never took his eyes off the corrugated metal fence that separated the two worlds, and Buffy also turned her attention in that direction. The twenty-foot-high barrier was topped by barbed wire and looked like a major problem, but the earth in this arroyo was mostly sand that shifted with every new rain. Angel surveyed the haphazard system of culverts and concrete ditches; they were in disrepair with large cracks and piles of rubble. Steel grates guarded the culverts, but they were choked with tree limbs, leaves, and debris, making the big pipes look like dangerous underground forests.

"I think we should hide this van," said Angel. "We don't want to scare them off."

"Scare *who* off?" asked Buffy. The area looked deserted to her.

"You don't feel them? Those houses across the street aren't empty," Angel said with certainty.

Buffy strode toward the back door of the van. "Let's do a scan for Machete, and then we'll go."

"Get in," Angel said urgently. "Somebody's coming, and this van is like a beacon. This is the place, I'm sure of it. Whatever is going down, it's here."

"All right," Buffy said, jumping back into the driver's seat and starting the engine. Angel hopped in beside her, and she lumbered back onto the dirt road. He craned his neck to watch the shanty village as it vanished in the dust and gloom behind them.

After driving half a mile, Buffy parked under a copse of palo verde trees, thinking this would have to do for camouflage. She wasn't going to question Angel's instincts, because he had a nose for bad things. The two of them jumped out and went to the rear of the vehicle, where Buffy grabbed a crossbow and a quarrel of wood-shafted bolts; she already had a stake in her belt, which fit over her gray sweats. Angel grabbed Sam's pistol, which was loaded with silver bullets, and hid it inside his new black leather jacket. "I don't like guns," he muttered.

"Me neither, but we can't fight that wolf hand-to-hand." She reached into her pocket for something and said, "I want you to put a tracer on yourself. I have one too. That way we can locate each other if we get separated."

"Good idea."

Buffy shrugged. "Riley's not here, so I'm trying to channel him."

She took the adhesive off a button-sized tracer and reached into his jacket to apply it to his chest. Touching his cool skin brought back a rush of primal memories, and it didn't help when Angel gently caught her wrist and said, "You're tickling me."

"You put it on," she answered, quickly withdrawing her hand.

"Shall I put yours on too?" he asked playfully.

"No, I already put mine on," she muttered. "Are we ready?"

"Let's find the drainage ditch and stay in it for cover," he suggested.

Buffy grimaced. "The ditch? You know, the shower in our room doesn't work very well."

"We can't just stroll down the road," he answered. "It's too wide open."

"Whatever," said Buffy. "It must be down this way."

She led him through the low scrub brush of the desert until they were close enough to see the massive fence along the border. Despite the wind and blowing sand, they had no trouble finding an overgrown drainage ditch that connected to the big arroyo. Crouching low, Angel and Buffy made their way through a morass of tree limbs, shopping carts, and rusty cans. Twilight had faded completely by the time they reached a section of the wash that was all concrete, with weeds growing through the cracks.

Angel motioned her to follow, and they climbed up the cement incline to the top of the ditch, where they had a view of the dirt road and the desolate shacks beyond. The howling wind combined with the creeping darkness to make every shadow a living thing. Buffy thought she saw creatures moving among the hovels, and she gripped Angel's arm.

"I see them too," he whispered.

The Slayer held her breath as the shadows took form and were clearly two-legged, manlike beings . . . with hunchbacks. They shuffled solemnly from the shanty town, crossed the gloomy road, and climbed down into the drainage ditch.

"Are they all named Igor?" she whispered to Angel. "They all have humps on their backs."

He shook his head. "No, I think those are backpacks."

"Backpacks?" Knowing Angel's vision was a lot better than hers, Buffy took his word for it. Despite the backpacks, this didn't look like a Boy Scout camping trip. "Where are they going?"

He shook his head. "When we see the last one go down, we'll follow them."

They waited as a seemingly endless stream of ghosts in backpacks emerged from the crumbling houses and vanished into the cement ditch. The street was finally empty again, except for the debris swirling in the wind, and Angel tapped her on the shoulder. They hauled themselves out of the filthy moat and jogged alongside it until they reached the culvert that led under the border. Angel held out his hand to stop her, and they listened to loud scraping noises. It sounded as if something heavy, like a manhole cover, was being dragged across an opening. Very close to the ground, there was a glimmer of light, which dipped lower and then disappeared.

"Look," Angel said, bending down to pick up something off the ground. He held up a small disc that glimmered in a pulse of lightning—for a second, it was as yellow and brilliant as the sun.

"Gold," breathed Buffy.

"A coin," said Angel. "A Krugerrand."

"Is that what's in their backpacks?"

"Maybe some of it." Angel motioned for her to follow him, and he slipped silently into the drainage ditch, bouncing over roots and rubble. With a bit more difficulty because of her shorter legs, Buffy managed to follow him. They stopped at the debris-encrusted mesh that covered the circular culvert, an overgrown pipe about four feet tall. The trapped debris was covered with its own slime and rot, and it smelled like the foulest plastic outhouse.

Angel gripped the grate with both hands and jerked it two feet to the side, making an awful grinding noise. Buffy looked at the weeds at the bottom of the opening and saw that they had been trampled recently. Like Alice, the smugglers with backpacks had vanished down the rabbit hole. "They can't crawl through this thing very far," she said with distaste. "If the border patrol camped out on the other side—"

"It wouldn't be that simple," said Angel. "Come on, we won't know where it goes until we see for ourselves."

He got down on his hands and knees and crawled through the grimy pipe, which was clogged with muddy leaves, twigs, and crud. With trepidation, Buffy followed him; she knew that if the rain promised by the lightning and dark clouds ever came, they could drown in this filthy run-off pipe.

Buffy had a flashlight in her pocket, but she dared not use it unless Angel gave her the go-ahead. If he was right, those mysterious shamblers were only a few moments ahead of them in this grimy tunnel. They had seen someone with a light, and they had heard him close the grate—so they weren't alone in here. *And if they heard us open the gate,* she thought, *then they know they aren't alone too.*

"What's this?" asked Angel. He stopped and pointed upward, where a crude hole a couple feet wide had been pounded into the concrete top of the culvert. It was hardly big enough to crawl through, and a person would need a boost or a pull to even get up there. Buffy had thought they were surrounded by solid ground, but that apparently wasn't so. Somewhere in the depths of this hole, a light glimmered.

Angel picked up a painted, circular piece of plywood that was dry and clean. "If this is shoved in that opening," he whispered, "you would never see it. Come on, I'll give you a lift." He cupped his hands like a stableboy helping his ladyship onto a horse.

"Me first?" Buffy said with a gulp. "Okay." She put

her foot into his cupped hands and let him propel her upward and headfirst into the hole.

"Whoa!" she cried, vaulting out into dark nothingness. At the last second she grabbed a wooden brace that turned out to be the rung of a ladder. She knew it was a ladder because her whole body crashed into eight or nine hard, wooden slats. The fall nearly knocked the breath out of her, but she held on.

Looking around, she could see where the light was coming from: a green glow stick about thirty feet below her. The child's toy weakly illuminated the bottom of this crude pit and the wooden ladder that allowed access. "Careful of the first step," she told Angel. "It's a lulu."

His head and shoulders appeared in the hole, and he looked around the rustic shaft before proceeding. Buffy followed his gaze and could see more as her eyes adjusted to the dim green glow stick. Uneven planks of wood, which looked like construction cast-offs, lined the walls, and there was a tunnel entrance on the muddy floor thirty feet below. This hole actually had a frame of two-by-fours and vertical beams holding it up.

Angel motioned her to go down, and she did. At the bottom of the pit her booted feet landed in gushy mud full of human trash such as soda bottles and bits of clear plastic wrapping. Buffy peered into the murky gloom of the new tunnel and saw that it ran off into unknown lengths. It looked like an ancient mine with crude support beams and paneling made from mismatched, cast-off lumber. The height of the tunnel seemed to vary, but it looked about four or five feet high, enough for a normal person to walk in a crouch. Unlike the surface, it was refreshingly cool down here.

Angel tapped her on the shoulder and showed her one of the torn bits of plastic. It was covered in a sheen of fine white powder. "Cocaine," he whispered. "That's what they tried to plant in your luggage."

"So we know they get it wholesale," answered Buffy. "What *is* this place?"

"A drug tunnel," answered Angel. "The border is riddled with them. This one looks as if it's been around for a while, and was built to last. Those are mules we saw—drug couriers."

Now it began to make sense to her. If the border entry points got too tight, and crossing the desert too dangerous, Raul and Machete had an underground route. But they couldn't use this tunnel for people-moving, because they couldn't reveal it to just anyone. It just piggybacked onto the actual, people-moving drainage pipe. "This is a secret that must never be told," she whispered.

"No kidding," agreed Angel. "But it's only half a secret until we find out where it leads." He motioned her into the abject blackness of the adjoining tunnel. "Ladies first?"

"Thanks," Buffy said, picking up the glow stick with one hand and hefting her crossbow with the other. She stooped over and peered doubtfully into the clammy, wood-paneled burrow, where the beams were slimy and wormy. "Don't we need some dwarves or elves for this?"

"We're fresh out," answered Angel. "But I'll lead, if you—"

His words were interrupted by the muffled sound of the grate moving high above them. *We left it open!* thought Buffy, and someone else had closed it. Anyone could be coming down the culvert. Angel looked at Buffy and motioned her to drop the glow stick light, even while squishy footsteps sounded in the pipe above them.

She quickly tossed the light back to the ground, leaving it for this new arrival. Taking a breath to ward against the stench, she and Angel scuttled crablike through the low, muddy tunnel.

CHAPTER FIFTEEN

Buffy spotted another glow stick twenty feet down the burrow, where it cast a greenish aura upon the decrepit beams and slimy wooden walls. Unfortunately, she could also see the shadowy shapes of the drug mules ahead of them—there were dozens, maybe a hundred. Burdened with their packs and bent over in the low tunnel, the stream of smugglers didn't make very good time. She and Angel would catch them in a few seconds, even while someone else came tramping behind them.

"Listen," whispered Angel, "just bend over and join the parade. It's too dark in here for anyone to get a good look at us."

So they fell in line behind the last mule, who paid them scant attention as he maneuvered his bulging backpack through the cockeyed tunnel. Just walking over the muddy roots and ruts was hard enough, and the intermittent glow stick provided only the most minimal light. At least the smell of decay wasn't quite as bad here as it was above, and it was cooler. Buffy paused to listen, and she let out a relieved sigh. Whoever had been behind them had stopped walking for the moment. Maybe the underground passageway had creeped him out; if so, Buffy could understand why.

As they crawled along the burrow like a couple of gophers, Buffy and Angel passed a side chamber—another dark space carved from the ground and buttressed haphazardly with old timber. It was hard to tell if this offshoot was a room or a separate tunnel, because there was nothing in there but darkness. With a motion of his hand, Angel kept her following the wordless shuffle of the mules down the main tunnel, and Buffy tried to stay close to him.

Sam Finn watched her husband pace the drab confines of the motel room, even while darkness claimed the parking lot and the rolling hills of the Sonoran Desert. Wind still hurtled tumbleweeds across the sands, but the rain had stopped; even the lightning had receded farther into the mountains, so far that she couldn't hear the thunder anymore. It was such a bucolic Western scene that Sam half-expected to see some longhorn cattle come meandering through the parking lot.

Riley stopped his pacing to peer suspiciously out the window, now that the night had settled into its rhythms. She knew what he was looking for, but she didn't think he would find it here.

"That's pointless, you know," Sam said, breaking the silence. "You can't take your mind off it by pacing."

"Off what?" he asked innocently.

Trying to not grimace, she dragged herself out of bed and walked gingerly to his side. "The deal. Something is going on out there, and you want to bust it."

He brushed her concerns aside. "Sure, I'm curious, but I know where I have to be."

"It's okay," she said, grabbing a loose pair of overalls from her drawer. "I'll get dressed and go with you."

"Wait a minute," Riley said with concern. "You're still recovering."

"I can sit in a car," she insisted. "I could probably drive. Believe it or not, I can even walk a short distance. Anything would be better than watching you pace."

At his downcast expression, she softened her own attitude and said, "I need to get out. Besides, how dangerous can it be? We have no idea where to go, so we'll just be driving around. And I can do that. I'll take the portable tracker, just in case Machete is on this side. Not likely, I admit."

"All right," Riley answered with a sigh. "But you're just going to sit and watch. If we see anything dangerous, we'll, um . . ."

"Call the sheriff," she quipped.

"No," he said with a chuckle. "You get dressed, and I'll get the car. And, uh, maybe we should bring the gun."

"You take it," she answered, grimacing at a sharp twinge of pain as she adjusted her sling. "I'll help you look for him."

The drug tunnel grew darker and darker between the pools of green radiance given off by the fading glow sticks. Without warning, Angel and Buffy stepped from the cramped tunnel into a large chamber, where they could stand up straight. Buffy knew this from the echo of her ragged breathing, which now boomed with a big echo. She tried to peer into the gloom, but there was only a distant glimmer of light. It looked like a natural cave, and smelled vaguely of rotten eggs. A black oil oozed up through cracks in the chalky ground, and the room was filled with dark shapes: somber, businesslike smugglers who murmured softly while they rested and waited.

"We're halfway there," said a familiar raspy voice in English. Buffy saw a dapper figure in a suit go sweeping through the crowd of shadows, exhorting them. "There will be a full share for every one of you. Whatever you want—cash, drugs, gold! Then we party—with *live* entertainment. Just come back here to see me, Raul, after your delivery topside."

His voice faded in volume as he moved away from Buffy. "The first group has gone ahead. I don't think we'll be piled up so much." Then he gave what she presumed was the same information in Spanish, ending with *"¡Vamos!"*

Buffy and Angel didn't *vamos* quite as quickly as the others, because they hung back until most of the mules had vanished down another rabbit hole at the far end of the cavern. Angel managed to hunch his shoulders and jacket in order to make it look as if he had a pack, while Buffy shifted her belt onto her back and tried to use Angel for cover. She heard a snuffling sound, so she turned to look behind her, but darkness had swallowed everything in the clammy depths of the tunnel. If there was anything following them, it was keeping its distance . . . for now. Angel tugged on her sleeve to move on, and she stooped down and followed him into the next segment of blackness.

Buffy was glad it was so dark, or else claustrophobia might have closed in upon her. As it was, the pools of sickly green glow sticks began to seem like islands of civilization. At this pace, they had probably traveled only a hundred yards total, but it seemed like miles of stooped scuttling. She couldn't help but wonder where this underground passage came out on the other side. Someone was going to have a lot of explaining to do.

Somebody bumped her and growled unpleasantly, but this person kept on staggering in the other direction. When it happened again, Buffy realized that the first mules in line must have reached their destination, delivered their loads, and were headed back. She pulled on Angel's hand to get him to slow down, and he touched her arm in acknowledgment. Being buffeted by strangers passing in the darkness, Buffy knew they couldn't talk to each other. *If we had any sense, we'd turn around and join the procession headed back to Mexico, but we both want to see what's at the end of the line.*

The two-way traffic continued for another stretch of time that went by at a crawl, until they finally saw what looked like a tiny skylight, which dropped a dusty beam into the gloom. Following the feeble light, they entered another chamber, where they could stand upright; here, the mules took off their backpacks and lined up to put them on a small elevator run by a winch. Two or three backpacks at a time vanished upward through a narrow shaft. A wooden ladder lined the pit, but there was no room to use it as long as the ersatz dumbwaiter was operating. Feeble light spilled down from somewhere about thirty feet above them on the surface, but it seemed like a spotlight down here.

Somehow they had to disable the dumbwaiter and climb to the top, she decided, to find out who owned this underground mule train. But that wasn't going to be easy with a cavern full of drug smugglers, especially when the light from above allowed them to see who was loading the little elevator: He was a lanky figure who wore a fringed coat with a long machete hanging from his belt. "Move it along!" he called out, waving them toward his loading point. "The sooner we're out of here, the better."

Buffy seldom ran away from anything, but she had an overwhelming feeling that they should get out of there. They had to return another night, when the numbers weren't so stacked against them. She tugged on Angel's coattails and tried to turn him away from the ominous light. Doing so, she bumped into a stocky figure behind her.

"Hello, my dear," said the silky, raspy voice of Raul. He eyed her appreciatively. "I thought I smelled a human. I must say, Angelus, I like your choice of company."

Buffy tried to draw her crossbow; but the vampire knocked it deftly out of her hands, and it clattered uselessly against the wooden wall. Angel whirled around, about to come to her aid, when he was suddenly surrounded by snarling vampires. Wherever they looked, the feral faces of enraged vampires bore down on them. With a gulp, Buffy realized that every single smuggler in the tunnel was a vampire. There had to be at least fifty of them.

"Ooops," she heard Angel say as half a dozen vampires leaped upon him.

Angel became a whirlwind of flying fists and feet as he carved enough space to draw his wooden stake and dispatch the closest bloodsucker. Raul tried to grab Buffy by the shoulders, and she jabbed him in the solar plexus, getting a look of surprise out of the vampire. As he tried to grab her wrists, she collapsed against Angel and drew a stake, and they battled back-to-back in a dark cavern filled with vampires.

"To the tunnel!" she urged Angel. "It will be too narrow for all of them to come at us!"

Getting back to the narrow tunnel was easier said than done, and Buffy was slammed against a vertical beam, which groaned ominously and dumped a ton of dirt on her head. She used the momentary confusion to smash past two more vampires, and she turned one of them into swirling dust. Buffy could hear Angel's grunts as he slugged his way through the throng of vampires. If anything, there were almost too many of the enemy to be effective, and they couldn't get coordinated to find the interlopers in the dim light. She heard Raul swearing and Machete urging his underlings to forget them and get the cargo loaded onto the elevator.

"If you don't have cargo, follow me!" shouted Raul.

Shoving bodies out of her way, Buffy staggered into the narrow tunnel, glad for once of the cramped space. Angel leaped in after her, kicking both legs like a real mule. The enemy kept coming, but only one or two of them could reach Angel at a time, and he was able to fend them off. Buffy peered down the length of the tunnel, trying to figure out if anyone was lying in wait. While Angel battled to secure their escape, she drew her flashlight and turned it on. There was no sense worrying about being spotted now.

Despite their ambitious plans to find the big boss, they were soon in full retreat down the tunnel. Buffy led the way with the light, while Angel dissuaded anyone from coming too close. After the enemy saw him dispatch a few of their comrades with his stake, they stayed in pursuit but kept a distance.

"We'll make it out," she said. "But then we'll be in the open again."

"I know," Angel answered breathlessly. "If we hold them off until daylight, you can get to the van without them following."

"What about *you*?" she asked in horror.

"I'll have to take my chances." He stopped and punched a grizzly vampire who had lunged for his leg. "Keep moving!"

She didn't have to be told twice to do that, and they broke into the big cavern where the mules had rested and regrouped halfway to their destination. Her flashlight illuminated a few mules waiting there, but they didn't know why these two were running pell-mell through their midst. By the time the pursuing vampires spilled into the cavern, Buffy and Angel were already scuttling down the next section of tunnel. She heard voices behind them, including the crackle of a walkie-talkie.

"Are they backing off?" she asked.

"No, they're still coming," muttered Angel. "I don't like this."

"What's not to like?" she asked, panting with exertion. "We've got every vampire in the Southwest in one place!"

"They seem to be letting us get away," he answered.

Buffy stopped suddenly, and he banged into her. "I'm sorry," she gasped with relief. "I saw something black ahead of us, but it's that connecting tunnel."

Angel sniffed the damp, fetid air. "There's something else down here," he said, grabbing her hand. "Come on, let's hurry."

They passed the gaping maw of the unexplored tunnel on their right and continued toward the exit, until Buffy heard a low growling sound just ahead of them. She froze, and so did Angel. Buffy aimed the flashlight beam down the twisting passageway, and saw crouched shapes moving toward them. Behind these attackers was something big and hairy, moving swiftly on four legs.

The wolf! And he wasn't alone.

"We're trapped between them," Angel hissed, drawing his handgun. He couldn't shoot the wolf because there was a phalanx of vampires in front of it, and shooting them would be a waste of bullets. So he grabbed Buffy and dragged her into the unknown blackness of the connecting tunnel.

In a crouch, they scurried into another burrow, with the only light being Buffy's bouncing flashlight beam. This hand-dug tunnel didn't even have wood paneling, and there were mounds of earth that hadn't been cleared out yet—they looked like burial mounds. Because it seemed like an unfinished tunnel, she worried there wouldn't be another way out. At least they couldn't be rushed from all sides in here—they would be able to fight like heroes in a kung fu movie, one villain at a time.

When she heard the pad of paws right behind her,

Buffy whirled the light around and caught the monstrous wolf, ready to leap. Angel twisted around, too, and squeezed off a shot, but the ferocious creature sprang at the same instant. The gunshot reverberated in the crude tunnel like an explosion, bringing a rain of dirt on their heads. The walls began to crack, and the wolf actually thudded into her before it sprang back toward the exit. Buffy and Angel held each other until the ringing and the shaking stopped, and both kept their eyes wide open, searching for the wolf to return.

The massive animal was gone, but Raul's silky laugh echoed from the depths of darkness. "I know you like tombs and cemeteries. I hope you like this one, because you may be here a while."

As his laugh faded, a real explosion sounded, and the shock force blew Buffy off her feet and showered her with smoke and debris. A cave-in started at once, and rocks and clods of dirt plummeted down on them. Angel pulled Buffy toward his chest, and she burrowed for cover under his broad shoulders as the drug tunnel collapsed around them.

CHAPTER SIXTEEN

"Can't stay here. . . . Keep moving!" Angel urged, yanking Buffy to her feet despite the ceiling raining down. Coughing and flailing at the dirt, Buffy blindly staggered deeper into the collapsing passageway. Twice, Angel picked her up and threw her several feet ahead of the falling debris, and she stumbled through the choking dust, finally plunging into an area free of the downfall. A second later, Angel came crawling into the clear, cuts and bruises all over his head and hands.

Buffy had somehow held on to her flashlight, but the beam was diffused by so much dust that she couldn't see anything. She felt Angel's banged-up body collapse at her feet, and she crouched down to hold him.

"Stay down," she cautioned. "It's behind us."

He nodded even as he gasped for breath. The downpour of dirt on the muddy floor lasted for several seconds, though no more large sections of tunnel collapsed. But the exit to the culvert and Mexico was now cut off to them by tons of dirt and rock. If there was no other way out, they were trapped in here. If there *was* another exit, it was also a way in, and the bad guys could send a surprise force to attack them. So either way, they were trapped in here.

With a groan, Angel dragged himself to his feet and looked back at the massive wall of rock and dirt that cut the tunnel in half. "I guess we have to explore the other way."

Bent over, Buffy scowled and cast her beam around the cramped blackness. "I was thinking that anything was better than the wolf, but now I'm not so sure."

Limping slightly, Angel led the way down the unexplored part of the tunnel, the only way they could go. Within about twenty feet, the tunnel dwindled to nothing, not even a rabbit hole, and they were stuck between two dead ends.

"Don't worry," Angel said, tight-lipped. "Vampires are very good at digging with our hands. We'll be out of here in no time."

"Angel, we're thirty feet under," Buffy said glumly, "not six feet under."

"Well, have you got a better idea?"

She took one of Riley's mobile phones out of her pocket and tried to dial their friends, but all she got was a recording that told her that there was no signal. "We're too far down," she grumbled.

"Then I'd better get started," replied Angel. He rose to his feet and found some firm ground a few feet away from the tapered end of the tunnel. Then he took off his coat and his shirt and began to tear dirt from the top of the tunnel with his bare hands.

"In some S and M fantasy, this would be really cool," muttered Buffy, "but I want out of here."

"Stand on the other side of me," he ordered. "I need to use this back part of the tunnel for the dirt."

"Dirt," she echoed, looking around in disgust. "We don't have a plan B, do we?"

"Well, we could dig out the collapsed end," said Angel. "Then we'd be right back with our friends." As he pulled down the ceiling with his bare hands, he added, "That sounds like more work than this."

Buffy stepped out of his way and halfheartedly kicked some dirt clods to the rear of the cave. More and more, that's what this place seemed like—a cave, where they were trapped by an old-fashioned cave-in. *So much for being the experts called in to crack the big case,* she thought gloomily. *Nobody knows we're down here. . . . We'll be lucky if we ever get out, dead or alive.*

Then Buffy looked at Angel and realized that he wasn't going to die. Even if it took him months to dig his way out, he'd be weak but still kicking when he made it to the surface. However, she was a different case. To allow her to survive without air, water, or food, in that order, Angel would have to turn her into a vampire.

Riley and Sam pulled up in front of the Río Conchas Resort in their new rented Buick, which looked much like the one they had abandoned at the Western-wear outlet store. Seen by moonlight and the twinkling fairy bulbs in the palm trees, the hotel and grounds were considerably more peaceful than they had been at the grand opening. No wedding parties, golfing foursomes, or hordes of retirees jammed the place. Seen on a midsummer's night, this island of stucco and brick had some appeal as an oasis of gentility in the middle of nowhere. Then he remembered that the surrounding desert was gone, replaced by lush fairways, artificial lakes, and pristine sand traps. The peace and quiet was probably an illusion, too. It was off-season, and the resort would be noisy and full by the time winter came.

"Are you up to a little stroll?" he asked.

"Sure," Sam answered as she surveyed the handheld tracking device they had brought with them across the border. "I don't see any sign of Machete here."

"I'm not sure he would go for the blue-hair crowd," replied Riley. He maneuvered the car into a parking space, turned off the engine, and opened his door. The brief rain had made the desert smell clean and new, and the lawn and flowers gave the warm air a hint of sweetness. "I'll come around and help you," he told her.

"I'll make it," Sam said, mustering a smile as she opened the door and eased herself onto the asphalt. He knew she was toughing it out without painkillers to keep alert, or perhaps it was to atone for being less than perfect. Letting the wolf get the better of her, then discovering she was pregnant—these incidents had made his flawless wife seem strangely human and endearing. He had never known her to be out of action before, and it pained him to see her moving at about 50 percent of her normal dexterity.

"Do we have an excuse to be here?" Sam asked, dropping the handheld tracker into her purse.

Riley scowled. "We came back because of the great service."

"Funny." Sam adjusted the sling on her left arm, but from her grimaces it was clear that she couldn't make it comfortable. "Don't they have a bar here? We could just be getting a drink. I'm walking like an old lady, anyway."

"Okay, sweetheart," Riley agreed, taking her right arm and helping her toward the curb. The young couple strolled unhurriedly up the lit walkway to the main entrance of the hotel. The bright lights were almost blinding after having driven through the opaque desert.

Riley saw something that made him smile, and he pointed it out to Sam. "They must have a leak in their new roof." To the left of the check-in desk, which seemed to be deserted, a large paint bucket was situated under a stain in the vaulted ceiling.

"Good help is hard to find," Sam said, glancing around the gleaming lobby. Sprightly Muzak played over the PA system, but nobody was in sight—not a single clerk or bellhop. "Where is everybody?" she asked.

"I don't know," Riley answered with a glance at his watch. "It's only ten thirty."

"Well, let's try the bar." Sam sauntered in that direction, and Riley followed cautiously. They passed the rest rooms and came upon some swinging saloon doors, reminiscent of the Old West. Beyond lay a dark oaken bar, and they could hear the drone of a sportscaster offering up scores. Riley pushed the swinging doors open, and they creaked authentically. Sam strolled past him and wandered through the empty bar toward some other voices. Riley followed her to the end of the bar, where they found another TV, which was tuned to an infomercial. Drinks and ashtrays lay scattered about on a few of the tables, leading Riley to believe that the customers had left within the hour. There was no half-eaten food in sight.

"Maybe the busboy is on vacation," suggested Sam.

They heard the squeak of the swinging saloon doors, and Riley whirled around. But he was too slow to get a good glimpse of the person who had just left, so he dashed out of the bar into the lobby. He arrived just in time to see the door of the men's rest room close shut. Riley was torn as to whether he should leave his injured wife or follow this mystery customer. He didn't know why, but he had a feeling he would lose him if he didn't stay in pursuit.

Riley quietly opened the door and slipped into the tasteful latrine. The first thing he saw was his reflection in a wide mirror on the opposite wall, and he could also see the row of urinals, hidden from his direct view by a partition. In the reflection, he couldn't see anyone using a urinal. *But a vampire is invisible in a mirror,* he told himself.

Riley slipped out before the invisible creature finished, and he rushed back into the bar—only to find no one there. "Sam!" he called urgently, trying to keep his voice low at the same time. "Sam, where are you!"

Feeling waves of dread wash over him, Riley rushed to the spot at the end of the bar where they had been standing. Discarded on the floor was the handheld tracker Sam had been using. The telephone behind the bar rang loudly, making him jump, and he looked around, half-expecting someone to answer the blaring instrument. *No,* he thought miserably, *the bell tolls for me.*

Fighting the urge to scream in anguish, he headed behind the bar and grabbed the telephone. "Hello?"

"Mr. Finn," came the familiar voice of Frederick Tatum. "We didn't expect a solution to our problems so soon."

"Bastard!" cursed Riley. "If you harm her—"

"You know how to avoid that," the rancher insisted, and Riley forced himself to shut up and remain calm. "You leave town and forget all about us," he said. "We don't have time to deal with you now. Get your sorry ass back to wherever you came from, and we'll release your wife, unharmed. If you hang around and give us grief . . . well, you don't want to go there."

"All right," Riley said, taking a deep breath. He was trying to listen to noises in the building, to figure out where they went. At the approach of footsteps, he whirled around and saw two uniformed deputies with riot guns approach the bar. Getting himself killed wouldn't help matters, he thought, so he relaxed his stance and said loudly, "Okay, Mr. Tatum, you are in the driver's seat, and your boys are here to show me out. You'll keep in touch, right?"

"You can depend on that," answered Tatum. "After we're left alone for a few days, you'll get your wife back. Then you can snoop around to your heart's content—there won't be anything to find."

"Whatever you say," Riley agreed through clenched teeth. He hung up the phone and nodded to the deputies as he walked toward the swinging doors. He gauged his odds of disarming one of both of them, and getting a shotgun to boot, but it was still too early in the game to do something stupid. He had to think of the desired end: to get Sam back.

Riley walked briskly out the door and made considerable pretext of climbing in his car, slamming the door, and driving away. He did so rapidly, with the hope that they wouldn't have time to follow him.

Riley didn't think he had a very long grace period before he truly had to leave, but he wanted to make the most of it. The operative pulled out a phone and tried to call Buffy and Angel, knowing that they were probably deep into it too.

The call went unanswered, which wasn't any help. *But since when did Buffy and Angel care much about keeping in contact?* He wondered how much he could depend upon his own organization for help. Even if they wanted to send the cavalry, it would be hours before anyone could reach them here in the remote Arizona desert; and that wouldn't be a snap decision on their part. So he considered his company the last resort, especially if he was forced to leave the area. The only local law enforcement was on the wrong side, so he was on his own.

He tore the big sedan along the two-lane blacktop and veered off onto the first winding dirt road he saw. Riley killed his headlights and his engine and rolled behind a hill, waiting for the deputies' squad car to streak past him. When it roared by a moment later in hot pursuit of nothing, Riley tried to breathe evenly and tell himself that he still had options. As long as they didn't know where he was or what he was doing, they had to stay on their toes and devote resources to find him. They also had to worry about still negotiating with him, and maybe that would keep Sam alive.

In truth, he had to admit to himself that she was dead—or would be soon. These weren't the kind of people to kidnap and release; they had too many secrets to keep. No, this was just a ploy to buy them some time, for whatever was happening tonight. Riley always believed in going on the offensive against monsters, and the taking of hostages was never supposed to change that strategy. It was a given that innocents were going to die in this war against ancient terror, because the enemy was ruthless, often immortal, and never considered surrender.

"Sam, it could've been good," he said hoarsely to the night. "But we got out of this madness a little too late." Although it was pointless, he called Sam's voice mail on the laptop computer and left a brief message, saying where he was going next.

Spying no more headlights on the road, he cautiously backed out of his hiding place and headed in the direction of Tatum's mansion and pecan farm. *Whenever possible, track the beast to its lair,* Riley thought grimly. He figured there was a chance to save Sam by getting Tatum before he issued the order to kill her.

At any rate, he was going to get Tatum.

As Riley neared the orchards, he again killed the headlamps on the rented Buick and coasted down into the lush hollow, where the pecan trees grew in stately, abundant rows. It was growing season, not harvesting, and the machinery was quiet even if the sprinklers were not. *What it must cost to keep this place in water,* he thought, *even though it is near a wash. Maybe this is really the breeding ground for the West Nile Virus.* Mosquitoes were not usually given much thought in the Sonoran Desert, because of a lack of water for their breeding. But where there was man, there was always wasted water.

On the access road where he had sneaked in several nights ago, the gate was now closed and locked, so Riley drove past Tatum's complex and parked the car under a low-slung willow tree. As an afterthought, he checked the handheld tracking device, which was set on Machete's tracer. Remarkably, the machine reported a distant blip near the end of the device's range. Riley frowned at this strange reading, then he checked his map, his notes, and a few sketches he had made of Tatum's sprawling acreage. As far as he could tell, the pointer put Machete in the pecan-processing plant. But the signal was barely detectable, indicating it might be coming from underground, and that was curious.

Riley got out of the car, still carrying the Beretta with the silver bullets, and a couple of wooden stakes. He hadn't actually seen the vampire in the men's rest room, but he knew it was still around and probably was involved in keeping his wife prisoner. He had to climb an eight-foot-tall wire-link fence to get onto Tatum's property, but he had plenty of adrenaline to get him over. There was no reason not to let the blips of Machete's tracer guide him onto the property. If left on his own, he would have checked the house first, but maybe the processing plant and giant picking machines were a good place to start. At any rate, they probably wouldn't be looking for him right under their noses.

And he wasn't going to stop until he found *them* . . . and what had become of Samantha.

Her body wracked with pain, Samantha groaned as she reached behind her neck and felt where the sting had caught her. At least it had felt like a sting—from a wasp or a killer bee—and that's all she remembered. Except now it was dark, and she was rocking gently in the backseat of a car. Beside her sat a sheriff's deputy, and he was asleep. In the front seat were two more men, so bathed in shadows that she couldn't recognize them. There was little to see out the window but vague silhouettes of giant saguaro cacti and gnarly yucca plants. All she knew was that they were driving down a very dark stretch of country road so deep in the desert that she couldn't see a single light.

"You fainted," said a voice from the front seat. "We have to take you to a hospital. Hope you're all right."

She looked around, wondering where her husband had gone. Last she'd seen him, he was headed to the rest room chasing a phantom who had gone out the swinging door. For some reason, that now seemed like a long time ago, and this car ride was very suspicious. Her knee hurt with fresh pain, indicating that she might have fallen on it when she'd lost consciousness. "And what happened to the man I was with?" she asked, rubbing her neck. "Did he faint too?"

"Your husband?" asked the driver. "Last I saw him, he was having a little talk with Mr. Tatum."

That was a polite way of saying that they expected Riley to behave himself while she was being held hostage. Sam looked around to familiarize herself with the door handles and layout of the car. It was a big Crown Victoria, like they often used for squad cars, but this one was either retired or unmarked. The doors were no doubt locked, and there didn't appear to be any reason for them to slow down on this dark stretch of narrow pavement. "Are you telling me there's a hospital out here somewhere?" she said.

"Just someplace safe," answered the front-seat passenger. "For you to recover."

"Where's my purse?" she asked with mild annoyance.

"The one with the stakes and crucifixes?" the driver asked with a chuckle. "One would think you were a gardening nun." The passenger laughed appreciatively. Even Sam giggled, trying to put these three bozos at ease.

The deputy stirred and looked sullenly at her. Despite the uniform, he was a lowlife thug, and he wore his service revolver on his right hip, facing her. They were just a bunch of cowboys.

"You know, I'm bleeding," she said matter-of-factly. "I think I tore one of my stitches loose."

"What do we look like, nurses?" the driver asked, still in a jolly mood. "You'll have time to get undressed and washed up." He said the last bit with

243

a hoarse voice, and Sam knew she was in trouble.

"No, seriously, I'm bleeding all over the place," she insisted, although it was too dark to see much of anything. With no street lights, not even passing light glimpsed into the car.

Still, Sam leaned forward, unbuttoning her blouse around her injured shoulder and showing a considerable amount of breast and bra. "See, look, it's all over me."

She had the deputy's immediate attention, plus the passenger was leaning over to look. The driver bobbed his head around, trying to sneak a peak with his mirror.

"Oops, there's some on the seat!" she said with a squeal, sitting closer to the deputy and getting behind the driver. For a moment, she felt the hardness of his holster against her thigh.

She pulled her clothing off a bit more and scooted more toward the left. "Man, you should see all these stitches. There's a big, nasty wolf out in this desert."

"We see him all the time," the driver said with a laugh.

Ignoring the pain and putting all her strength into one burst of action, Sam suddenly lifted her legs and kicked the front seat forward. That slammed the driver into his steering column and caused him to cream the brakes, while his air bag exploded in his face. At the same time, Sam reached for the deputy's gun, and his reactions came a split second too slow to stop her. Although he wrestled her for it, she got the gun out of his holster and fired a round into his leg.

Now it was complete chaos inside the car, with the exploded air bag blocking the front seat, a deputy screaming, a woman grappling for a gun, and the car screeching sideways down the road. Sam wrenched the gun away from her captor as they swerved off the road and plowed down an embankment, and she glimpsed the front-seat passenger trying to draw his own weapon. Reversing the gun in her hand, she whacked him across the head, and he slumped forward as the car bounced into the desert. The driver, after the collision with his dashboard, was slowly coming to. Using her legs, Sam shoved herself away from the screaming deputy and looked for his door handle. She hit the handle with one foot and the deputy with the other, popping open the door and spilling him out of the bouncing car and into the dirt.

Before the driver could gather his wits, Sam cracked him with the butt of her pistol; the two thugs in front slumped against each other, wrapped by the remains of the air bag. By the time the car had rolled to a stop, several of Sam's stitches *had* popped open, but she couldn't worry about that. She used the last of her strength to push open the door and stagger onto the desert. Still waving her revolver, she followed their tire tracks in the crusty sand and found the deputy unconscious.

Sam limped back to the car and pulled both

unconscious men from the front seat. The gun might be used to trace her, so she wiped it down on her dress, then tossed it into the sand beside their bodies. She felt a pang of guilt over leaving them here, but they had kidnapped her. Plus she had a child coming; she couldn't let these scum get their way. Sam ransacked their pockets until she found a mobile phone and a couple of wallets. Both men were retired deputies, although they didn't look older than forty, and both were listed as security officers at Río Conchas. She took their cash and any keys and cards that looked as if they might operate a security checkpoint.

Sam tried to call Riley on the cell, but the owner had the keypad locked. Besides, there was no signal way out here. Sam eased herself onto the bloody seat and started the car, then she made a U-turn in a broad swath of desert. The Ford was banged up but was still roadworthy, and she followed their tire tracks back to the pavement. Shifting in her seat, trying to accommodate all her individual aches and pains, Sam drove back the way they had come. It was time to find her husband.

CHAPTER SEVENTEEN

With her hands and feet, Buffy shoved dirt back into the dead end of the unfinished drug tunnel, while Angel tore it down from above. *Never underestimate how much dirt a determined vampire can move,* she decided, because Angel was a terror digging his way out. At times, he unconciously reverted to his vampire features, and she tried not to look at him then. He also amassed a pile of dirt under his feet, which he needed to stand on, but he could make a lot more progress if he had a ladder, she decided. Despite all their frantic work, her flashlight batteries were failing, and they were still about twenty-five feet underground. She didn't have a lot of hope for their survival, unless they took drastic measures. "Angel," she said, broaching the subject, "it may not be thirty feet of digging if we go through the cave-in."

"You're right," he said, panting as he kept working, "it may be *fifty* feet that way. A lot of dirt fell down there. It's six of one, half dozen of another, Buffy. Until we decide to do something else, I'll keep digging. In the meantime, see if you can find me anything else to stand on—rocks, big clumps. Drag stuff from the cave-in site."

"All right," Buffy said, rolling up her sleeves as if this new action were going to do the trick. "Can I take the flashlight?"

"Go ahead, I can see," he answered, straining with exertion.

Buffy crept back toward the cave-in, guided by her feeble yellow beam and trying not to think how desperately thirsty and afraid she was.

Riley sampled the air with a wet finger and discovered that it was blowing northeast, so he positioned himself downwind just south of the mansion and north of the pecan plant. There were no dogs to worry about, not with that primeval wolf on the loose. But there were vampires, and they could smell almost as well as dogs. He got down in a crouch behind a conveyer belt and observed for a few minutes, which he always found useful for collecting his thoughts and planning his next move.

He checked the tracking device and found that Machete was indeed inside the biggest building in the compound; and he was at least one story underground. This puzzled Riley, because people in this part of the country were not known for digging basements in their hard soil. They built expansive ranch houses and Santa Fe–style mansions. But maybe this structure had some underground storage—in what appeared to be the southwest corner.

However, getting in the plant would not be trivial, because he suspected that the windows and doors were all alarmed. It was really a glorified barn, mostly wood frame, one story but high, with a sloped metal roof. He could see what looked like steam coming from a pipe on the roof, probably from a boiler or heater. Riley decided to search the roof for access, unless another option presented itself.

While he mulled over his next move, a figure walked boldly around the northeast corner of the building and kept moving in a counterclockwise sweep. Riley didn't duck right away, because he didn't want his quarry to see any movement. This was clearly a guard, but he was also unarmed, which indicated to Riley that he wasn't human. The guard stopped before he rounded the northwest corner in order to sniff the swirling night winds. The air was mostly hot but had some cool currents, thanks to the brief rain. Riley all but decided that his first guess was correct—his nemesis was a vampire—and he hefted a stake in his right hand.

A moment later the sentry turned the corner and moved out of sight. Riley looked around for a drainpipe, a box, one of the tall, mechanical rakes—anything he could use as a ladder to reach the roof. He also listened, because he was sure he would hear the crunching footsteps on gravel before the guard reappeared. Then he remembered there was a water tank, or some large reservoir, on the eastern side of the building—he had made a note of it on their earlier visit.

Having spent a lot of time thinking, Riley was forced to wait until the sentry returned, which he did, walking more slowly and talking in Spanish on a walkie-talkie. He heard the noise of an engine and turned around to see a truck marked with the golden logo TATUM PECANS coming from the house. It rumbled down the concrete drive and pulled around to the south side of the complex, away from Riley. He was glad for the distraction, because the vampire strode past him and also headed south in pursuit.

Riley looked around for more of the trucks, but he remembered they were all parked farther north, near Tatum's mansion. So he dashed from his position, across open ground, and slumped against the wall, hidden by a big harvesting rake with a tractor hitch. He stayed there only long enough to catch a breath and make sure nobody was on this side of the building. Then he ran clockwise to peer around the northeast corner. There was the water tank, as he'd remembered it, and it was only surrounded by a chain-link fence.

Being in the open was the most dangerous time, so he wanted to get across the space as fast as he could. Keeping low and in the shadows, he dashed to the chain-link fence and grabbed it. If it was alarmed, he would be detected, but he had no time for subtlety; he was ready to run like hell, meet the silver wolf, or whatever happened next. But no, this fence wasn't live—it was intended to keep animals away from the tank, which turned out to contain cooking oil waiting to be recycled. He scaled the fence and jumped atop the big rusty tank, where he held on, unmoving, waiting to see if his climb had been observed.

Now he heard the crunching of boots in gravel, which made him hang on all the more tightly and quietly, waiting for the guard to pass. He couldn't risk moving to look at the sentry, so Riley held perfectly still and listened to his footsteps fading in volume. When the sound was gone, he scrambled to his feet and swayed before getting his balance on the curved top of the tank. As soon as he had some footing, he took a leap onto the slick metal roof and dug his foot in the rain gutter to stop his slide down the incline. This was the noisiest of his maneuvers, and he held his breath waiting to see if there would be any repercussions.

When he heard running footsteps, he crawled on his belly a few inches away from the edge of the roof, until he found a crack in the white elastic paint where he could hang on with his fingernails. The sentry stopped and paced several times, as if unsure where the sound had come from. Riley wished he could make a cat noise or something to throw him off, but all he had was the will and patience to stay quiet. The guard finally moved on, grumbling to himself and sniffing the wind.

Riley let out a breath, thinking that he had reached his first objective: the roof. He had to avoid making unnecessary noise, but at least now he could circumnavigate the building and find a way in, without being spotted. The noise of the trucks and the loading would probably cover the minor bumps he might produce. Riley crawled up to the peak of the roof, where he took stock of his surroundings. A pipe was giving off steam, plus several more gave off nothing; one looked like a chimney, or laundry room vent. There were two large evaporative coolers, also called swamp coolers, which were cheaper to operate than air conditioners. Of course, they might have the A/C compressor on the ground. He looked for skylights and could only find small ones, in the corners.

He checked the tracing device and found Machete's bug, still active and somewhere under the southwest corner of the plant. Walking would be faster, but much noisier, so he inched along in that direction, covering the slanted steel like a worm.

Through the feeble beam of her flashlight, Buffy stood looking at an immense hill of dusty rubble, which seemed to have taken over the collapsed tunnel. Water came seeping down from above, turning some of the rocks, roots, clods, and clay into gummy mud. Walking anywhere was treacherous. The explosion—probably a grenade—had widened the tunnel an instant before filling it with tons of debris from above. She shone her flashlight beam up the mountain of clutter, trying to find its peak, but all she saw was a bit of blackness at the top. It might not mean anything, but it might be a slight opening.

She rushed back to catch Angel taking a breather. Seeing her, he instantly tried to stand on his tiptoes to pull more dirt from his upside-down hole.

"Angel," she said nonjudgmentally, "there's something I want you to see. It might not be anything, but then again, it might be something. Anyway, if you want a pile of rubble to stand on while you dig, this one is already pretty high."

With a heave of his big shoulders, Angel wiped the dirt off his face and chest, then he grabbed his shirt from the ground. Sounding tired, he muttered, "I guess I could take a short break. But I don't see how we can go out that way."

"Not out the part that fell down," she answered, leading him through the treacherous passageway. "I want to climb out, not dig out—I'm talking about going *over* it. There seems to be an opening above the cave-in."

"Above it?" Angel asked curiously.

They had to clamber over a lot of rocks and dirt just to get to the main site of the collapse, where they had almost been buried alive. She could understand why Angel didn't want to move all that dirt, or even look at it, but she pointed her light beam to the top of the pile. It wasn't dramatic, but she could plainly see a slit of blackness where the dirt had possibly left a pocket.

"Let me check it out," Angel said, gingerly wading into the debris and trying to climb upward.

Until she watched his struggle, Buffy hadn't realized how difficult it would be to move on the freshly fallen rubble. Not being packed down, it was treacherous. She tried pushing on his leg, which only made him slip farther. With a grunt, he seemed to spring on all fours to the top of the pile, then he had to crawl on his stomach to reach the opening. He waved down and said, "Give me the flashlight."

She had to climb a few feet herself in the slippery dirt in order to hand over the light, and she slipped down immediately.

"Weird," he finally said. "Either there's a branch of a small cave up here, which is possible, or somebody carved a teeny-tiny tunnel on this level."

"Can we get out?" Buffy asked excitedly.

He shrugged as he continued to peer into the blackness. "Well, we can get out from where we are to this cavity up here, but we'll still be underground. There's hardly any room to move—this tunnel makes that one down there look like Grand Central Station."

"Sounds great! What are we waiting for?" Buffy asked with a gulp.

"Stand back," said Angel. "This is my impression of a dog kicking a lot of dirt."

Buffy jumped back and watched him dig. "Atta boy, good Angel," she said under her breath.

After finding her way back to Verdura, Arizona, Samantha Finn fought the temptation to return to Tatum's resort, where she had last seen Riley. She had been taken from there, and they would have chased off Riley, too. After all, the whole point of her abduction was to get them out of the way for whatever was happening tonight—let the devil take tomorrow. Instead of searching blindly for her husband, she drove back to the Bates Motel, where she had clean clothes and a few weapons. For what it was worth, that was also their base, and most good operatives would return to their home base when they were separated from one another. Of course, Riley wouldn't be nearly so calm as to come here and sit; he was probably looking for her now, and not expecting to find her.

After a quick drive through the darkened parking lot, Sam parked the stolen Crown Victoria at the far end of the motel, away from their room. Moving as swiftly as her wounds would let her, she slipped through the shadows until she reached her door. After letting herself in, she made a quick inventory of what she had to work with: her laptop computer, a spare phone, some wooden stakes, and two gas grenades that she had grabbed from the van. A gas mask went along with the grenades, and they were her only real weapon. Riley had the pistol with the five silver bullets, and she hoped he had an opportunity to use it.

Sam awakened the laptop from its slumber, hoping that Riley had used the wireless network to leave her a text message or a voice mail. "Speak to me, Riley," she chanted. "Please speak to me!" She had to enter a password and some encryption data before she was allowed full access, and she held her breath when she saw that she had recent voice mail. With a trembling finger, she clicked the mouse button.

"Sweetheart," came a hurried voice, and she almost dissolved into tears. "I don't know where you are, but I'll tell you where I'm headed—to the place where Angel first met the wolf. I don't know what else to say. . . ." His voice grew hoarse when he added, "See you at sunrise."

"See you at sunrise," repeated Sam, echoing a phrase they used in their organization. When you hunted vampires, sunrise was the end of the working day. It was also a euphemism for the last round-up, in case you didn't make it. Shaking off her raw emotions, Sam began to remove her bloody clothes as she rummaged in her drawer for clean ones. Several of her bandages were oozing fluid from popped stitches and scabs, but the pain kept her mind sharp and focused.

She looked at her flat, grimy stomach and wanted to place her unborn child in a safety deposit box—to be reclaimed later, after the danger was over. Of course, life didn't work that way. Even while Sam came to grips with producing a new life, she might have to take two lives that night. Maybe someday she could appreciate the awful irony, but right now Sam Finn was at war, fighting to keep her family alive.

Riley held his breath as he approached the first skylight in the southeastern corner of the pecan plant, because he could hear voices on the ground only a few feet away. He saw another truck roll up to the back to take delivery, but he couldn't see the cargo or the people loading it, although he could hear them talking in a combination of Spanish and English. They didn't sound too concerned about anything, which was a good sign that he had gotten this far undetected. Riley listened carefully for any mention of Sam but didn't hear anything about a woman—just the "cargo." So he crept over the skylight and looked down.

The lights were on, and he was staring straight into a pair of sinks in a public rest room. The skylight was old and had a film of dirt on it, so he couldn't see much detail—but he could see that nobody was there at the moment. The opening was about two feet square and was set on an incline, which meant it was big enough for him to fit through, barely. As he watched, the door opened and someone walked through and went to the stalls. He got a glimpse of a man in street clothes, dressed not much differently from himself. He waited while the man finished his business and went back to work.

It was tempting, but this lavatory was too bright and too close to the action. So Riley crawled across the roof toward the first skylight on the southwest side. This one was situated over a dark room, which was more to his liking. The agent took out his pouch of lockpicks and tools and found his glass cutter. He applied a suction cup with a handle to the glass, to keep the pieces from falling, and went immediately to work. When he was finished cutting the glass, he had to snip away a screen of wire mesh, but it was old and fragile. Steeling himself, Riley stuck his legs into the now-open square and dropped eight feet onto plush carpet.

This was not a rest room but a well-appointed office, from what he could tell in the dark. He found a coatrack upon which hung a white laboratory coat and a construction hardhat. He put on the helmet, deciding that it would partly hide his face and make him look as if he fit in. To complete his disguise, he grabbed a clipboard from the desk, then he marched out the door as if he owned the place.

This wing of the plant was mostly offices, although the musty smell of pecans, shells, spices, and cooking oil permeated even here. Since the rooms were dark, he doubted that Sam was being kept here, although Machete was still nearby, possibly in an underground storage room. Sticking his tools and handheld tracker in his pockets, Riley followed the corridor east until he got back into an area of lights and activity.

Rounding a corner, he suddenly saw workers moving ahead of him. Their backs were to him, but he could see that they were carrying what looked like backpacks, the same as any schoolkid would carry. Another one with a backpack stepped out of a lounge marked EMPLOYEE BREAK ROOM and joined his fellows in their strange procession.

Although they were coming and going, this corridor was not going to be deserted for a while, and Riley had to see what was in that room. There was nothing to do but walk right past them and try to look like part of the team. He consulted his clipboard as he entered the employee lounge, saying to no one in particular, "How's the cargo? Good condition?"

"What you think, *cabron?*" responded a grizzled worker. "Colombia's finest." He picked up two backpacks and dragged them out.

Riley tried not to look surprised to see that one of the soda machines and a fake chunk of floor had been pushed aside to reveal an impressive shaft dug straight down into the earth. The pit was about three feet square, timber-lined, and had a ladder on one side. They had positioned a portable winch over the hole, and an operator was using it to lift a small elevator packed with backpacks from the depths of the earth. The ominous hole did appear deep, stretching into the reddish soil like a primitive well, or a mine dug by greedy gnomes.

"How many more?" Riley shouted into the pit.

"That's almost it!" called a voice from below that

sounded chillingly familiar. He could swear it was Machete. "Just two more loads."

"Is security okay?" asked Riley. No matter what an organization was doing, if it was secret, security was always an issue.

"It's okay now!" answered Machete. "You heard about our visitors earlier, right?"

"Right," answered Riley. "That was quick thinking." He watched the worker bring up another load of illicit cargo in backpacks.

"Yeah, our watchdog chased 'em right where we wanted, then I finished them off with a grenade." Machete laughed. "You were never going to use that west branch tunnel, were you?"

"Not really," Riley answered with a friendly chuckle. "We handled our problems, too!"

"So Raul told me." There was some discussion in Spanish, then Machete yelled up, "We're done. I want to go settle with my people. You'll need some diggers and repair people down here, okay?"

"When things have died down," answered Riley. "Catch you later." He made a point of scribbling notes on his clipboard, while returning mules carried off the rest of the bundles. In a few seconds the big worker dismantled the winch and coiled his chains and ropes for the next time.

The hole was open, and Riley didn't waste time thinking about his next move. Before anyone who was really in charge showed up, he stepped onto the wooden ladder and began to climb down into the pit.

He was operating on pure adrenaline and emotion, not caring about what risks he took. The reason to be careful was gone.

He climbed down into the musty, loamy dirt, wondering if they would push the soda machine back over the hole and effectively trap him down here. Of course, there had to be a way out of this secret tunnel at the other end, but that might not land him in the friendliest environs. The bad guys had been interrupted by visitors from the Mexican side, and that had to be Buffy and Angel. Machete may have thought he'd taken care of them, but Riley knew that those two were hard to kill.

Buffy hadn't felt such claustrophobia since she was dead and buried, but at least she could keep moving as she crawled like a snake through a rank, muddy burrow hardly bigger than herself. There was no way for her to turn around or even look around—she would have to back out. Not only that, but there were some metal tracks under her stomach that made her movements all the more uncomfortable. Her flashlight didn't make much difference, because there was no way to go but straight ahead, and that looked worse with the light—it was better to crawl in darkness, just checking the gopher hole every now and then. Buffy was beginning to think that Angel had been right, because this hardly seemed like progress. "Whose idea was this?" she muttered.

"Yours," Angel answered from behind her. He

sounded as if he were a mile away, not just a few inches. "You know the track underneath us?"

"I'm getting to know it intimately," she answered.

"They probably had a little wagon loaded with stuff, which they put on this track and pulled on a rope by hand through the tunnel. This is a drug tunnel, too, an older one."

"Who dug it, prairie dogs?" she asked disgruntledly. It didn't help to find out that people weren't supposed to actually crawl in here—that it was only for little wagons.

Angel replied, "It has to lead somewhere. This is better than digging."

"It is?" she asked, spitting dirt out of her mouth. Nevertheless, she kept her appendages moving and wriggled another few inches down the filthy passageway.

Riley jumped off the ladder onto hard-packed dirt at the bottom of the shaft; it was barely illuminated by the square of light from above, and he wondered how long that would be left open. The drug tunnel was professionally but hastily built, with wooden beams and timber keeping most of the dirt out. The only other feature was a green glow stick about ten feet away—*the only light*, he supposed. Here was the secret that must never be told.

Riley knew he should keep looking for Sam and not worry about this drug tunnel, but it was all related. He checked his pocket tracker and found that Machete was very nearby, perhaps thirty feet away. He heard a scraping sound, and the light above his head slowly disappeared, leaving him in darkness except for the eerie green glow stick.

He heard footsteps in the darkness. "I don't know you," said a threatening voice.

Riley lifted the stake from his back pocket. "I know you," he answered. "You're Machete."

"Well, that does put you at an advantage," said the voice. The footsteps stopped, but Riley still couldn't see the vampire. "You don't work for Tatum, do you?"

"Of course I do," Riley answered, inching closer to the ominous presence. "Doesn't everybody in this hick town?"

Machete laughed. "You got that right. But we're not always going to be his lapdogs. This is underground— that's *our* domain."

Riley's handheld device suddenly started beeping, and he glanced at it to find that there were two more tracers having just come into his range. They were preprogrammed, the ones he had left with Angel and Buffy, and they were also underground.

"What have you got there?" Machete asked, sounding angry. A dark, lean figure moved into the outer rays of the glow stick.

"I've been tracking you with this thing," Riley answered matter-of-factly. He slipped a wooden stake just under the tracking device a second before he stepped into the light. "We put a bug in your jacket— a tracer. As long as you wear that jacket, we can find you. Hey, what is that language you speak with Raul?"

Snarling with rage, the vampire tore off his fringed leather jacket and threw it into the darkness, and his face thickened into that of a berserk bloodsucker. He charged Riley, flying through the tunnel in a single leap.

The young man was ready. He lowered his head to let the hardhat take some of the blow, and he let himself be bowled over as he jammed his hidden stake upward into the monster's chest. The snarling fangs were inches from his neck when the enraged vampire turned into a cloud of reeking dust, which covered Riley like a bad case of dandruff.

The man breathed in the stench and thought it smelled pretty good. They had lost their unwitting spy in this den of thieves and monsters, but they had gained something. The vampire hunter ditched his helmet, stood up, and strode down the dark tunnel, where he stopped to pick up Machete's aged-leather jacket. Had he been wearing the fringed finery, it would also be dust, but this way it was a perfect disguise for the dim lights down here. Riley put on the jacket and it fit perfectly, feeling like a second layer of skin. It was surprisingly heavy, too, like a vest of leather armor. He felt where a tear had been stitched and repaired in the front, and he imagined that this thick jacket had saved Machete's undead life a time or two. Tonight, it had not saved him from final death.

Now Riley consulted his tracking device once again. Discounting his own blip, he found the other two and saw that they were remarkably close. Perhaps they had moved even closer. Following these tiny beacons, he crouched down and scuttled along the dingy passageway, looking for the next feeble pool of green light.

In due time, Riley heard raucous voices ahead of him—it almost sounded like a party. Well, he had come this far on pure gall, and there was no point stopping now. He walked toward the voices and found himself entering a chamber where he could stand upright. There were a number of people here, although he wasn't sure they were people. Giving everyone a good look at the familiar jacket he wore, he put his head down and strode through them. There was a body in the corner, and they seemed to be drinking from it; others were counting coins and small bundles of loot. He noticed what looked like pre-Columbian art as well as jewelry.

As much as Riley would have liked to break up this hellish gathering, he had to get through here. He forced down the gag in his throat and kept walking.

"Hey, Machete!" called someone.

He grunted and waved, never slowing down. Before he left the chamber, Riley spotted a shovel leaning against the wall, and he grabbed it. Shovels made good weapons in a pinch. Not looking back, he ducked his head and plunged onward down the grimy passageway. When he felt he had put some distance between himself and the revelers, Riley took out the tracking device and consulted it again.

Now the blips seemed to be ahead of him and above, like on another level. He rushed down the tunnel until they were directly above him, which made him stop and consider what to do. Were Buffy and Angel above him, on the surface? That couldn't be, unless the surface was only a few feet away.

When he saw that the blips were moving off, he had to act fast, so he rammed the shovel straight up into the wooden plank above his head. It echoed loudly in the tunnel, although the sound probably didn't travel very far. He waited until he heard a slight thud in response. Not knowing what else to do, he banged against the wood several times in Morse code, spelling out "A-n-g-e-l." If anyone behind him was listening, maybe it would just sound as if he was digging; after all, they had seen Machete with a shovel. He hoped the vampires had enough to do in their lair to occupy themselves.

Riley made some more banging and scraping sounds on the timber, spelling out "B-u-f-f-y" this time. He was answered by frantic pounding—it sounded as if somebody was trying to dig down to him. Riley stuck the shovel between two boards and pried one loose. A rain of dirt fell down on him, plus some old rotten timber, but he kept digging.

Suddenly an arm struck through the dirt ceiling and waved down at him. He started scraping away more dirt, being careful what he hit with the blade of the shovel. With the two of them working together, they had soon caused enough dirt to fall to allow a strange reversal of form. Riley watched in awe as a determined vampire dug his way downward and fell from the ceiling instead of rising from the ground.

Angel coughed as he staggered to his feet, then he pointed upward. "Let's get Buffy down."

"How did you get—?"

"Later," Angel answered hoarsely. The vampire grabbed the shovel from him and began to dig furiously while Riley wandered a few more steps down the tunnel, intending to keep a lookout. Angel was making so much noise, he couldn't hear anything from the far end of the tunnel, the part he hadn't seen. He rushed back to Angel just as a slim, blond shape tumbled from a hole in the ceiling. Angel caught Buffy and set her gently on the floor of the tunnel, amidst more mounds of freshly dug dirt.

"They bragged that they'd killed you," whispered Riley.

"They tried," said Angel.

"Am I glad to see you!" Buffy rasped, grabbing Riley and using him to haul herself to her feet. She still looked wobbly as she wiped the dirt from her face and hair. "Where's Sam?"

He shook his head grimly. "I don't know. They kidnapped her and are holding her somewhere. If I don't cooperate—"

"You saved us—now let's save her." Angel pointed down the tunnel behind Riley. "There's no sense going that way, back to Mexico. Unless you think that's where she is."

"I don't know, but I doubt it."

All three of them stopped to think, and Riley listened for voices but didn't hear any. "The other way," he said, "goes to Tatum's house and the pecan plant—that's where the tunnel comes out."

"No kidding," Buffy said, her jaw clenched in anger. "That guy has a lot of explaining to do, especially about Sam. I say we go rattle his cage."

"Sounds good to me," Angel said, turning on his heel to survey the dark tunnel.

"Wait," Riley warned, "a cave's down there that's full of vampires. There might be a couple dozen of them."

"Good," Buffy answered with determination. "We know the place. By the way, I like your jacket."

Angel brushed some dirt off the weathered leather. "I take it Machete didn't lend it to you."

"No," Riley answered with a grim smile. "But he won't be needing it anymore."

"A lot of them won't be needing their clothes anymore," said Buffy. She reached down and picked up two shards of splintered wood from the planks they had destroyed. Brandishing a stake in each hand, the Slayer took off down the tunnel while Angel and Riley shuffled to keep up in the low-ceiling tunnel.

There was no more planning, no more stealth and guile. Buffy stormed into the earthen den full of vampires, who were too busy counting their loot and feeding on half-dead victims to notice her at first. Riley and Angel moved to either side of the Slayer, but they let her handle this undead mob. These were the moments when Buffy was in her element.

"Party's over!" she announced to the vampires. "Put down the gold, because, like they say . . . you can't take it with you."

CHAPTER EIGHTEEN

The vampires spread out, forming a half-circle around the trio of Buffy, Angel, and Riley. Angel tried to count the number arrayed against them in the dimly lit cavern, and it had to be eighteen or nineteen. Down in this drug tunnel, it was always night—a perfect place for vampires to feel at home. Riley looked nervous, as he kept glancing at the doorway where they had just entered, and Buffy looked pissed. The bloated bloodsuckers were amused by the petite blonde and her two boyfriends who had ventured into their lair armed with a few sticks of wood.

The dapper Raul stepped forward, a smirk on his

face. Angel could see a smear of blood around his lips and a dusting of white powder on his nose. "Can you believe this? Room service couldn't be more accommodating! And we were just about to send out for refreshments."

The vampires laughed appreciatively, and Raul added, "Do you see how many we are against you?"

"You know," said Buffy, "when I'm fighting demons or counseling high school students, I daydream about stuff like this on my lunch break."

Raul chuckled at her brazen courage, until his eyes got a good look at the jacket Riley was wearing. "You!" he bellowed, shaking a finger at the young man. "Where did you get that jacket?"

"He took it off a pile of dust," snapped Buffy. "Somebody you knew?"

That sent Raul into a rage, and his face instantly distorted into fierce vampire visage. Taking a cue from their leader, several of the other vampires also changed into their vicious state. Raul didn't wait to organize a charge—he flew at Buffy and dodged her first swipe at him. But that was just a feint on her part to fling him over her shoulder into Angel's clutches. As Raul fell against Angel, the soulful vampire buried one stake in his foe's back and another in his chest. With a howl of anguish, Raul turned into the dust he should have been long ago.

Soon Angel and Riley were fighting back-to-back as the vampires converged on them, and Buffy was a whirlwind of kicking legs and punching fists. Angel had been in many frenetic battles with Buffy at his side, but he couldn't remember a more insane melee than this. Perhaps it was the darkness or the close quarters, but he was never quite sure who he was punching or stabbing with a stake. Seeing which way this was going, one or two vampires tried to escape, but Riley cut them down at the doorway. Angel protected Buffy's back, which allowed her to do what she did best: slay.

They vanquished vampires for what seemed like hours, until finally there were no more. The three of them stopped, bent over from exhaustion, the humans panting for breath. From the entrance to the far tunnel came the sound of a pair of hands clapping. Then a powerful searchlight went on, blinding them. Angel shielded his eyes as he watched about eight men armed with crossbows enter the cavern from the far side. Frederick Tatum was one of them; Clete Barton was another, and he was wearing his wolf skin like a cape, ready to invoke its powers. The rest of them were thugs who looked too nervous to be anything but humans; they took their courage from their sinister leaders.

"That was impressive," said Frederick Tatum. "Thank you for eliminating them. The vampires were becoming quite a liability, especially Raul and Machete. In fact, we were coming down here to deal with them, but you saved us the trouble."

Sheriff Barton glanced at Riley in his new jacket and smiled. "I guess we don't have to worry about Machete anymore. Did you get Raul, too?"

"Yep, and you're next," Buffy blurted, standing her ground.

Tatum's smiled faded, and his demeanor grew grim. "By now you know that we can't let you see this tunnel and live. We thought the vampires could keep secrets, but the fewer people who know, the better." He hefted his crossbow and aimed it at Buffy. "It's a good thing this old weapon works equally as well on humans as vampires."

"My wife doesn't know about the tunnel," said Riley. "Let her go."

"All of that is immaterial now," Tatum answered with a sneer. "Sheriff, let's end their suffering."

"Right," Clete Barton growled, lifting his crossbow and setting his sights on Angel. "Men, aim your weapons. Make sure you get the vampire on the—"

Suddenly a metal canister came lobbing into the chamber, and it exploded in a great plume of sparks and blue-gray gas. The cloud spread rapidly, squirting from the device, and it overcame every human in the cramped cave in less than a second. Coughing and wheezing, Tatum slumped to the earthen floor, as did every one of his men. Their searchlights clattered to the ground, shooting odd angles of light into the spreading cloud. Buffy and Riley grabbed Angel for support, but they also succumbed. Five seconds later, Angel was the only one standing.

He still sensed danger, and it was a good thing he drew Sam's Glock pistol, because a huge silver wolf came bounding out of the smoke. It lunged straight for

273

Angel, blood in its golden eyes and drool on its feral fangs, and he squeezed off a shot just as the monster's claws landed on his chest. Angel hit the ground with a loud "ooomph" that knocked the wind out of him, and he struggled against the weight of the ferocious beast. It roared in rage and raked mammoth claws across his chest, just as he buried the gun in its hairy hide and fired two more shots. The velocity of the shot propelled the animal off of him, and it lay thrashing on the floor of the cave, roaring and whimpering.

Angel sat in stunned silence as the primeval thing, a creature from a bygone era, churned and twitched in its death throes. With a strangled roar it lay still, pools of blood forming in the brown dirt. He heard footsteps and turned to see a shapely apparition in a gas mask and yards of bloody bandages come limping to his side. Sam stared at the fallen creature, too, because it was undergoing a startling metamorphosis. It shrank and twisted like a fallen leaf caught in a time-action photograph, until the being was much smaller and less impressive than the great wolf. It was a wizened dead man who looked very old, as if time had caught up with him. Angel hardly recognized him as Sheriff Barton, except for the ill-fitting uniform that draped his thin body.

"Who do you think he really was?" Sam asked, her voice sounding muffled in the gas mask.

"I don't know," answered Angel. He looked up at her gratefully, shaking his head in amazement. "I'm glad to see you're all right."

"I would think so," replied Sam. "Listen, I pulled some strings and have got the DEA, FBI, CDC, and half of Washington on their way here. Most will be slow, but somebody is liable to show up quickly. This tunnel will make the evening news, and everyone in here is going to jail. So why don't you pick up Buffy and run like hell back to Mexico?"

"Good idea," he answered. Angel rose to his feet, brushed his clothes, then bent down and picked up the sleeping Slayer. He marveled at how little she weighed for being such a potent force in the world. He turned back to the figure in the gas mask and said, "So this is good-bye?"

"I think so," she answered. "This is the best way for both of you to stay out of it. Don't worry, I've got another gas bomb to keep them quiet until the cavalry gets here. I know we couldn't have busted this bunch without you, and they really needed busting. Sincerely, thanks a lot. Go on now, Angel, before I get mushy."

"If you ever want to live in Los Angeles," he said as he carried Buffy into the tunnel, "I've got a job for you."

"I don't know," answered Sam. "How are the schools? Can we get a baby-sitter?"

"I've got lots of experienced baby-sitters," Angel replied as he disappeared into the inky burrow that led to Mexico.

Buffy stirred out of her sleep, wondering where she was. It was a strange antiseptic smell that brought her fully awake, and she heard the faint sound of music. Somewhere farther off, a coyote howled plaintively, as if complaining that the night was not as wild as it used to be. The cushioned comfort told Buffy that she was in a bed, which felt wonderful on her tired, bruised body. She remembered something about dispatching a couple dozen vampires, crawling through muddy holes in the ground, and seeing a dazzling cloud in a cave. That last part was very fuzzy, but it had been quite a dream, all right. Some of it took place in Mexico, and Riley Finn was in it. Quite a dream . . .

Then a rooster crowed, and that sounded very real and not something she would hear in Sunnydale. Buffy forced her eyes wide open and touched a hand to her aching head, then looked around at a drab hotel room. Then she remembered—this really *was* Verdura, Mexico. She hadn't been dreaming, and Angel was staring down at her.

"Hello, Sleeping Beauty," he said with amusement. "I'm glad you're awake, because my travel time is running out. Or didn't you hear that rooster?"

"I heard him," she muttered, sitting up. "Uh, what happened back there . . . down in the mine?"

Angel picked up his jacket and suitcase and glanced worriedly out the window. "Well, you killed half the vampires in the Southwest, and Sam saved us with a gas grenade. Sam caught the bad guys too. Actually, the most amazing thing is that you and I both got paid for this. The second most amazing thing is that I've decided to put up with Riley, since he's married to Sam."

"That's big of you," Buffy said, feeling vaguely cheated. But that was always the way she felt with Angel. "And the wolf?"

"I plugged him with your silver bullets," answered Angel. "Without that skin, he was an old man." He started for the door. "Sorry to leave. You've got plenty of money to get home. You can catch a bus to Tucson and get a flight from there."

"You could stay one more day," she replied. "I mean . . . we could both . . . stay."

Angel stopped in the doorway and gazed fondly at her. "I wish I could, Buffy. I've been addicted to blood and violence and immortality—but the hardest addiction I ever had to break was the one to you. It would be too easy to start again . . . and too impossible to quit. The Powers wouldn't let us be happy."

"I know," she replied with a wistful smile. "Be good."

"Always," he assured her. With that, Angel was out the door and gone.

Rubbing her eyes, the Slayer slumped back into the cushy bed, guessing that she would sleep the rest of the day away. But this scene was too melodramatic: A man had just walked out the door, leaving her alone in a flophouse in a Mexican border town. She couldn't end the adventure like this, especially with a bunch of cash in her wallet.

If she were sensible, she would take the money home and pay a few bills, or put it away for Dawn's college. *But what fun was that?* A couple more nights in Mexico wouldn't do any harm, but not Verdura.

Back to the beach house in Puerto Peñasco, she decided. There were swank hotels there, with room service, parasailing, discos, cabana boys, and spas. She still had Riley's van, and he wouldn't miss it for a few days. *It's not like I get a paid vacation every week!*

So Buffy hurriedly packed her bags, checked out, and caught the first white van to the coast.

ABOUT THE AUTHOR

John Vornholt has had several writing and performing careers, ranging from being a stuntman in the movies to writing animated cartoons. After spending fifteen years as a freelance journalist, John turned to book publishing in 1989. Drawing upon the goodwill generated by an earlier nonfiction book he had written, John secured a contract to write *Masks*, number seven in the Star Trek: The Next Generation™ book series.

Masks was the first of the numbered Star Trek: The Next Generation™ books to make the *New York Times* best-seller list and was reprinted three times in the first month. John has seen several of his Star Trek books make the *Times* best-seller list. Since then, he has written and sold more than fifty books for both adults and children.

Theatrical rights for his fantasy novel about Aesop, the fabulist, have been sold to David Spencer and Stephen Witkin in New York. They're in the process of adapting it as a Broadway musical. In addition, *The Troll King* was just published by Simon & Schuster, and John is working on two sequels, which will be published in August and December of 2003.

John currently lives with his wife and two children in Tucson, Arizona. Please visit his Web site at www.vornholt.net.

"Are you bad now? Am I the good one now?"

FAITH

She's been called many things: Dark. Rogue. The
Other One. Murderer. But above all: Dangerous.

"Want. Take. Have."

Catch up with the Other Slayer in these adventures:

The Faith Files
The Book of Fours
Buffy / Angel: Unseen trilogy
Wisdom of War
Chosen (Finale Tie-In)
Chaos Bleeds

Available now from Pocket Books
Published by Simon & Schuster